CAT
CRIMES
TAKES A
VACATION

edited by
MARTIN H. GREENBERG
AND ED GORMAN

New York

Contents

Author Notes

BARBARA PAUL has written several notable mystery novels and in the process has won herself an ever-growing number of fans. Barbara can work well in virtually every form of the mystery story, including a few which she probably invented.

GILLIAN ROBERTS writes wry and sometimes melancholy mysteries about the pleasures and perversities of modern life, especially as endured by decent, everyday people who occasionally get confused by it all.

BILL CRIDER has worked in virtually every genre of modern popular fiction, and has done so with skill, style, and great good humor. He is especially winning when his beat is the vanishing American small town.

MICHAEL COLLINS usually walks the dark side of the mystery street, using his award-winning novels and stories to chart the bleaker aspects of modern American society. Here he turns his remarkable skills to a tale in a lighter vein.

GARY A. BRAUNBECK is a young Midwestern writer who is just now beginning to receive some recognition for his quiet but effective stories about life in Middle America. He is now completing several novels.

DANIEL B. BRAWNER is another young Midwestern writer who is

also just starting out on what we hope will be a long career. His stories combine the best aspects of the traditional mystery with just a hint of the harder stuff.

BRUCE HOLLAND ROGERS was nominated for an Edgar for his first *Cat Crimes* story. Here he hands in an equally strong story about life in the world of felines. We hope soon to see a novel bearing the Rogers by-line.

TRACY A. KNIGHT is a psychologist who writes with grace and style about some of the darker aspects of the human psyche. His story here, however, recalls Agatha Christie more than Raymond Chandler.

CATHERINE DAIN has written several mysteries that critics have found fast-paced and amusing. She works the same vein here in a piece of accomplished storytelling and wry human observation.

KRISTINE KATHRYN RUSCH is a novelist, short-story writer, and editor (*The Magazine of Fantasy & Science Fiction*) of great renown and accomplishment. She works in a variety of voices and styles, all of them first-rate.

ED GORMAN has written seven mystery novels and twenty-five mystery stories.

JAN GRAPE is one of the most distinctive new writers on the mystery scene. She works in a style and manner all her own, writing about her native Texas in a fashion that fuses the traditional mystery with the harder-boiled. She's somebody to watch.

BILL PRONZINI is the creator of Nameless, one of the truly classic private eyes (and private eye series) in this half of the century. He is one of the major mystery voices of our time, and here he shows why.

TERRY BLACK is a screenwriter and teacher who occasionally writes short stories, and darned good ones. His work recalls the playful novels of the forties, *Mr. and Mrs. North*, perhaps, or any number of Craig Rice characters.

DOROTHY CANNELL is a major star in today's mystery world, a writer as skilled at short stories as she is at novels. With each book her audience grows, as does her esteem in the eyes of the critics.

Introduction

Ever notice that look of betrayal in the eyes of your cat when you're leaving on vacation? She knows you're going to have a cat-sitter come in or, even worse, board her for a few weeks.

How can a person enjoy a vacation knowing that her feline is back home having a horrible time?

Well, the writers in this book have managed to combine cats and vacations. In some cases, this means taking the family cat along. In others, it means encountering different cats in glitzy lands abroad.

That's the operative word here. *Glitzy.*

We wanted to show you as many fabled vacationing spots as possible. Real upscale places. Not a Howard Johnson's to be found anywhere.

And lots of cats.

Enjoy yourself. With us you don't need passports or sunblock or beach towels.

All you need is a nice quiet nook where you can read our book—and there you'll be. Balmy breezes. Spectacular sights. Exotic settings.

And one more thing about vacationing with us: you won't make your cat mad.

He can sit in your lap as you read.

And you can scratch his head.
And pet him.
And tell him how smart he is.
And how honored you are to be in his presence.
And make sure his food bowl is full.
And make sure his drinking water is fresh.
And make sure his litter box is clean.
And then you can relax.
He's ready. You're ready.
Finally.
So turn to the first story and enjoy yourself.
After all, you're on vacation.

—MARTIN H. GREENBERG and ED GORMAN

Midnight Sun

Barbara Paul

Fur-ruffling breeze: a sniff of winter. Good and bad. Good: warm fireplaces, warm laps, warm chocolate in her saucer. Bad: feet-freezing white stuff on the ground. Playing in the snow was for kittens and humans.

The visitors grew fewer every day . . . the young ones and the old ones, the white ones and the yellow ones and the brown ones, the ones that talked funny and the ones that didn't talk at all. The ones with bad eyesight who had to look through little black boxes that flashed a light before they could see.

Ingvald hunkered down, stroked her long fur. "You smell winter coming, don't you, Takki? Hm?" Carefully he looked over the fenced-in medieval village maintained as an open-air museum, making sure everything was in order. No one lived in the village now . . . except Takki. Ingvald's house was her winter home, but the village was where she lived in summer.

The beefy-chested man approached them, Lars, who helped take care of the place. "Anything scheduled for today?"

Ingvald stood up. "A private party of six, coming by limousine from Lillehammer around three o'clock. Arne's bringing in a tourist bus at four. But that's all . . . other than the usual drop-ins."

Lars nodded. "The private party—Americans?"

"Yes, I believe so."

"They'll think this is a Viking village. Vikings, the Middle Ages . . . it's all the same to them."

"I know. But at least they come."

Lars looked at the leaden sky. "Storm. Big one."

"Not for hours yet." The two men moved off, talking.

Takki felt the breeze lift her long fur again, a little more insistent this time. Not yet prepared for the cold, she padded toward her favorite house in the village. Small rooms, small furniture, low ceilings . . . cozy and comforting. Ingvald had to stoop when he went through the doorways. Takki automatically avoided the wooden cradle. The one time she'd tried to sleep there, that particular piece of furniture had proved remarkably unstable, actually rocking beneath her every time she moved.

She leapt to a wooden bench, found a patch of sunlight shining through the window, and curled up for her after-lunch nap.

The sound of car doors slamming roused her. Instantly awake, Takki stood up and stretched; her patch of sunlight had disappeared. She dropped lightly from her bench and trotted outside.

All the buildings in the village had been constructed on pilings that raised them several feet above ground level, offering some rudimentary protection against both wild beasts and deep snows. The beasts were all gone now, but the open spaces beneath the buildings made good hiding places for a kitty intent on checking out these newest guests in her village.

This was an older crowd, autumn visitors who'd waited until the students and the lovers and the families with small children had all ended their sampling of Norway's fjords and mountains and lush summer valleys. All six of them were dressed in colorful summer clothing, as if determined to hang on to a season that had already served notice that the end was in sight.

And they were a vocal bunch, talking loudly at one another even as they spread out to see what the village had to offer. "*Smørbrød,*

smørbrød," one man in his fifties was complaining. "If I go into one more hotel that serves us *smørbrød,* I think I'll puke."

His wife raised an eyebrow. "You never complained about open-faced sandwiches at home."

"At home I don't have to eat them every goddamned day."

She laughed shortly. "Vince, we haven't had them *every* day."

"Seems like it," Vince growled. "These people don't exactly knock themselves out for you, do they?" He glanced over to where Ingvald was courteously answering questions put to him by another of the tourists. "Look at that guy, Millie. A cold fish if ever I saw one. Real remote, these people."

But Millie had grown tired of his complaints. "If you wanted to be fawned over, you should have stayed at home."

He shot a look toward her, but she had her back turned, heading toward the nearest village building. Vince muttered under his breath and went hunting for something to look at.

Another couple had heard the exchange. "Vince and Millie are at it again," the woman said with poorly concealed glee. "I don't think Vince travels well."

Her husband sighed. "Vince thought he was flying in to Oslo for meetings with the Nordstrom people and then would fly straight back home again. Mr. Hysinger sprang this little vacation trip on us after we got here, remember?"

"Uh-huh. And neither one of you suspected a thing? Even when Mr. Hysinger said 'Bring your wives—I'm paying'?"

"We've talked about this before."

"Yes, we have, haven't we? I told you before we left that this trip is by way of being an audition."

"Deb, Mr. Hysinger as good as promised me the position."

"Then why is Vince here? And why is Charlotte Evers here?"

"Vince is a branch manager. Who better to advise when we're opening a new branch? And Charlotte is Mr. Hysinger's statistical analyst. He doesn't make a move without her."

Deb looked at him meaningfully.

"Oh, don't read anything into that." He laughed dismissively.

"She's your real competition, you know. I think Vince has already struck out. He's obviously having trouble adjusting to this country. Charlotte's the one you should be worrying about."

"Charlotte's administrative experience is minimal. You're seeing roadblocks where there are none," he insisted. "I'm going to be running the Norwegian branch, count on it."

She stared. "Jerry, sometimes you can be so naive I can't believe you. Don't you see? Hysinger is playing you off against each other."

"No, he's not," Jerry said firmly. "Mr. Hysinger doesn't operate that way. You've misunderstood the situation completely. Relax a little, Deb. Try to enjoy our vacation."

With an effort she bit back what she wanted to say. "All right. We'll play it your way." ———————

"Good." He smiled. "Oh, look at that—there's a cat peeking out at us from under the house." He moved closer to the open space beneath the building. "Hello, kitty . . . what are you doing under there? Come here. Here, kitty kitty!"

Takki just looked at him, didn't move.

Deb gave a will-he-never-learn sigh. "Jerry, European cats don't know *kitty kitty*. You have to say *puss puss puss puss puss.*"

He tried it, but Takki still didn't move.

Ingvald came up to them. "Ah, there she is. I was wondering where she'd got to."

"How do you call her?" Jerry asked. "I can't get her to come out."

"I usually just call her by name. Come on out, Takki."

Takki oozed up to Ingvald, butted her head against his shin.

"Takki, huh?" Jerry said. "I'm a sucker for cats myself."

"I found this one huddled by the door to my office when she was still so young she had to be fed with an eye . . . ah." Ingvald groped for the English word. "Eye dropper . . . she took milk from an eye dropper. I have no idea where she came from."

"She reminds me of a long-haired cat we once had. Deb, do you remember Mitzi?"

Deb looked at him as if he were simpleminded. "Of course I remember Mitzi. She lived with us for six years."

Ingvald changed the subject. "I'm afraid I have bad news. I just got a call from the weather station in Trondheim, and a storm is moving in faster than was expected. It would be better if you all returned to Lillehammer."

"But we just got here!" Jerry protested.

"I know, and I'm sorry. But there's a low stretch of road about a kilometer from here where the Lågen River always overflows its banks following heavy rains. You could be cut off. And we have no facilities for overnight guests here."

The other man sighed. "Well, it will be up to Mr. Hysinger. It's his party."

"Which one is he?"

"Totally bald, you can't miss him. Last I saw him, he was going into that building over there."

Jerry was pointing toward the long hall, the communal building where those long-dead villagers had taken all their food and drink together, had met to thrash out shared problems, or just had gathered for the warmth of fellowship during the long Norwegian winters. Takki scampered ahead as Ingvald headed toward the hall.

The hall contained the largest single room in the village. Pairs of crossed iron-headed axes faced each other from opposing walls, but other than that the room was quite bare. The villagers had poured their yearning for beauty into their church and into their homes, where every lintel was meticulously carved, where every piece of furniture was decorative as well as useful, where artfully woven tapestries picturing religious and outdoor scenes were hung on the wooden walls, where every surviving box or ale-bowl or wooden chest had been lovingly painted with bold colors and vigorous lines. The whole village was a monument to folk art. But the hall where those people had spent most of their time together—they'd left that stark and barren, even bleak. The two small windows let in only enough daylight to throw the shadows into prominence.

Ingvald walked in on what was clearly a private conversation. The bald-headed man named Hysinger was talking earnestly to a well-groomed woman in her late thirties, the youngest member of the party. "Don't tell me Nordstrom wants to keep all its personnel, I *know* that," Hysinger was saying—and then broke off to look at Ingvald. Impervious to the tension in the room, Takki jumped up on the table to see if either of the two visitors wanted to pet her.

Neither did. Ingvald apologized for interrupting and repeated his warning about the storm. "I've had to cancel a tourist bus that was due in later this afternoon. And it would be better if your party returned immediately, before the rain starts. If you're driving through the lowlands when the Lågen overflows, it could be dangerous."

Hysinger swore mildly. "Well, if the man says we gotta go, we gotta go."

"I did not see your driver," Ingvald said. "Where—"

"Jerry drove the limo," the woman interposed. "There are only the six of us."

"Round them up, will you, Charlotte?" Hysinger said casually. "I'll be along in a minute."

Charlotte clearly didn't relish being made an errand-girl, but she got up to do as Hysinger asked. She passed Ingvald without a glance.

When she'd left, Hysinger cocked his head to the side. "I don't know your name."

"Ingvald Gunnarsson."

"Well, Ingvald, let me ask you something." He paused to push Takki away. "I want to build an executive retreat within driving distance of Oslo. A posh place, where we can bring potential clients. But it's gotta have a spectacular view. Anyplace like that around here?"

"Several," Ingvald answered. "But they are all part of this national preserve. Not for sale."

"Everything's for sale. But I gotta know where to look. You know this country around here, and I'd kinda like the retreat to be near some sort of tourist attraction like this little village you got here. Give the clients something to do if they get bored. Tell me a coupla places to look at."

Ingvald shrugged mentally and gave him directions to two scenic spots in the area. Hysinger pulled out a leather-bound notebook and used a gold pen to take notes.

When he'd finished, he put a hundred-dollar bill on the table. "A little something for your trouble."

Ingvald fixed his gaze on one pair of the iron-headed axes mounted on the wall. "Thank you, Mr. Hysinger, but national preserve employees are not permitted to accept gratuities."

Hysinger laughed. "A man of principle, huh? I like that." He pocketed the hundred.

Feeling patronized, Ingvald said, "Now you must excuse me. I have to see to the others." He scooped up Takki from the tabletop and left.

Outside, there wasn't another person visible anywhere. Even Lars, whose help Ingvald could use just then, was nowhere in sight. He glanced up at the sky, now an ominous pewter color. When Takki started wriggling in his arms, he put her on the ground and started a systematic search of the village.

Ingvald tried the church first, as it was the most engaging building in the village. No one. He checked the restrooms. Empty. He worked his way through the small homes, the prettiest one first, Takki's favorite. Not a sign of anyone. Where had they all disappeared to?

He finally found Vince and Millie at the *stabbur*, the storehouse for communal food and clothing that had no precise equivalent in American towns; America had had no Middle Ages. Vince and Millie were sitting on the removable steps to the second floor entrance of the *stabbur*, puffing away on cigarettes. And arguing.

"Fer gawd's sake, Millie, we'd have to *live* here. In a foreign country. Let him give the job to Charlotte."

"Or Jerry."

"Jerry's a weak sister. He'll pick the yuppie, you'll see."

"If he does, it's because you're not *trying*, Vince! You're the only one here who's ever managed a branch—you're the obvious choice! What would be so terrible about living here?"

Vince caught sight of Ingvald just in time. "Oh, er, hi there."

"Smoking is not permitted," Ingvald said expressionlessly and watched as they quickly stubbed out their cigarettes. For the third time he explained about the storm and led them back toward their limousine.

Charlotte had located Jerry and Deb. "Let's get out of here," she said nervously. "I don't like the look of that sky."

"Where's Mr. Hysinger?" Millie asked.

They all glanced around, as if expecting to spot him hiding behind a tree. "I left him in the long hall," Ingvald said.

"He's probably waiting for someone to come fetch him," Deb said. The five of them avoided one another's eyes, none of them wanting to play the sycophant before the others.

Hiding his irritation, Ingvald said, "I'll get him." Anything to be rid of these people. He took off toward the long hall at a trot.

And was surprised to find the door to the hall shut; all the doors in all the village buildings were kept propped open during tourist season. As he lifted the latch, he heard a plaintive mew from inside.

"Takki?" he said, pushing the door open. "How did you get shut up in here?"

The cat darted between his legs and disappeared.

Ingvald stepped inside and called out, "Mr. Hysinger?" As soon as his eyes adjusted to the dim light, he saw what had frightened the cat.

Hysinger lay slumped at the end of the long table, one of the iron-headed axes from the wall buried in his skull.

The rain was a solid wall of water, pounding down hard and cold; the storm had come shrieking in just as Ingvald was telling the others that Hysinger had been murdered. Ingvald demanded the keys to the limousine from Jerry and then directed them all to take refuge in the church—a small building, but still the next largest in the village after the long hall. Then he and Lars had hurried away to close all the doors and window shutters.

It was as if someone had turned off the sun. The five tourists groped their way through the darkness, getting their bearings through the brief illumination provided by the occasional flash of lightning. Inside the church was pitch black, until a new lightning flash showed four small windows open to the rain, the wooden shutters banging against the outside walls in the gale. Ducking their heads against the wind, Jerry and Deb closed and latched the shutters.

Then they were in total darkness—scant comfort for the five cold, wet, anxious people. Vince and Millie flicked their cigarette lighters, and they all made their way to the carved wooden pews that had first seen service some six hundred years earlier.

Then they sat there invisibly, listening to one another breathe. Someone's teeth were chattering. "I thought this was supposed to be the Land of the Midnight Sun," Vince complained.

"It's the storm," Deb said impatiently. "It's been light enough to read by most nights since we got here."

"Well, it's not light now."

A sound of annoyance. "Vince, you can always be counted on to state the obvious."

"Well, excuse me, Miss Know-It-All!"

Charlotte spoke up. "Oh, stop it, both of you. We've got a bigger problem than a little temporary discomfort."

"Poor Mr. Hysinger," Millie murmured.

"Poor Mr. Hysinger?" Charlotte repeated in astonishment. "Hasn't it sunk in on you yet? Someone right here killed him! We've got a murderer sitting here with us!"

That put an end to the talk for a while. Eventually Jerry cleared his throat and said, "I know we're all feeling uneasy, but I doubt that we're in any danger. We can't see a thing in the dark, but neither can the killer. Surely he wouldn't attempt to, er, strike again under these conditions."

"Why would he want to?" Millie asked, bewilderment and fear in her voice.

"How do you know it's a he?" Vince said gruffly.

"Why kill Mr. Hysinger anyway?" Jerry wanted to know. "Who benefits?"

They were still mulling that over when the church door roared open, letting in a blast of rainy wind. "Why didn't you light the candles?" Ingvald asked them.

Deb laughed shortly. "Candles. We are in a church, aren't we?" No one had thought of it.

Ingvald and Lars had brought oilskin-wrapped blankets, which Ingvald distributed to the cold and wet tourists as Lars moved around the small interior, lighting the thick candles in their iron sconces. The glow of candlelight on old wood created the illusion of warmth where there was none, and the growing light revealed the five visitors sitting as far apart as possible.

"Takki," said Ingvald with a smile. "I knew you'd be all right."

Sitting majestically at the base of the altar, Takki looked out at them through slitted eyes. She was the only dry one in the place.

Vince huddled miserably in his blanket. "Some vacation."

Jerry said, "The road to Lillehammer . . . where does it go in the other direction?"

Lars answered him. "It goes to small lake. No houses." Ingvald got a whiff of his breath. Lars was a good maintenance worker but not much good with people; as soon as the tourists had showed up, he'd retreated to his bottle.

Deb made a suggestion. "I say we try for Lillehammer. The longer we wait here, the more chance the river will have to flood."

Ingvald stood in front of the altar and faced them. "It has already flooded. I called the police in Lillehammer. They instructed me to keep you here until they can get through."

"Keep us here?" Jerry raised both eyebrows. "You can't keep us here if we want to leave."

This part was touchy; Ingvald had to make sure everyone understood. "Excuse me, I have the authority to make arrests," he said. "All directors of state preserves do. There have been problems elsewhere with public drunkenness and vandalism."

"Oh?" Charlotte smiled at him sweetly. "And how many arrests have *you* made?"

"None." Ingvald let his eyes travel over them. "You will be my first."

They got the message. Millie said, "Then we'll have to stay here . . . until the water recedes. How long will that take?"

"We need wait only until the storm passes. Then the police will send a boat up the river."

"Well, that's not too bad," Millie said, determined to find some bright spot.

Deb asked, "Any idea how long this storm will last?"

"No. The phone went dead before I could ask." Ingvald took out a notebook and pencil he'd picked up from his office. "Please, information you give me now will save the police time later. Three of you were employees of Mr. Hysinger, is that correct? What is the name of his company?"

They all stared at him. "You've never heard of Hysinger Furnaces?" Vince demanded.

They were here to sell furnaces? "Your full names and addresses, please."

True Americans, they all insisted Ingvald call them by their first names and assumed he would welcome the same familiarity in return. Hysinger Furnaces' corporate headquarters were located in Chicago, where three of the suspects lived. Ingvald no longer thought of them as tourists.

Jerry Swann was vice-president in charge of marketing. His wife Deb ran an art gallery in Chicago that she oh-so-cleverly called Swann's Way. Charlotte Evers was the company's director of statistical analysis. She was married to a cellist in the Chicago Symphony Orchestra, which was currently playing in Rome—the reason Charlotte's husband had not accompanied them to Norway.

Vince Taggart managed the St. Louis branch of the company, so he and Millie were residents of Missouri. Millie Taggart was what the Americans so dismissively called a housewife. And almost unconsciously Ingvald had pretty much dismissed her as a viable suspect. Fiftyish, a little on the plump side, she walked as if her feet hurt her. Not exactly a daring axe-murderer type. Besides, Millie was the only one who seemed genuinely upset that a man had died. The others were all thinking of their own skins.

Hysinger had bought out a business called A. R. Nordstrom Company, a heating supplies concern based in Oslo. The buyout had been friendly; Nordstrom would become Hysinger's Norwegian branch.

"And possibly even more than that," Charlotte added. "Hysinger was considering making Nordstrom his European headquarters. More than just a branch managership was involved here."

Jerry waved a hand dismissively. "That was just talk, Charlotte."

"You think so?" She smiled slyly: *I know something you don't know.*

Ingvald watched them carefully. There was more than just money at stake here. Ego, prestige. Status. "Hysinger was going to put one of you in charge of the Norwegian operation? Is that why he was killed?"

"That doesn't make any sense," Deb snapped. "Why kill the goose that lays the golden eggs?"

"Unless he had made his choice," Ingvald pointed out. "If he informed one of you that he or she was no longer on the running—ah." He corrected himself. "*In* the running. But if Hysinger were dead, then no one need know the killer had been passed over. Who will decide now who is in charge of the Norwegian branch?"

Jerry said, "That'll be up to the board of directors. Or else they'll appoint a new CEO and let *him* decide."

"Or her," Charlotte murmured.

"So the killer would still have a chance at the job, you see," Ingvald concluded. "With Hysinger out of the way, there'd still be the possibility of promotion. Perhaps Hysinger had even fired the killer. Perhaps the killer saw getting rid of Hysinger as the only way to save his career."

"That lets me out, then," Vince said. "I didn't even want the damned job."

Deb hooted. "Like hell you didn't! We've all seen you play coy before, Vince."

"I tell ya, I didn't want it," Vince insisted. "No offense, Ingvald, but I don't want to live here."

Charlotte looked thoughtful. "You didn't want the managership of the St. Louis branch either—but somehow you let Hysinger talk you into it."

Jerry's eyes widened. "That's right . . . you said you didn't want to live in Missouri. I remember."

"That was different. Hey, what is this? How come you're all fingering *me*?"

Lars was standing by the door with his arms folded; he and Ingvald exchanged a look as the five Americans quarreled among themselves. Ingvald felt a small head butting against his leg; Takki had been ignored for too long. The man sat down in the first pew; the cat jumped up on the seat next to him to make it easier for him to scratch behind her ears.

The five suspects had argued themselves into a state of sullen silence. Ingvald picked up his notebook again. From the time he'd left Hysinger in the long hall to the time they all gathered by the limousine couldn't have been more than twenty-five minutes or half an hour. He'd spent that time looking for the Americans, until he finally came upon Vince and Millie sitting on the steps of the *stabbur*. But one of them had used the time to kill Hysinger. Could Vince have murdered a man and then calmly sat down and had a cigarette with his wife?

But he hadn't been calm, Ingvald remembered. *He'd been arguing with Millie.*

The wind was rattling the wooden shutters at the windows with a violence that made all of them uneasy. Lars moved quietly from one window to the next, checking the latches.

Ingvald turned sideways in the pew so he could face the others. "Now you will please tell me where you were in the thirty minutes before I found Hysinger's body. Everyplace you went. We start with Mrs. Taggart."

"Millie," she corrected automatically. "Well, I spent some time right here, in the church."

"How long, please?"

"Oh, ten minutes, about."

"Did anyone else come in?"

"No, no one. Then I went into that funny little storage building. I was looking out at that tiny balcony when I saw Vince coming. You remember, we were having a smoke when you found us. Why does a storage building have a balcony?"

Ingvald said, "It's strictly ornamental. The people who lived here thought even a storage facility deserved to be decorative. Now then, Mr. Taggart—Vince."

"Oh, hell, I don't know where I was," Vince said. "I looked into two or three of the buildings. These people sure were small, weren't they? Small rooms, small furniture . . . I got claustrophobic and went outside and just wandered around until I saw Millie poking her head out on that balcony."

"You never went into the long hall?"

"That's where Hysinger was killed? Naw. And I didn't see anybody go in, either."

A crash of thunder made them all jump; the storm was still going strong. Ingvald quickly asked Charlotte what she had been doing during the crucial half-hour.

She shrugged. "You know what I was doing. I was looking for the others. I found Jerry and Deb and you found Vince and Millie."

"Did you look in the *stabbur* . . . the storage building?"

Charlotte frowned. "I think that was one of the places I checked early. Millie must not have gotten there yet."

"Where did you find Jerry and Deb?"

"Oh, Jerry was wandering around looking lost and Deb was in one of the homes."

"I was not lost," Jerry said with irritation. "I didn't actually go into any of the buildings. I walked around the perimeter of the village—I was more interested in the architecture of the place."

"Did you see any of the others?"

"Not a soul. I must have just missed, er, everybody. Then Charlotte found me and told me we had to leave."

"But you already knew you had to leave," Ingvald pointed out. "I had told you so myself, before I went to speak to Hysinger."

"Sure, but we'd come all this way and I wanted to get a quick look before we left."

That sounded reasonable. Ingvald looked at Jerry's wife. "Deb?"

She said, "I spent all my time in the same home. I don't know how to identify it . . . it has an almost rococo mantelpiece, and a hand-carved wooden cradle . . ."

Takki's house. "I know the one." Ingvald suppressed a smile at her use of the term *hand-carved*; how else would a cradle be carved in the Middle Ages?

"Well, I stayed there the whole time," Deb said. "That place is just full of goodies! Ingvald, are any of those items for sale? The cradle, that enormous wooden spoon with the elaborate carved handle—"

"I am sorry, nothing is for sale. Everything here is the property of the state."

Unhearing, she said, "You know I run an art gallery." Deb stood up and made her way back toward the church door, clutching her blanket around her. Lars moved aside to give her room as she ran her hand down a painted door panel that showed some mythical plant blooming out of an urn poised precariously on an abstract geometrical design, a design that was repeated in reverse at the top of the panel. "Look at that!" Deb said appreciatively. "Do you know what I could get for that in Chicago?"

Vince growled. "Fer gawd's sake, Deb, the man's trying to conduct a murder investigation!"

"Yes, Deb," Millie agreed. "This is not the time."

Ingvald asked, "Did anyone else come in while you were there?"

"Just Charlotte. I left with her."

Ingvald regarded her closely as she stood possessively by the door. "Are you sure you never left that one building?"

"Yes, of course I'm sure."

"Not even once?"

All restless movement stopped; the others sensed something in the wind. "I told you," Deb said, "I stayed there the whole time until Charlotte showed up."

Ingvald dropped a hand on the napping Takki, whom he'd been looking for as well as for the Americans. "I checked that building. No one was there. No one."

Deb turned white. "You must be mistaken! Did . . . did you check that room in the back? I was—oh. Wait a minute. I did leave to go to the restroom, over by the office. But I wasn't gone more than five minutes and I went right straight back to the same building."

A silence grew. Then: "You know," Charlotte drawled, "that rest-room story might be a tad more believable if you'd thought of it *before* Ingvald said he'd checked that building out."

Vince snorted. "A little credibility problem there, Deb."

"I had to pee!" Deb cried. "That makes me a murder suspect?"

Jerry exploded. "This is absurd! Do you really think Deb could swing a big heavy axe like that? That's ridiculous."

Lars surprised everyone by speaking up. "You do not have to swing the axe. Just let it fall. The iron head does all the work."

The Americans were momentarily taken aback, but then Jerry persisted. "I doubt if Deb could even lift it."

"How do you know the axe is big and heavy, Jerry?" Ingvald asked quietly. "If you never went into the long hall, as you say— then how do you know how big the axe is?"

Jerry sighed impatiently. "You're telling me the axe was tiny and light? *All* axes are big and heavy, Ingvald. I doubt that even in the Middle Ages they made them any different."

Again, a reasonable-sounding response. Jerry was quite good at that. And that made Ingvald suspicious. And while Jerry had come to his wife's defense . . . he'd not done so immediately. But that meant nothing; maybe he just enjoyed seeing her squirm.

Ingvald stood up to stretch his legs. Deb had indeed been in Tak-ki's house; otherwise she wouldn't have known about the cradle and the other things there. But how *long* had she been there? She could have slipped in right before Charlotte found her. There would have been time to kill Hysinger first.

In fact, they all would have had time. Even Charlotte could have gone back to the long hall and done the deed while she was sup-posed to be looking for the others. She and Hysinger had not seemed very friendly when Ingvald walked in on them. Jerry and Vince also had the time. Even Millie, although Ingvald didn't believe she was guilty. For all his questioning, Ingvald had not been able to remove a single name from the suspects list.

"I've got a headache," Millie announced.

"Because you're hungry," Vince told her. "Hell, *I'm* hungry. Hey, Ingvald—you got any vending machines in that office of yours?"

Ingvald said no. "But we can make coffee."

"Coffee," Charlotte said, her eyes lighting up.

Lars cleared his throat. "I have *bakverk* from my wife."

"A kind of pastry," Ingvald explained.

"Oh, that sounds marvelous," Millie said.

"Yes, it does," Charlotte agreed. "We all need something on our stomachs."

That was an idiom not familiar to Ingvald, and he had a fleeting vision of the five Americans lying flat on their backs in the pews, balancing pastries on their stomachs. Lars was shrugging into one of the oilskins they'd brought in wrapped around the blankets, preparing to brave the storm in search of *bakverk* and coffee.

"Thank you, Lars," Ingvald said. Lars grunted and left—probably glad to be out of there. Deb closed the paneled door behind him.

They were all on their feet now except Millie, moving around in the limited space with their blankets wrapped about them toga-style, trying to get their circulation going. It would take Lars a while to brew up enough coffee for seven people, and they were all fidgety anyway; walking was good. Millie's face was pinched; Ingvald wished he'd thought to tell Lars to bring back some aspirin.

A creaking floorboard woke Takki up. She yawned a little and stretched a little and then noticed all the people moving about. She stood up on her hind legs to get a better view, resting her front paws lightly on the back of the pew.

Ingvald moved over to a window and lifted the latch. He slowly eased one of the shutters open until he felt a blast of wet air in his face. Even so, the wind was not as strong as it had been earlier, and there'd been no sound of thunder for some time. The worst of the storm had passed. The rain was still coming down solidly; it smelled clean and good. Ingvald closed the shutter and dropped the latch.

He leaned his back against the closed shutter, watching Takki watch the Americans. There was another mystery there. The killer had closed the door when he or she left, shutting the cat inside. But what was Takki doing there in the first place? The long hall was not one of her special places in the village; she'd gone in earlier that day only because that's where Ingvald was going.

But why did she go back a second time, the time Hysinger was killed? The only notice Hysinger had taken of the cat was to push her out of the way. Takki wouldn't go back to a man who'd dismissed her like that; some cats might, but not Takki. There seemed to be only one explanation: someone had picked her up and carried her inside. Someone who just liked cats. And there was only one of the Americans who had paid any attention to Takki at all.

Jerry.

Jerry the smooth talker, who always had a sensible explanation for what he did. Jerry who claimed he'd never been inside the long hall but seemed familiar with the murder weapon. Jerry who'd been led to think the Norwegian branch was his. Jerry, whom Vince had called the "weak sister" in the three-way race for the new job.

There'd been remarkably little blood; the killer either hadn't been splattered or had had time to go to the restroom and clean up. But clearly it was an impulse murder—not planned ahead of time. Had Jerry gone berserk when Hysinger told him he wasn't getting the Norwegian branch? Had he just grabbed the first thing that came to hand—the axe—and hit Hysinger? And then, realizing what he'd done, he'd wandered around outside "looking lost," as Charlotte said, until she found him. It fit; Jerry could have closed the door in a trance, automatically, not thinking about it. And Takki had been trapped inside with the dead man.

Ingvald didn't have the slightest notion of what to do about it. The police would never arrest a man because a preserve director said his cat wouldn't have gone into a certain building on her own. An impulse murderer might not have had the presence of mind to wipe fingerprints off the axe handle, but Ingvald wasn't counting much on prints. The handles of those axes had been partially wrapped with leather thongs, to make gripping easier; it was doubtful that enough smooth surface was left to take a print.

A thumping at the door announced Lars's return; Vince let him in. Lars was laden with thermos jugs, paper cups, pastry, even milk for Takki. And he'd thought to bring aspirin for Millie. "Wind's dying down," Lars said.

The Americans were soon gulping down hot coffee and devouring

Lars's pastry. *You'd think they'd never missed a meal before*, Ingvald mused to himself. He fed a little piece of pastry to Takki but didn't eat any himself.

Then they waited, talking only desultorily or not at all. Ingvald and Lars kept a close watch on the weather. Once the wind was gone, the swollen Lågen River would be less dangerous to navigate; the Lillehammer police could well be here before morning. The candles were burning low in the church, but a supply of fresh ones was kept stored behind the altar.

Ingvald left the weather-watching to Lars and sat down in one of the pews, twisting sideways to stretch out his legs on the seat beside him. He'd barely got settled when Takki leaped up to his lap and kneaded his stomach with her paws a few times. Ingvald dropped a gentle hand on her back and started to stroke her—and scratched himself.

Curious, he parted her long fur and found what looked like a silver earring. Takki hissed, but Ingvald held her still until he'd worked it loose. It was an earring, all right, one of those that clamp on; Takki's fur had caught in the hinge.

Ingvald's heart thudded as he realized what that meant. One might argue that Takki could have picked up the earring anywhere, that it had been dropped on her or she'd lain on it just about anyplace. But he didn't think so; there just hadn't been time. When Ingvald had opened the door to the long hall, Takki had scooted out between his legs and out of sight. The cat would have known a storm was coming; she'd have headed straight for the nearest shelter—which was the church. The fact that Takki remained dry while all the people got soaking wet meant she didn't linger waiting for the rain to start. No, she'd acquired the earring in the long hall.

Ingvald looked at the earring cupped in his hand. Two intertwining silver spirals, a double helix; very distinctive. Casually he turned his head to look at the three women in the church. Both of Millie's pearl earrings were in place. Neither Deb nor Charlotte was wearing earrings.

Deb or Charlotte.

Charlotte had been in the long hall talking to Hysinger when

Ingvald went in, so she could have lost the earring then. Ingvald closed his eyes and tried to visualize the scene, but gave up in frustration. He just couldn't remember whether she'd been wearing earrings or not. If she had lost it then, innocently, then he was back to square one, as the Americans liked to say. But if she'd gone back later and lost it then, or if the earring belonged to Deb . . .

Ingvald looked at Millie. The pinched look was gone from her face; the aspirin had done its job. He decided to take a chance on her. Easing Takki from his lap, Ingvald stood up and went back to where Millie was sitting.

He bent down and said into her ear, low, so only she could hear: "Will you please come with me to the altar, where the light is better? There's something I want to show you." She looked startled, but agreed readily enough.

The church was small enough that his speaking to Millie could not go unnoticed. All eyes were upon them as they made their way to the altar.

When they were there, Ingvald said, "Please keep your voice low." He opened his hand. "Do you know whom this belongs to?"

She didn't even have to stop to think. "Why, that's Deb's. Where did you get it?"

"Are you sure? Could it possibly belong to Charlotte?"

Millie shook her head firmly. "I have never once seen Charlotte Evers wearing earrings. Not once."

Ingvald felt like kissing her. Instead he thanked her and asked her to return to her seat. Then he went over to the window where Lars was watching and told his assistant to go stand by the church door in case anyone tried to bolt.

The Americans were all watching him expectantly. Ingvald took a deep breath, steadying himself to make his first arrest. He walked down the narrow center aisle until he reached Deb's pew. He cleared his throat and said, "Would you care to change your story about never going into the long hall?"

She was indignant. "No, of course not! Why should I?"

"Because you left a calling card behind." He held up the earring. "That's not mine," Deb said quickly.

Charlotte got up for a closer look. "Yes, it is, Deb. You were wearing those this morning. What did you do with the other one? Throw it away?"

"You're imagining things! I ought to know my own earrings!"

Ingvald felt an enormous relief. If she'd said yes, that was her earring but she'd noticed it missing when they first got here—well, he wouldn't have a leg to stand on. But by lying, she'd only dug herself in deeper. Ingvald said, "Two people have now identified this earring as yours. You were in the long hall and you lost your earring there. That places you at the scene of the crime. That is sufficient for an arrest."

"You're crazy!" Deb screamed. "I didn't kill him!"

Ingvald stood up straight. "I am now arresting you for murder." That didn't sound right, but he couldn't remember what words he was supposed to use.

"Jesus H. Christ." Vince's mouth was hanging open.

Frightened, Deb looked at her husband. "Jerry?"

But he was already on his feet, protesting. "Ingvald, you're out of your mind! Deb didn't kill anyone. You call that evidence, one flimsy little earring? The *real* police will laugh in your face." He turned to his wife. "Don't worry, Deb, they won't even charge you. And if they do, I'll get the best lawyer this country has to offer." Back to Ingvald. "Better think what you're doing, Ingvald."

"You'll *what*?" Deb said to Jerry, rising from her seat.

"I don't know Norwegian law," Jerry went on, "but I'm sure you have something equivalent to our false arrest. Do you want to get sued, Ingvald?"

"Wait a minute, wait a minute," Deb interrupted. "Did you say you'd get me the best *lawyer*?"

"The very best there is. Don't worry, now, you—"

"Why, you son of a bitch," Deb said, furious. "You're going to let me be arrested?"

Jerry was making little calming gestures with his hands. "Now, Deb, don't say anything until I get the lawyer. I mean, don't say *anything*. Just keep quiet and everything will be all right."

Right then Deb looked as if she was capable of murder, with her husband as her intended victim. "Oh, no, you don't. I've put up with a lot from you, Jerry, but now you go too far! I am not going to prison for you!"

"Now, Deb, think what you're saying—"

She turned to face Ingvald. "Jerry hit Hysinger with that axe. I was there, I saw him do it, and I'll testify that I saw him do it!" Jerry moaned and sank down on a pew.

So it was Jerry after all? Well, well. Everyone was staring at the accused man. "In that case," Ingvald said to Jerry, "I am now arresting *you* for murder." He looked back at Deb. "You are still under arrest. You knew who killed Hysinger and lied about it. I'm sure there's a law against that."

"Good God," said Charlotte. "What happened?"

Jerry buried his face in his hands, didn't answer. Deb said, "We went to see if Hysinger had made up his mind about who'd get the job. He had. He told Jerry he was out of the running." She sighed. "He said the job was Vince's if he wanted it and Charlotte's if he didn't. But Jerry was out."

"*I don't want the goddamned job!*" Vince roared. "How many times do I have to say it?"

"Then what?" Ingvald asked Deb.

She said, "Jerry went nuts, completely nuts . . . that's the only way to describe it. I've never seen him like that. He was like a wild man. He pulled that axe off the wall and buried it in Hysinger's skull."

Millie was sniffling. "Oh, this is terrible, just terrible!"

Ingvald asked Deb, "What did you do?"

"I tried to stop him, I grabbed one arm . . . but I don't think he even knew I was there." She touched her ear. "That must be when I lost the earring, during that useless little tussle. It was all so fast . . . anyway, then I ran. I was terrified! I ran until I was out of sight of that building, and then I ducked into one of the little homes . . . the one with the cradle and the other nice things. Then I just sat there, trying to think what to do."

"You should have stuck together," Charlotte said dryly. "Alibi each other." Deb shot her a look of pure venom.

Ingvald said to Jerry, "Then what did *you* do?"

Jerry sat slumped in his pew, not looking at anyone. Unbidden, Lars had moved into the pew behind him and stood there towering over him. Jerry glanced over his shoulder at him. "I was in a daze," Jerry said to Ingvald. "I don't know where I went. I was just wandering until Charlotte found me."

Ingvald nodded, satisfied that the picture was now complete. "Then the storm intervened. When I was at last able to start questioning you, you'd had time to put your thoughts together. And Deb had decided to say nothing."

"I hadn't *completely* decided," Deb said in her own defense. "But I hadn't had a chance to talk to Jerry alone since . . . since it happened."

A silence developed. Then Jerry looked up at Ingvald, a sadly wistful smile playing around his lips. "Aren't you going to put the cuffs on me?"

Ingvald was embarrassed. "I don't have any."

"That's all right," Deb snapped. "He's not going anywhere."

There was no more to be said. The other four Americans all avoided looking at Jerry, and Charlotte was even smiling. Ingvald thought he knew why: with Jerry arrested for murder and Vince withdrawn from the competition, the new job was hers by default.

Less than an hour later, Lars opened the church door and announced, "Rain has stopped."

The three innocent Americans practically fell over themselves getting outside, freed at last. Lars planted himself in the open doorway of the church, a warning to Jerry and Deb not to try running. Outdoors, the cool air was heavy with moisture, and broken tree limbs and other detritus of the storm lay scattered on the muddy ground; the only one who minded the slippery footing was Takki. The blackness brought by the storm was completely gone; the familiar light of Norway's night sky was back.

"There's your midnight sun, Vince," Millie said.

He wrapped an arm around her and gave her a hug. "Some vacation, huh? Missouri's gonna look damned good."

Charlotte drew Ingvald aside. "I was impressed by the way you handled this problem," she said. "You had none of the resources of the police at your disposal, but you still managed to arrive at the truth. You were *very* impressive."

"Thank you." He didn't know what else to say.

"When this new branch in Oslo gears up, we're going to need a security chief. Someone who can think on his feet. I'm going to recommend you for the job. You're wasted out here, Ingvald."

He wasn't expecting anything like that. "Ah, I thank you, but I must decline. My life is here."

"Don't you ever want a little change in your life?" she asked, surprised. "You'd be making a lot of money working for us. You'd be in the city, right at the center of what's happening—not stuck out in the middle of nowhere. Do you live alone?"

Thinking the question impertinent, he nevertheless answered it. "I live with Takki."

"The cat? Way out here with nothing but a cat for company? What kind of life is that?"

"It is my kind of life. Thank you for the offer, but the answer is no."

She raised an eyebrow. "You prefer cats to people?"

Ingvald smiled. "The cat is never vulgar," he said.

The Shrine of Eleanor

Gillian Roberts

Nothing was as irritating as not finding a good objection to any idea her husband had. "But . . ." Eleanor Morris spluttered. "But . . ." Still, for the first time ever, her cupboard of objections, complaints, and oppositions was bare.

"It's a lifelong dream," Frederick Morris said. "You know that. Paradise on earth, they say. I want to see it."

"But . . ." Eleanor spluttered.

"It's our time, El," he said. "We've scrimped and saved and put off so many good things, luxuries . . ."

The boat. That's what he was talking about. The stupid sailboat he'd wanted for years. All those outdoor conventions he dragged her through, even the talk about building his own boat. Was it her fault she got seasick? A boat was impractical, not for the likes of them, and sailing, a waste of time that could be better spent taking care of chores and meeting responsibilities. Eventually, Frederick understood, or at least stopped talking about it. Until now.

Or, good Lord, was it about the stupid RV? See the USA, all that nonsense. No way was she going to be imprisoned in a metal box with wheels on its outside and Frederick on its inside. Who needed it, anyway? No place like home was her philosophy. She hated the funny way people talked in other parts of the country, hated the weird things they cooked, the stupid ways they built their houses. And why leave when you could see everything you needed on TV anyway?

". . . and no vacations while Mickeyboy was growing up or since."

"Nonsense—you always took your two weeks off, even though you could have gotten time and a half if you'd skipped them."

"But we stayed home. Painted the house or fixed the decking, which was important, of course, but all the same . . . now the house is painted, the decks are fine, the boy's a grown man, and I want to see Bali before I die. Let's do it."

"But . . ." She just plain didn't want to go to Bali. Didn't, for that matter, want to go anywhere with Frederick. Didn't want Frederick. "What about your cats?"

"Margaret told me she'd gladly take care of them while we're gone."

"She'll steal them, Frederick." Not that Eleanor would care. "She'll alienate their affections."

"Nonsense. She loves them. They'll be happy, and even if they run home here by mistake, she lives down the street, so she'll know where to get them. The Mickeys will love it."

"They'll be spoiled rotten by the time we get back."

"Cats are born spoiled. What's Margaret going to do that I don't already do? I've always had a soft spot for my Mickeys."

She gritted her teeth. His Mickeys were pampered jerks, lording it around the house and eating only gourmet delicacies, costing them a fortune.

Everything about the Mickeys irritated her, starting with their names. Forty-two years ago, when she was a newlywed, a tiny mewling black and white stray that gave Eleanor the willies, but that Frederick found charming, the way he found every cat on God's earth charming, appeared at their door. He named it Mickey, because of its coloring. "Mickey Cat, not Mouse, get it?" he'd said. "See the little white gloves?"

The Mickey joke was one of many early clues that her groom was not as much of a prize catch as she'd thought he might be.

And she didn't like cats. They shed. They got fleas. They ruined furniture. And they liked Frederick, not her.

He'd named every cat since then—and there had been numbers of them—Mickey. Mickey Two, Mickey Three, and so forth. It didn't matter if they were black with white gloves. They were Mickeys. Currently, Mickey Eleven and Twelve lived with them, and Frederick still found the names amusing and the cats adorable, and she still found Frederick, his cats, and their names repugnant.

He even called their son Mickey even though his name was Stephen. At least there was no need to number him. One pregnancy and childbirth was more than enough for Eleanor. Their one and only offspring was called by his father Mickeyboy.

Not that it mattered any longer what they'd called him. Stephen-Mickey, no longer anything like a boy, lived fourteen hundred miles away. Their relationship consisted of his having his dreadful wife send Christmas and anniversary gifts. Always in bad taste.

Oh, he visited when Frederick had the heart attack and surgery, she'd grant him that. And he even brought that witch of a wife and his ninny of an eldest daughter, but they left the second Frederick was on the mend.

She didn't care. Stephen had turned out to be too much like his father. Spineless, ambitionless, impractical.

And in absolute truth, she could understand his leave-taking when his father was disconnected from the machines. She, too, liked Frederick hooked up and inert. Not that she wished him ill— she wasn't really that type—but when the doctor said that her husband was in grave danger, that his heart attack had been serious, that all his gaskets and valves and pipes had to be repaired, she hadn't been exactly distraught. There'd been instead a giddy reaction the nurse called "nerves." Eleanor would have called it dizzy relief. Her marriage to a man with one stupid joke and jackets covered with cat hair had gone on long enough. It had seemed that Nature agreed and was granting her a reprieve.

Except Nature reneged and Frederick recuperated. He became a fanatic about diet and exercise and keeping a benign outlook on life. "Healthier than ever," the doctor said.

Forty-two years tied to such a man was excessive. And the thought of traveling halfway around the world with him to a stupid island where the women barely covered their parts was unbearable.

"It's too far," she told her husband. "Bad for your heart. Too dangerous. The doctor would never allow it."

"But I already asked and he said it was fine. Just to take it easy, take it in steps, don't overtax myself. So I thought we could stop in Hawaii, and Hong Kong, and Singapore. And maybe stay awhile in Java, too. Just saying the names of the places makes me need to sit down! Exotic ports, different cultures, a whole new world, Ellie."

"Ridiculous," she said. "At our age—"

"At our age we *have* to do things like this. We should have been doing them all along. But now—when else are we going to live out our fantasies, the things we've dreamed of all our lives?"

"I dreamed of staying put and finally getting some peace and quiet!"

"Bali is the very heart of peace and quiet," he answered.

"Not when it involves packing and getting on and off planes and winding up in a heathen country with bare-breasted—"

"They cover themselves up nowadays," he said.

She thought he sounded sad about that.

"They aren't heathen. They have their own blend of Hinduism, Buddhism, and animism. It's quite a lovely religion, too. It's a different world there—not just far away, but different. For starters, art isn't a separate thing—it's part of their religion, of their daily life. After the rice fields, they dance, they sing, they play music and make masks."

Another jab at her, just because he had once had delusions about being a singer. He had a nice-enough voice, she would admit that, but show business was no profession for a married man, particularly one with a child on the way, so he'd done the right thing and gotten the job at the plant. Was that her fault? Was she to blame that there wasn't time to work and sing, the way he said the Balinese did? That she needed his help in the evenings instead of having him gallivant off to perform in a bar or at a wedding?

"The Balinese live differently than we do," Frederick said in his mild voice. "Less competition, less stress. It would be good for me to be with them, to learn from them. Therapeutic. And good for you too."

"Me? What are you insinuating? I don't need to travel halfway around the world to gape at happy-go-lucky natives who lounge around singing all day."

"They don't. They work the rice fields, work hard, but they—"

"You listen now, Frederick. I don't need to get away to escape stress. I wouldn't have any stress in my life if only you'd grow up and stop indulging in these ridiculous flights of imagination."

Frederick's chin looked solid and set. Forty-two years and she had never seen his face wear that expression before. "I am quite grown up," he said in his customary quiet voice, although it sounded steelier, more solid than she remembered. "And I want to see Bali before I am so thoroughly and completely grown up that I'm dead."

She tried out different avenues of protest. The trip was too expensive, she said, but he asked what they were supposed to do with their savings, anyway. To tell the truth, every time she watched the Home Shopping Network, she saw lots of fine ideas for those savings, but Frederick was becoming too selfish to understand.

She relented a bit and said she'd consider going if they were part of a tour. Travel seemed safer, easier, and cheaper—and less confined to Frederick, although she didn't say that part—if they were in a group.

"No," he said. "I want to be on my own. On our own. All my life I've felt like somebody on a package tour. I've been one of the gang, the guy who goes along. But not this time. No leaders, no itinerary, no rules, no time limits."

He already lived with no time limits. Almost with no clocks. They'd tossed away the alarm clock after the surgery. The doctor had said that he was to wake up gently, with no shock to his heart.

Worst thing you could do for the heart was to be jolted awake. Not that they had to be up at any particular time, but it wasn't right to live this way. Loll around, wake up whenever. Wasn't decent.

"I don't want to talk to people I don't like." He was still going on about why he wouldn't be part of a tour.

She faked pain in her ankles and feet, claimed arthritic damage that made walking painful if not impossible. The doctor—in front of Frederick—said that the equatorial heat of Bali would probably do her aches and pains a world of good.

She insisted that the diet in Idonesia would kill Frederick. After all, he was supposed to eat low-fat foods, wasn't he? Lord knows, his damnable cardiac cooking requirements took up half her days, and what did those heathen people know about health?

"Did you ever once see a fat Balinese?" Frederick asked her.

She had never once seen a Balinese of any shape, so she kept her lips clamped together.

"Their mainstay is rice, which is fine, and vegetables, and tiny bits of meat. Tiny. And fruit. A perfect diet. Much better for me than ham and eggs or American take-out."

He was casting aspersions at her cooking. The doctor had made her change every single thing she knew and liked about food, just for Frederick's sake. Now, because of him, they weren't permitted to have any of her favorite foods. And no rest for the weary cook. No fast foods. Frederick required slow food. Her food, slowly made by hand. Frederick got to retire and lord it over her and her very kitchen, while she slaved on without a break. It just wasn't fair.

When they reached an impasse concerning the trip, Frederick resorted to guerilla warfare, telling everybody he met about his dream and the difficulties he was having attaining it, enlisting their support. This was extremely abnormal behavior on his part—he had never been one to complain or air their dirty laundry. She suggested that he was losing his mind, and insisted he see a therapist.

The psychologist said he was doing the right thing, letting out his feelings. That, in fact, bottling them up all along until now had helped give him a heart attack.

In the end, exhausted, she realized Frederick had boxed her in so that she had no choice. She had to give in. This was not a form of behavior she had much experience with. Her giving-in muscles were flabby from disuse, and ached constantly. It pained her to see Frederick tote home travel books. It gave her psychic muscle spasms to watch him outline itineraries, clip hints from travel columns, and collect ideas from anyone he met who'd been in the general vicinity of Indonesia.

And although she'd hoped that time itself would take its toll, nature proved perverse. Instead of wearing himself out, Frederick seemed to gain strength and vitality with each day that brought them closer to the distant island world. "I feel young again," he'd tell people who inquired after his health. "I feel reborn. Invigorated. I have something to look forward to. The only bad part is leaving my Mickeys, but maybe they need a vacation, too, and I know they'll be well taken care of. I'm practically delirious about this." Eleanor thought that delirious people should be put in straitjackets and carted off.

And then one day, when the lady who lived behind them once again asked Frederick about this wonderful trip of a lifetime he was planning, Eleanor began to think in a new direction, emphasis of that lifetime of his, and that trip of it.

Okay, she thought. Fine. If he was so eager to see Bali before he died, she'd grant him his wish. Both his wishes. He'd see Bali and die. Having had no other trips, and having no life beyond this one, this would definitely be the trip of *his* lifetime.

Frederick made all their arrangements and was pleased when he saw Eleanor dipping into the travel books stacked on the coffee table. She soon gave up, however. The books weren't sufficiently detailed for her purposes. She would have to wait until she was there and she got the lay of the land before she could finalize ideas.

Eventually, they packed a suitcase apiece with lightweight clothing and took along a satchelful of Frederick's heart medications. They stopped mail and newspaper delivery, moved Mickeys Eleven and Twelve to Margaret's, locked the house, gave the neighbor who'd promised to water the philodendron a key, and set off. Frederick was elated and couldn't stop talking about what was ahead.

Eleanor was exhausted by the preparations, and by worry over the future of her philodendron.

Hawaii was nice enough, although Eleanor wasn't one for sitting around and doing nothing on a beach. Hong Kong was neon lights, crowds, and skyscrapers, and she'd seen those things before. Singapore was boring and scary, with fines for things like chewing gum on the street or not flushing a public toilet. Eleanor, who always flushed and never chewed, was nonetheless glad to get out of there.

They tried Java, particularly two enormous monuments, one Buddhist, one Hindu, built God knew when and still partly in rubble. Frederick could not get over the reassembled parts, the carvings, the massive size of the places, the years and years it had taken pretechnological people to build them, the story of the Buddha painstakingly carved in panels that spanned the huge monument.

Eleanor had nothing but contempt for the places. Their stone steps were so uneven and dangerous that her feet hurt nearly as much as she said they did, the figures in the carvings silly nonsense—a man with an elephant's head, of all things. What was the point?

They went to the famous Bird Market, where, as Eleanor made a point of saying loudly, almost everything but birds were being sold. Peculiar foods she wouldn't touch with a stick and hideous Komodo dragons and panther kittens—over which Frederick, of course, went gaga. And as for the birds—most of them were *pigeons.* "For God's sake!" she shouted. "I had to travel around the world to see pigeons in cages?"

"Very expensive," the guide said, with reverence. He explained how they had contests, the pigeons wearing whistles in their tail feathers so that their swoops and arcs made lovely airborne sounds. A truly excellent racing pigeon could cost a year's salary.

"Back home, we call them rats with wings," Eleanor said.

So they left for Bali, a short flight away. "This better be good," Eleanor said. "I've had it with people who talk funny and can't build a smooth staircase—"

"Those steps were twelve hundred years old," Frederick said. "People's feet wore those stones down."

"That isn't my problem," Eleanor said. "They should fix 'em!"

Bali would have no wretched stairs she had to climb, Frederick promised. And the cab ride to their hotel was pleasant enough, she admitted as they drove through green and flowering lanes. They passed a group of women in bright, tight sarongs. They wore towering tiers of fruit and flower offerings on their head.

"How beautiful," Frederick said with awe. "Just as it's been for thousands of years."

"You'd think by now they'd have heard of shopping carts and tote bags," Eleanor snapped.

And then they arrived at their hotel. Several times she had to warn Frederick to calm down or he'd have another heart attack. He could barely contain himself. "I picked this hotel because it's authentic Balinese," he said. "Right on the rice fields."

She looked at rows of free-standing cottages with thatched roofs and bamboo rails and woven walls and was singularly unimpressed.

And when they got to their room, she became nearly incoherent. "Where is the *bedroom*?" she demanded.

"Here, Madame," the small man in the sarong said with a bow.

"No, I mean—where is the *inside*?"

"Excuse me? This is your room, Madame," he said with another bow. "Deluxe. The bathroom is behind that door."

"This is a *porch!* Frederick, tell him—this is a porch! Ask him where the *room* is!"

Frederick smiled. "This is a sleeping pavilion, Ellie dear," he said. "Surely you see the bed. Balinese homes are built this way. The high ceiling keeps it cooler and breezes can come through the open side. What use would windows be?"

It didn't matter what fancy names he gave it. She knew a porch when she saw one. He had condemned her to an extremely high-ceilinged hut with woven half-walls and no glass or screens or anything—except insects and animals who lived in the woven ceiling and grunted and chirped if she lit the bathroom light at night. And right outside the porch were the rice fields, a grid of squares in various stages of growth and cultivation, separated by raised grassy walkways. She could not believe that she'd come halfway around the world to camp out in an infested hut on a field.

Frederick was enchanted by everything, no matter how ridiculous. "Look there," Frederick said the next morning. He stood at what should have been a window but was instead open space overlooking the rice fields. "The duck herder. I read about that, but it seemed too unbelievable. Never thought I'd see it for myself."

Outside, an ancient man made his way across the rice fields. He carried a pole with a bright banner attached. A flock of brown ducks followed him until he planted his flag in the middle of an empty-looking field. "They'll eat the last bits of loose grain that didn't get harvested," Frederick explained.

The old man walked away. The ducks stayed in the field, near the flag. "They'll stay there all day, until he comes and leads them back," Frederick said. "Isn't that incredible? Isn't it charming? Exactly what I'd hoped for. I don't know if I've ever been happier. I want to stay here forever."

"It already feels like forever," Eleanor snarled. "If I'd wanted to visit a farm, I could have gone to Iowa." Her sleep had been torn to shreds by the bleats and snorts and barks and moos, crows and bellows of dogs, roosters, cows, birds, frogs, and possibly the old man's ducks.

In the light of dawn, with yet another chorus of roosters deafening her, it had become painfully obvious that this unbearable trip—and Frederick—had to be terminated as quickly as possible.

The logistics of ending Frederick were tricky, however. For a moment, she was optimistic about the night noises. The squeaking, squealing barnyard outside had startled her awake a dozen times in precisely the manner that supposedly would do Frederick in.

But the calls of the wild outside their porch did not jolt Frederick. The few times their sounds roused him, he seemed delighted, chuckling at the cackles and caws.

As the days rolled on, hot and boring and impossibly foreign, she searched for other options. Aside from the insanely reckless driving that took place on the main street—the only street, as far as she could tell—Bali was entirely too mild for murder. The people seemed constitutionally incapable of it, with perhaps one serious act of violence a year for the entire country, and that included acts involving foreign visitors.

Eleanor hadn't seen a police officer since she arrived. That was the good news. Surely, if they existed, she could outwit them. They'd be too unpracticed to be much as detectives.

But the people in general were too smiling, too gentle. Eleanor was going to have to be mighty careful if she wasn't going to upset them with sudden moves. She couldn't, for example, simply push Frederick in front of a car, which had been her first idea. The passersby would notice. Nobody rushed, nobody scowled, nobody pretended you were invisible the way they did back home. Plus, the drivers, recklessly insane though they might be, were also tricky and quick-witted and would probably swerve in time.

For one wild moment, she wanted to disguise Frederick as a dog, because they were the single exception to the rule of gentle kindness. Nobody swerved for them. Nobody hurt the dogs deliberately—nobody here seemed to hurt anything deliberately. But neither did drivers try to avoid the mangy wraiths who wandered into the streets. Dogs were considered dirty, earthbound creatures who scavenged for the offerings left outside to appease the wrathful gods each day. It was up to dogs to react quickly and scram.

For a few blissful moments, she imagined stuffing Frederick into a Saint Bernard suit and putting him on the road where he'd be squashed flat by a careening taxi. Of course, she realized with regret, even in a land of reckless drivers and some belief in magic, this would be a stretch.

The long, lean cats who roamed the island, leaping up onto thatched roofs and staring down at Eleanor, were, to Frederick's delight, not reviled the way dogs were. Cats were less earthbound, less crass, more celestial and discriminating, and they were tolerated with affection. And much to Eleanor's disgust, Frederick befriended a gold and white slip of a cat who'd taken to sitting on their porch and keeping them company. He even invented a new and equally dismal joke for this one. It, at least, wasn't called Mickey. It was called "Balicat, you get it? Instead of alley?" Frederick's sense of humor had not improved over the years.

She gritted her teeth and wondered if a person could break another person's neck by swinging a cat directly into the jugular. But she guessed that even if she could, it would be difficult pleading that it had been an accident or a completely innocent act.

She was living on a porch with no walls. She couldn't do anything that would arouse suspicion, raise Frederick's voice, or be observed by somebody gleaning rice out in the fields.

And where they were there were no natural hazards to speak of. At least none that she heard about or saw. They weren't warned against snakes, vipers, wild animals, or black widow spiders. Frederick was rigid about not drinking unpurified water or eating food washed in it, so he didn't even get a stomachache. It was not a land of guns the way home was, so even if she could find one, using it was out of the question, let alone getting somebody else to use it.

She eyed the machetes used to harvest the rice, but they were really too awkward to steal, and what would be her excuse for swinging one anyway?

The days rolled on. They took excursions to black sand beaches, walked the rice fields, watched men painstakingly carve masks. Went to the dance. To many dance performances. Too many. Night after night they sat on uncomfortable chairs around an ancient palace and listened to peculiar music and watched people enact old stories. Frederick was entranced by the diminutive, stylized Balinese dancers.

Eleanor found them excruciating. "They call themselves dancers," she sneered, "and they never lift a foot. Where's the pirouettes, the leaps? What did we pay good money for?"

Of course, Frederick had his defense and explanation. He was always on their side. Again it had to do with earth and sky and good being above, bad below. "The hands," he said. "Watch them. And the eyes. It's a different aesthetic, that's all."

It was no use. She knew what it was really about. It was about ogling dark-haired, dark-eyed, honey-skinned girls. Eleanor knew she looked like a piece of suet in this heat, her blonde hair slicked to her pale forehead. The Balinese didn't even sweat. Watching these performances was about drooling over tiny foreign slips of girls and then not liking good solid American bodies. Thinking she wasn't graceful enough, either, because she couldn't make her hands bend backward.

She was well and truly sick of the dancers and of Frederick and of being compared—even silently—to ten-year-old unsweaty girls. Even the damned cat was slender and the color of light honey, a constant reminder of how large and clumsy she was. She'd watch Frederick snuggle and drift off to sleep, the golden Balinese intruder in his arms and a smile on his face, and she'd feel stranded and betrayed and she'd hate him even more.

One month into their trip, Frederick made an announcement. "I have never been this happy," he said. "I understand why people have always considered this paradise. I want to stay here. Forever. And try as I can, I can't think of any reason to go back."

"The Mickeys," she said.

"Yes. I miss them. But I know they're happy with Margaret. She always adored them, and vice versa. I'm going to write and tell her to keep them and to put the house up for sale."

There was no time left to dither. He had to be gone; and soon, or life as she'd known it would be gone.

And then one morning Frederick decided to visit an old master crafter of instruments, but Eleanor, who could not get used to the sound of the gamelan music in the first place and didn't want to hear what an old man had to say about its creation, refused. "I'm too tired," she said. "All this gallivanting. I'm not one of your ten-year-old dancing girls, Frederick. I don't have endless resources of strength."

He looked as if he understood. "Then rest up, dearest. I'll see you later."

"You mean you'd still go?" she said. "Without me? You're going to abandon me here?"

Frederick laughed, as if she'd made a fine joke, and left. Never, ever had he done anything like that.

She sat on the porch, out of the midday sun, her lips clamped together with resolve. Frederick's cat, Bali, lay dozing on their bed. Frederick's books about this country, its people, its customs, its history, lay in a stack on the table. One of Frederick's sarongs, to be worn when visiting holy sites, lay on a chair.

Frederick was everywhere, but he wasn't the Frederick she'd known for four decades. Her relatively agreeable husband had disappeared and been replaced by somebody who lived precisely the way he wanted to, with no regard for her. Somebody selfish and independent, someone she could not abide.

She had to find a way. A safe way. The perfect crime. The perfect weapon.

And there it was. As it had been for a while now. Across a rice field, near a wall, a skinny brown cat mewed in her direction. Eleanor was sure it was the same pesky cat that had nearly tripped her the day before. She had no idea what it wanted of her, or why it had chosen her to torment. But there it definitely was. Eleanor allowed herself a smile.

Bali opened one eye, seemed to consider the mewing, then sighed and returned to her snooze.

Eleanor, on the other hand, put on her straw hat and her sandals and walked to the market, humming all the way. The open-air stalls normally revolted her. What these people needed was a supermarket with freezers and aisles and tidy stacks of cans and boxes. What they had instead were cramped rows of tables holding peculiar grains and pods and unidentifiable meat with only flapping awnings as protection from contamination.

Fish would have been best, but these idiot people didn't eat much fish. They lived on an island but avoided the sea, and when she commented on the pure lunacy of this, Frederick, who thought they were so wonderful, explained again the religious basis, about how high, as in mountaintops, was worshiped, and low, as in the sea, was avoided. Demons lived in the sea. Hence, little fishing.

Eleanor surely didn't care why. Smelly, oily fish bits would have been the most effective. But she would make do, anyway. She always did.

A wizened woman with black-stained, betel-nut teeth nodded at her, and Eleanor swallowed hard and pointed at a duck back. The woman gestured at other, more succulent segments of duck, but Eleanor shook her head and pointed again at the back, and the woman wrapped it in paper and exchanged it for a bit of money.

On the way back to the porch, she saw the brown cat. It kept its distance but eyed her, as she was sure it had done for days. It looked tougher than its kin, belligerent in some way. One of its ears was jagged, as if it had been ripped and poorly healed, and she could clearly see the outline of its ribs.

She had never seen anyone call it, or invite it inside a compound where it could find kitchen scraps and a child to cuddle it. "Hey, Mickey," she whispered, and she lay the duck back by the side of the path where the cat stood.

After a few wary glances and tentative steps forward, the cat seized its bounty and busied itself with it. Eleanor heard its purr as she walked back to her hotel.

The next day, Frederick announced that he wanted to learn to make batik and he'd signed up for a five-afternoon beginner's class. He didn't ask Eleanor if she wanted to come along. Of course, she didn't—why ruin her nails with inks and hot wax? But all the same, he should have asked.

Each afternoon for five days, while Frederick was at the workshop, Eleanor went to the market and bought a morsel of duck meat. She knew that if this were any other place in the world, the woman at the market stall would eventually testify against her. But not here. First of all, no one would suspect what she had done. Second of all, this was not a land of finding and questioning witnesses. And third and most important of all, Eleanor wasn't going to do anything. Her weapon would do it for her.

After she left the market, she looked for the Mickey—he'd be number thirteen, she realized. How appropriate. Each afternoon, she found him alone, slightly hunched and defensive-looking, but less and less wary.

Each day she let him follow her a few more paces, and then she'd place his daily duck part on the edge of the path. Further from the wall where she'd first seen him. Closer to her room. The last afternoon, she tiptoed down from the porch, carrying her bit of duck, and placed it directly under the woven wall of their sleeping pavilion.

Frederick's batik class ended. He proudly presented her with a black and blue square of cloth, drips and blobs marring whatever design he'd intended. "Sarongs by Frederick of Bali," he said with a smile.

That night, the moon was full, casting a clear white light into the room, onto their bed. She looked at her husband and the Balicat curled into his arm, and she sighed. A tremor of regret stirred her.

But all the same. If she weakened, let sentiment take over, she'd be stuck on this stupid hot island forever. Besides, it was Frederick's own fault.

If he'd found them a more normal American kind of room with walls and windows, she wouldn't be able to do this.

If he'd been more sensitive and not left her all alone all those days, then she probably couldn't have spent the time establishing a relationship with the Mickey.

If he hadn't changed so drastically, they wouldn't be here in the first place and Frederick could have lived out his allotted time in peace.

With those thoughts, she got out of bed quietly, although very little disturbed Frederick's sleep these days and she probably could have clumped and thumped her way across the room.

She stood by the half-wall and looked out into the bright moonlit scene. The symmetrical squares of the rice fields looked surreal, green-black shadows pooling dark along their edges.

And below her, staring up with yellow eyes, was the Mickey, a smart little cat who knew which side his bread was buttered on. Or would, if this heathen land had bread.

Eleanor waved the piece of meat like a magic wand. She watched the skinny cat's head swivel as it followed the figure-eights she made above it.

She put the meat on the sill of the half-wall and waited. She watched as the cat climbed the woven bamboo wall, nails digging into the dried fronds. When he was onto the sill, purring with anticipation, rubbing against her hand, Eleanor quickly lifted the duck breast and tossed it halfway across the room, onto the center of the bed.

In a single dramatic leap, the Mickey arced halfway across the room after it, and onto the sheet.

Also, alas, onto the Balicat, who understandably resented the pain of the pounce, the interruption of her night's sleep, and worst of all, the intrusion onto her private turf, and expressed that resentment by a horrific yowl and a leap that tried to eliminate the Mickey, who in turn expressed keen resentment of her interference with his duckfest. The cats screamed and hissed and spat and swung at each other, rolling, flailing, and making the worst noise Eleanor had ever heard—even in this country.

Frederick sat bolt upright, gasping as the cats leaped against him, screaming cat imprecations and insults at one another. "What? What?" Frederick said. "Who—what?"

Eleanor raced around, looking as if she were trying to do something, taking swipes at the cat. "I can't stop them!" she wailed, just in case Frederick survived this and she needed to look as if she had cared. "Oh, God, you're not supposed to ever be shocked awake—this could kill you!"

She was accurate. Frederick gasped a few more times, grabbed his chest, and died, even as the cats continued to fight bitterly around and on him.

Eleanor calmly watched her husband's final moments. It wasn't her fault that their room had no telephone with which to call for help. It wasn't her fault that as far as she knew there were no nearby hospitals, no advanced emergency techniques for heart attacks, no ambulances. Frederick was the one who'd wanted to come to a country were things were completely different from the way they were at home.

Frederick's expression softened into one of great peace. He had, after all, gotten what he wanted. The trip of his lifetime.

And she'd committed the perfect crime. Her hands were clean, if a bit greasy from the duck meat. Whom could they blame, except the Mickey cat?

Eleanor lifted the duck meat off the sheet and tossed it over the window ledge.

The Mickey was too engrossed in his battle to notice that the prize for which he fought would be his if he'd only leave. Fur flew and the yowls continued. Eleanor lost whatever patience she'd had. "Enough!" she snarled, scooping up the brown cat.

He writhed, balefully looking at her with yellow eyes, his fangs showing, his claws still pursuing the Balicat, and as Eleanor released him at the window ledge, he swiped one last time, leaving a scratch on her arm from her elbow to her wrist.

"Ingrate!" she hissed into the night. "See if you get another ounce of food from me! You can starve from now on for all I care!"

She put on a cotton wrapper and a pair of bedroom slippers and made her way to the night manager. "My husband," she sobbed. "I think he's . . ."

The gentle Balinese treated the widow with compassion and care. The hotel manager said she could stay, rent-free, until the arrangements for her husband's return to the States were completed. Briefly, she considered letting Frederick rest in this land he so loved. He had said that he would love to stay here through eternity. But it wouldn't have looked right. This Buddhist-Hindu-animist country buried their dead and waited years until they could exhume them when they could finally afford an extravagant send-off into the next life, a lavish cremation ceremony. She didn't care what the Balinese would think if she buried Frederick here, although there didn't seem to be any proper place to do it, but she did worry about what people back home would say.

Unfortunately, there was a whole lot of Indonesian and U.S. red tape to cut through, and the cutting took an inordinate amount of time. And even more unfortunately, during that time the conditions that had made Eleanor's victory so easy still prevailed. There continued to be an absence of advanced medical facilities, and so when the cat scratch swelled and itched, Eleanor applied the ointments she'd brought from the States and never wondered whether a land so lush and exotic might also breed interestingly different organisms.

It turned out that it did. And the organisms were as ecstatic about

Eleanor's arm and vital organs and as ravenous for them as the Mickey cat, their former host, had been for duck meat.

Microbes move much more quickly than bureaucrats. Slowly, the red tape was sliced. Quickly, the microbes multiplied. Eleanor felt poorly.

On the day that Frederick's body was finally released to be shipped back to the States, in care of his son, Eleanor, her plane ticket in hand, gasped, put a hand to her chest, and breathed her last.

No one knew what to do with her remains, which were in dreadful shape, given the appetite of those internal microbes. So in a last act of gracious gentle kindness, the Balinese kept Eleanor with them in paradise, buried on a hillside, halfway between the demons of the sea and the gods of the mountains.

After a while it was said that the American man whose remains had been flown away had mourned the loss of Bali and so had returned in his next life as a duo of cats, one a sleek gold and white and the other brown with a ripped ear. Together, the cats and eventually a small tribe of gold and brown kittens, all with white paws, made the long trek to visit the grave on the hill each full moon, rubbing against the headstone and, in an odd final gesture, using the marker as their private, gigantic emery board so vigorously that as time went by, the stone developed grooves that looked almost like writing, like *Miki*, but of course that didn't mean anything.

The grave of Eleanor the Cat Lady made it into the guidebooks as a tourist attraction. "If we believe as animists that everything has a spirit or soul," the tour guide said one moonlit night, "we might think those cats—and perhaps her dead husband—had a bit of a problem with Eleanor, and are reminding her remains throughout eternity—perhaps taunting them with this news?—of how well all of them are thriving."

The tourists smiled at each other and were glad they'd traveled around the world to visit this funny, quaint country. What a great place. Had to buy a postcard of the Eleanor the Cat Lady Shrine and remember this funny superstition. Wasn't Bali adorable?

How I Found a Cat, Lost True Love and Broke the Bank at Monte Carlo

Bill Crider

1

Actually, the cat found me.

I was in the market section of Monaco, between the hills that support the royal palace on the one hand and the casino section of Monte Carlo on the other. It was a lovely day in early fall, the kind you read about in tourist manuals. The sun was bright, and the sky was a hard, brilliant blue.

The market was so crowded that I could hardly move. Flower vendors offered red and yellow and white blossoms that overflowed their paper cones, while food vendors hawked fish and vegetables, fruit and pastries. Shoppers swirled around me, and the street was packed with cars and vans.

The smells of roses and freshly caught seafood mingled with the odor of coffee from the sidewalk cafés, and I was thinking about having a cup of mocha when the cat ran up my leg, digging its claws into my jeans and hoisting itself right up to my waist.

For some reason I've never understood, cats find me attractive.

I settled my glasses on my nose, gently pried the cat loose, and held her in my arms. She was mostly black, with a white streak on her nose, a white badge on her chest, and white socks on her legs. Her eyes were emerald green and her heart was pounding as if she were frightened, but in that mob it was hard to tell what might be scaring her.

"What's the matter, cat?" I asked. Maybe that's why cats like me. I treat them as if their brains were larger than walnuts, though they aren't.

The cat of course didn't answer, but she did seem to relax a bit. Then a dog barked somewhere nearby and the cat tensed up, sliding her claws out and through my shirt, into the skin of my chest.

"It's all right," I said, squirming a little. "I won't let the dog get you."

The cat looked wide-eyed out over the heads of the crowd for the source of the barking. There was no dog in evidence, and though the cat didn't appear entirely convinced of my ability to protect her, she withdrew her claws from my shirt.

I hadn't come to Monaco to adopt a cat, as attractive as that idea might seem, so I looked around for someone to take her off my hands.

That's when I saw the woman.

She wasn't just any woman. She was *the* woman. Even in that crowd of the rich and beautiful, she stood out. She was tall and lithe. Her hair was midnight black under a pink sunhat, and her eyes were as deeply green as those of the cat I held in my arms. And she was walking straight toward me.

I was in love.

I opened my mouth, but nothing came out. Truly beautiful women affect my nervous system. They might not often be attracted to me, but I was certainly attracted to them.

"Hello," she said in English. She had that unidentifiable continental accent that I'd heard a lot in the last few days, but somehow it seemed much more charming from her than it had from anyone else. "Are you American?"

I managed to get my mouth to work. "How did you know?"

She laughed, though it was more like music to me than laughter. "You Americans are all alike. There is such an innocence about you."

She reached for the cat and rubbed a white hand along its dark coat. The cat began purring.

"That is why animals trust you," she said. "They can sense the innocence."

"I wondered about that," I told her.

"I'm sure that you did. True innocence never knows itself."

She took the cat from me. It went quite willingly and settled into her arms as if it belonged there.

"I thank you very much for rescuing Michelle. My uncle and I came to the market for fish, and she escaped my car when I opened the door to leave. There was a dog nearby, and I suspect that his barking may have frightened her."

"We heard him," I said.

She started to turn away, which is usually the case with women I meet. But then something unusual happened. She turned back.

"Would you like a cup of coffee, perhaps? Michelle would like to repay you for the rescue."

"What about your uncle?" I asked. Somehow I managed it without stuttering. "Won't he be worried about the cat?"

"He won't mind. He'll find us, I'm sure."

"I'd love some coffee," I said.

It was just as noisy at the small table where we sat under a striped umbrella as it had been in the market, but somehow we seemed isolated in an island of quiet where the only sounds were our two voices, along with the occasional mew from Michelle, who sat on a chair beside her owner, whose name was Antoinette Sagan. Tony to her friends, of which I was now officially one.

I had already told her to call me Mike.

"And what are you doing here in Monaco?" Tony asked me as she sipped her coffee.

"I came to break the bank at the casino," I said, pushing up my glasses.

Tony set her cup down and laughed. "As so many have. And how do you plan to do so?"

"Roulette," I said. "I have a system."

Tony winked at the cat. "Do you hear that, Michelle? The American has a system."

Michelle wasn't interested. She was watching some kind of bug that was crawling along the walk just beneath her chair.

Tony looked back at me and smiled. The green of her eyes was amazing. I think my heart fibrillated.

"Everyone has a system," she said. "For cards, for dice, for roulette. They come to Monaco daily. But no one has ever broken the bank."

"You'd never know if someone did," I said. "They'd never tell, and the banks here know how to keep a secret. Anyway, I don't have to break the bank, not really. I'd settle for a few million dollars."

Michelle had lost interest in the bug. She stepped up on the table and walked across it to me. She climbed into my lap, turned in a circle, and lay down, purring loudly.

"I believe you've made a conquest," Tony said. "And what is your system, if I may ask? Or is it a secret?"

I told her it wasn't a secret. I took one of my pens out of my pocket protector and pulled a napkin across the table.

"Do you know the game?" I asked.

Tony shrugged. The white shirt moved in interesting places, but I tried to ignore that.

"Of course," she said.

"Then you know the odds favoring the house." I jotted them on the napkin. "In American roulette, the house edge is five-point-two-six percent; in the European version it's two-point-seven-oh percent because there's no double zero on the wheel."

"So of course you'll be playing the European version."

"Of course. Now. Have you ever heard of the Martingale system?"

Tony made a comic frown. "Who has not? Many millions of francs have been lost with it. You make your bet. If you win, you take your winnings and begin again. If you lose, you double the bet. Lose again, double again." She took the pen from my hand and began scribbling on the napkin. "Say that your bet is one hundred francs on red. Seven times in a row the wheel comes up black. That means that your next bet will be twelve thousand eight hundred francs, but you will have already lost twelve thousand seven hundred francs. Should you win, you win one hundred francs, should you lose . . ." She shrugged again. "The croupier will be overjoyed to have you at his table."

Her figures were correct, and of course the house odds defeat everyone in the long run. I was going to beat the odds.

I told Tony that I was a math teacher at a community college in the States. That I'd always been fascinated with odds and statistics. And that I'd recently won fifty thousand dollars in the state lottery.

"Winning such a large amount was very lucky," she said. "And you have come to Monaco to lose it all at the roulette table? That does not seem practical."

"I'm not practical, and I don't think I'm going to lose."

I tried to elaborate on my system, which I explained was an elegant variation on the Martingale, involving shifting the bet to different locations, avoiding the low payoffs like red or black while never trying for the larger payoffs like the single number bet, and even dropping out of the betting occasionally.

"And if all else fails," I said, "maybe I'll get lucky."

"It has happened," she said.

"Right. About eighty years ago, black came up seventeen times in a row on one table. Anyone starting out with a dollar and leaving it on black would have won over, let's see . . ." I worked it out on the napkin. "One hundred thirty-one thousand seventy-two dollars. It could happen to me."

She looked at the cat, which was still lying comfortably in my lap.

"You seem like a nice man, Mike. I hope it does happen to you, and that you pick up your money before the eighteenth spin of the wheel."

Her smile made my knees weak.

"I could share it with you if it happens that way," I said, hardly caring that her answer could pose a real problem for me if it was the one I wanted to hear.

She opened her mouth to say something, but I never found out what it was. She saw someone behind me, and her eyes darkened. She closed her mouth.

I looked around. A very large man stood there. He wore a white shirt and dark slacks, and he had a dark face that was pitted like volcanic rock. I suppose you could call him ruggedly handsome if you liked the type.

Tony said, "Hello, André. This is Mike. He has found Michelle."

I picked up the cat in my left arm and began to turn. Michelle growled low in her throat, and the hair ridged along her back.

"Stupid cat," André said. His voice was like Michelle's growl.

"André is my uncle," Tony explained. "He and Michelle are not mutual admirers."

I could see that much. I could also see that André was not at all interested in meeting me, much less in shaking hands. I dropped the hand that I had been about to extend.

Tony came around the table and took Michelle, who had stopped growling, though she didn't look very happy.

"Thank you so much, Mike," Tony said. "André and I are both grateful."

Sure they were. André had already turned his back and was walking away. He was wide as a billboard.

"I hope you win at the casino," Tony said over her shoulder as she turned to follow André.

I watched them move through the crowd. André didn't look like anyone's uncle to me, and I wondered if Tony had lied. I suppose that it didn't make any difference.

Besides, if she had lied, we were even. After all, I hadn't won the lottery. I wasn't even a math teacher.

2

Cammie was waiting for me in a little café not far from the market. She was drinking black coffee and smoking a Players. She knew I didn't like cigarettes, but she didn't bother to snuff it out when I sat down. No one else minded. It wasn't like an American café. There were lots of smokers.

It was a little after noon, and I ordered a sandwich. Cammie didn't want one. She was too wired to eat.

"You look really dorky in those glasses," she said. Her voice was low and slightly husky, a quality I attributed to the cigarettes. "And where on earth did you get the pocket protector? Elmer's Plumbing? Give me a break."

"I thought it was nice touch," I told her.

She took a deep swallow of coffee. "You probably think that stupid part in your hair's a nice touch, too, but it isn't."

"It should fool the croupier," I said. "He won't know he's seen me before."

"I guess. If you want to risk it."

"I'm willing. What did you find out?"

She blew a spiral of smoke and looked around. No one appeared interested in us.

"I think you were right," she said, grinning.

She looked good with a grin. Short blonde hair, blue eyes, a small mouth and nose. Sort of the gamine look. Not that she looked as good as Tony, but she looked pretty good.

And like me, she could look quite different when the occasion called for it, as it had lately. Yesterday she'd looked like a fashion model on vacation, and the day before that she'd looked like a harassed mother who'd misplaced her three kids.

We'd been watching the wheels in Monte Carlo's famous casino for four days, and a couple of days earlier we'd settled on the one at table four. My theory was that a system wasn't good enough. It would help if you could find a wheel that was just slightly out of balance.

It didn't need to be out of balance much. Hardly any, in fact, and the odds against finding one were quite high in themselves. Casinos generally go to a lot of trouble to make sure that everything is perfect, but now and then someone slips up. It doesn't happen often. Hardly ever, in fact. But it does happen.

We'd been looking for weeks. Monte Carlo wasn't our first stop, and it wouldn't have been our last had we not found the right wheel. It looked as if we had.

All we needed was a wheel that turned up one number more often than any other. To be sure that we'd found one, we had to watch it for at least twenty-four hours. We'd been watching for forty-eight, spread out over three days, in our various disguises. Cammie had just come off the final shift.

"So it's the five?" I said.

She crushed out the cigarette. "It's the five, all right. Table four."

The odds of any single number coming up are one in thirty-seven. The red five was coming up more often than that, more like one time in thirty. That was more than often enough to offset the house odds on a single zero wheel.

"So if they don't adjust the wheel before tonight, we use the system on the five," she said. "At table four. And you're the player."

"That's me. Joe Nerd."

"You're not going to wear that get-up. Not really."

I told her that I wasn't going to change much, and that I had a good reason. When I told her why, she wasn't happy with me.

"You idiot! You actually *told* someone we had a system?"

"Not *we*. I told her that *I* had a system. She doesn't know about you. And I didn't tell her anything at all about the wheel. So don't worry."

Cammie showed instant suspicion, one of her less attractive qualities. "I should have known it was a woman. You always talk too much to women. What does she look like?"

The waiter brought my sandwich, and I took a bite to avoid answering. After I'd finished chewing, I said, "She looks good. But not great."

Cammie narrowed her eyes. I could tell she didn't trust me, not that I blamed her.

Cammie and I had met two years earlier in Las Vegas, where she'd been dealing blackjack. I'd made a bundle at her table, and we'd gotten out of town just before anyone figured out how I was doing it, a little matter of a trick that involved her help and that was in violation of every casino rule in the book. We'd made a little money since, here and there, enough so that I had a pretty good stake, and then I'd come up with the idea of finding a roulette wheel that was just slightly out of whack. I'd never expected to find it in Monte Carlo, really, but I was just as happy that we had.

"So why did you tell her?" Cammie asked. "I thought you were nervous around women."

She knew me pretty well. I'd been nervous around her too, at first, and talked too much, though if I hadn't had a drink or three too many, I'd never have tried to con her into helping me with the blackjack scam. As it turned out, she didn't need conning. She was eager to help.

"I found her cat," I said. I told her all about Tony, the cat, and Uncle André.

"Uncle, my Aunt Fanny," she said. She got out a Players and lit it with a disposable lighter from her purse. "You should've kept your mouth shut."

"Not really," I rationalized. "That's the beauty of it. She seems to know her way around here, and when word gets out that some geek broke the bank, she'll remember me and tell people about my supposed system. People will think I got lucky. No one will ever know we had a fixed wheel."

"It isn't fixed. It's just a little out of balance."

"You're absolutely right. And they certainly can't blame us for that."

She blew a smoke ring and stuck her finger through it. "Describe this André for me again."

I did.

"Dark hair?"

For some reason I don't usually notice men's hair, but now that she mentioned it, I remembered.

"Yes," I said. "And a little curly."

"I think I've seen him around the casino. Do you think he could be security?"

He was certainly big enough, but I didn't think they'd use anyone that obvious.

"Probably just another gambler," I said. "And remember what we just discussed. It's not our fault if the wheel's out of balance."

She took a deep drag from the cigarette and turned to blow the smoke away from me. Or maybe she just didn't want me to see her face.

"I'll remember," she said.

3

I went to the casino just as night was falling. I had to walk, because parking in the crush of automobiles there is almost impossible, but I didn't mind. The casino is an impressive sight, worth looking at as you approach it from nearly any angle, especially at night when the floodlights are on.

The floodlights brighten the ornate casino facade and throw into obscurity the high-rises that suffocate the area around it. Once Monte Carlo must have been a beautiful place, but now it looks a lot like any city anywhere.

Across from the casino, boats lined the harbor, and there was just the faintest tinge of azure still in the sky where it met the dark sea.

I had on my thick-rimmed glasses, and I was wearing a dark three-piece suit that was about four years out of style, loafers with tassels, and a paisley tie. I was worth a second glance from the man who checked my passport, but no more than that. He didn't care how I dressed as long as I had on a tie.

He returned my passport, and I walked into the American Room, which is filled with tourists who seem to want to lose their money fast. The smoky air was noisy with the sound of the 120 slot machines and the balls clacking around the American-style roulette wheels.

I walked right on through, with only a glance into the Pink Salon, the bar where Cammie would be waiting for me. The ceiling was painted with floating women, most of whom were nude and most of whom were smoking. I didn't see Cammie.

As I paid my fee to enter the European Room, I had a qualm or two about the tie and about the tassels on the loafers; the standards here were somewhat higher than for the first room in the casino. But apparently I passed muster. I was allowed to enter.

Besides being classier, the European Room was much quieter than the American Room. Nearly everyone was better-dressed than I was, and everyone looked quite serious about the business at hand, which was gambling. The *chefs* watched the tables from tall wooden chairs, their eyes bright and alert for any sign of trouble.

I wasn't going to be any trouble. I was just there to win a large sum of money. I exchanged a huge wad of francs for chips and walked up to the table, which was set up a bit differently from an American table. There are layouts for betting on both sides of the table, and in this room there were padded rails not far away so that onlookers could lean at their ease and get a few vicarious thrills by watching the real gamblers.

I approached the table and put five hundred francs down on the black ten. I thought I might as well lose a little to begin with.

Almost as soon as the money was down, one of the croupiers said, *"Rien ne va plus."* The *tourneur* spun the wheel and dropped the silver ball, which whirred and bounced and clicked. I took a deep breath and waited for it to drop.

I don't know when Tony arrived. I noticed her about two hours into the game, standing at the rail directly across the table from me. She smiled when I looked up, and my concentration broke for a moment.

That was all right. I needed a little break. I was almost fifty thousand francs in the hole. It wasn't as bad as it sounds at first, since a dollar is worth five francs, but ten thousand dollars is still a lot of money. In fact it was about a third of my stake. Things weren't working out exactly as I'd planned.

The five hadn't been coming up, not often enough and certainly not when I had money on it. My real plan—as opposed to the one I'd told Tony about—had been to move the money around at first, putting a little on the red five now and then so that no one would be suspicious when I started playing the five exclusively. I'd win a little, lose a little, then get hot and break the bank.

It had seemed like a good plan when I thought of it, but obviously it wasn't working out. I was losing more than I was winning. Maybe the wheel wasn't out of balance after all. Or maybe I was just un-lucky.

There was a TV commercial in the States when I left, something about never letting them see you sweat. Well, I was sweating, and if something good didn't happen soon, they were going to see me doing it.

The break was over. I wondered if Tony's appearance at the rail might not be an omen. What the hell, I thought. I shoved all the rest of my chips out on the table, onto the five.

The *tourneur* gave the wheel a practiced spin and flipped the ball in the opposite direction. Time suddenly slowed down. The ball glided like mercury on tile, and then it began bouncing. Every time that it bounced, it seemed to hang in the air for several seconds before striking the wheel again.

I looked at Tony. She was still smiling; it was as if she hadn't moved at all.

I glanced back at the wheel, and things suddenly snapped back to normal. The ball bounced once, twice, three times, and landed in the five.

As the croupier called out the number, I let out a breath that I hadn't even known I was holding. I'd put nearly twenty-five thousand francs on the number, at odds of thirty-five to one. That meant I'd won almost one hundred seventy-five thousand dollars in one spin of the wheel.

I straightened my glasses. "Let it ride," I said. It was time to go with the flow.

The croupier called to someone, and a man dressed better than most of the gamblers came over to the table. There was a whispered conversation.

I thought about the time all those years ago when the ball had landed in the black seventeen times in a row. I didn't need seventeen times in a row. I just needed to hit one more time. The odds against it happening were huge, but not as bad as you might think. The wheel didn't know that the red five had just come up. I had the same chance of hitting it again that I'd had the first time. And if the wheel really was out of balance, maybe the chance was better than it should be.

The croupier was looking at me as the well-dressed man whispered to him. I tried to keep my voice level and repeated, "Let it ride."

The man was finished with the croupier. Now he wanted to talk to me. I didn't blame him. If I hit, I was going to win something like six and a quarter million dollars. I was sweating a lot more now than I'd been when I was losing.

The man was very polite, and he didn't appear to be as nervous as I was. Probably he dealt with large sums of money more often than I did.

"Are you enjoying yourself, *monsieur*?" he asked.

"Very much," I said, taking off my glasses and cleaning them with a tissue from my suit pocket. My heart was about to jump out of my chest, but my hands didn't tremble. Much.

"Do you realize the value of your bet?" His voice was as calm as if he were discussing the beautiful autumn weather we were having.

"I believe I do," I said, settling the glasses on my nose and returning the tissue to my pocket. I patted my hair just to the right of the part and smiled at him.

"You have won quite a sum of money already. Are you sure that you want to risk it all on one spin of the wheel?"

I shrugged. Casual Joe Nerd. "Easy come, easy go."

He mumbled something then that might have been a reference

to "stupid Americans," but I didn't quite catch it. I wasn't meant to.

I looked around at the crowd. There were a lot more people watching now than there had been only moments before. All of them were observing us expectantly, Tony among them. She licked her lips in anticipation, and my heart beat even faster.

"Everyone's waiting," I said. "I hope the casino won't let them down."

The man didn't bother to look at the crowd. For that matter, he didn't bother to look at me. Six million dollars wasn't really that much money, not to him and the house. It wouldn't break the bank, though it would come close enough to satisfy me.

The man nodded to the croupier, who said, *"Rien ne va plus."* The room became as silent as an empty cathedral.

When the *tourneur* spun the wheel, it seemed to roar like a jet plane on takeoff. The ball zipped around like an Indy racer, and when it bounced it sounded like a skull ricocheting inside a marble cavern.

I couldn't watch. I closed my eyes. I may even have crossed my fingers.

About ten years later, I heard the croupier.

"Rouge." There was a pause of nearly a century, and I could hear the blood pounding in my head. Then he said, quite calmly, *"Cinq."*

I opened my eyes. There was a clamoring and shouting like you might hear when an underdog wins the Superbowl. Men were pounding me on the back and women were trying to kiss me. My knees were weak, but I was rapidly gaining strength.

I craned my neck above the sea of heads, trying to find Tony, but she was gone. I didn't wonder about her for long. Instead I looked back at the wheel and the silvery ball nestling in the five.

I'll admit it. There was an instant when I actually thought about saying, "Let it ride." If I hit again, I'd win over 214 million dollars. I really would break the bank at Monte Carlo, or come very close.

Would the well-dressed man have let me take the chance? Probably, in the hope that I'd lose; the odds were certainly against me, unbalanced wheel or not. Or maybe he'd hustle me outside, unwilling to allow me the opportunity to win.

It didn't matter. I told them to cash me in.

"Follow me, *monsieur*," the well-dressed man said. I did, after making sure that the croupiers and the *tourneur* had nice tips. I could afford to be generous.

I couldn't resist looking back, though, to see where the ball landed on the next spin.

In the black, thirty-two.

It was just as well I'd stopped.

4

Cammie was in the bar when I arrived carrying a black leather case.

"My God," she said. "You won."

I nodded.

She crushed out the cigarette she had been smoking, a sure sign that she was excited. "How much?" She didn't wait for an answer. "Was that cheering I heard in there for you? I thought it might be, but I couldn't bear to go in and find out."

I said that the cheering had been for me.

"Oh my God! I can't believe it! How much?"

I told her.

She stared at the leather bag. "And it's all in there?"

"Not all of it. They don't keep that much on hand, or if they do, they don't give it out to guys like me. But there's a lot. I told them I'd take a check for the rest."

"My God." She fumbled in her purse for her cigarettes, then gave it up. She looked back at the bag. "Everyone in that room knows you won. How are we going to get it to the hotel without being robbed?"

I turned and gestured toward the doorway. There were two large men in tight suits standing there.

"The casino was kind enough to provide an escort. No one wants to see a lucky gambler lose his winnings to a footpad."

"A footpad?"

"Cutpurse, mugger, what-have-you."

"You talk funny when you're excited."

"If you think I'm excited now, wait until we get to the hotel. I've always wanted to play Scrooge McDuck. You know. Throw it up and let it hit me on the head. Burrow through it like a gopher."

"Now's your chance," she said. She hooked an arm through mine. "Let's go."

We arrived at the hotel without incident, and the bodyguards left us without a word, except to thank me for the tip. I was about to have the bag put in the hotel vault when Cammie stopped me.

"Scrooge McDuck," she said. "Remember?"

I didn't suppose it would hurt anything. She deserved to see the money. And the check. We went up to the room.

When we opened the door, we got quite a surprise.

Tony was sitting in an armchair, waiting for us. So was Michelle, who was curled in Tony's lap, asleep.

And so, unfortunately, was Uncle André, who was holding a very ugly pistol in his right hand. A Glock 17, ugly but very accurate, or so I've heard.

"Shit," Cammie said, glaring at me. I didn't blame her.

"Close the door," André said, moving the pistol barrel just slightly.

I did what he said.

"Who's your friend, Mike?" Tony asked.

"Inspector Lestrade, Scotland Yard," I said, but no one laughed.

"You're a very lucky man, Mike," Tony said, stroking Michelle's back. The cat began to purr so loudly that I could hear her across the room. "Didn't I tell you he seemed lucky, André?"

"If I were lucky, you wouldn't be here," I said, thinking that it was really too bad. She was such a beautiful woman, and I'd been halfway in love with her. If she'd asked me nicely, I might have given her the money; after all, in a way, she'd helped me win it. Then again, maybe I wouldn't have.

André didn't seem to care one way or the other. "Give me the bag," he said.

"It won't do you any good," Cammie said. "There's no money. It's a check."

"I'm afraid we don't believe that," Tony said. "You see, we've been waiting around for days for someone like you, Mike. André is a terrible gambler, and I am not much better, but I could tell this morning that you were different. Did I not say so, André?"

André said nothing. He just stared at me with eyes like black glass.

"I had to ask André to wait. He wanted to take you for a little ride this morning and relieve you of your stake, but I told him to wait. I told him I had faith in you. Is that not true, André?"

André didn't answer the question. "Give me the bag," he told me, "or I will shoot your woman."

Cammie was furious. With me, for having told Tony I had a system, and with André for calling her my woman.

"He won't shoot," she said. "If he does, half the hotel will come running to this room."

"That is true," Tony said.

She got up, carrying the cat along with her, and walked to the bed. She picked up one of the pillows and took it to André.

"Use this," she said.

André muffled the pistol with the pillow. "Give me the bag."

I tensed just a little.

"And don't throw it," André said. "I'll shoot your woman."

"Shoot me then, you son of a bitch," Cammie said, throwing her purse at him.

When she did, I swung the bag as hard as I could at Tony. I hated to mess up her beautiful face, but I didn't hate it as much as I hated the thought of giving them any of my money.

The bag hit Tony at just about the same time the pistol went off, and made just about as much noise.

Even noisier than the pistol was the cat, which had jumped from Tony's arms and was yowling in the middle of the floor, its back arched, its tail puffed to three times its normal size. The air was filled with feathers from the pillow. I couldn't see Cammie. Maybe she had taken cover in the bathroom.

Tony had fallen back across the bed. Her nose was bleeding, but I wasn't worried about her. I was worried about André, who had started toward me. He wouldn't need the pistol. He could break me in half with his bare hands if he wanted to.

He might have done it, but he made one mistake. He didn't watch out for the cat. Maybe he didn't see her because of the feathers.

Michelle didn't like him anyway, and when he ran into her, she fastened herself to his right leg, sinking her claws into his calf and trying to bite through his pants.

He was hopping on his left leg and pointing the pistol at her when I let him have it with the bag. His face was one I didn't mind messing up.

I connected solidly, and André staggered backward. Michelle released him and ran under the bed, which was just as well. When I hit André again, he wobbled against the french doors that led to a tiny balcony.

The doors weren't locked, and they hardly slowed him down. Neither did the low railing outside. I have to give him credit. He didn't yell as he went over, or even on the way down. I heard him crash into some patio furniture.

I went outside and looked down. André was sprawled atop the remains of a metal table. Our room was on the third floor, not so great a distance from the ground. Maybe he'd even survive.

I heard a noise and turned back to the room. Tony was still on the bed, but now Cammie was sitting on top of her, straddling her waist. Tony was struggling to get up, but Cammie had pinned her arms and all she could do was thrash around.

"Let her go," I said. "She won't bother us without André around."

Cammie got off Tony, though I could tell she wanted to do a little more damage first. She stood beside the bed, disheveled and glowering. Her nose was no longer bleeding, however.

"Are you all right?" I asked Tony.

"You brogue my dose, you sud of a bitch."

Cammie, either because she felt sorry for Tony or because she didn't like the sight of blood, got her purse from the floor and dug around until she found a couple of tissues. She handed them to Tony.

"Sorry about your nose," I said. "You were trying to rob me, after all. Is that what you and André do for a living? Rob innocent tourists?"

She crumpled the tissues. "Iddocedt? Whod's iddocedt, you sud of a—"

"Never mind," I said. "And you don't have to call us names. We're not going to turn you in."

"We're not?" Cammie said.

"We don't want to cause any trouble. We just want to go on our way and enjoy our money. And we have lots to enjoy."

Tony sat up. She was wearing a white blouse, and there was a lot of blood on it. I wondered what the hotel staff would make of that, but I decided I didn't care.

"I cad go?" she said.

"Sure. Don't let us keep you. And you might want to check on your friend. I'm not sure, but I thought I saw him moving."

She stalked across the room. When her hand touched the doorknob, Cammie said, "Don't forget your cat."

"André has never liked Michelle," Tony said. "I do not think he will want to see her again."

And then she was out the door and gone.

Cammie took a deep breath. "You always talk too much to women," she said.

"And you smoke too much. I'll try to quit talking too much to women if you'll try to stop smoking."

I still had the bag in my hand. I walked over and put it on the chair. I thought it would be a good idea to put the money in the hotel safe now. I was no longer in the mood to play Scrooge McDuck.

"Why all the sudden concern about my smoking?" Cammie asked.

Michelle came halfway out from under the bed and stared at us. After a second or two she walked over and started rubbing against my leg and purring.

"Secondhand smoke," I said, reaching down to stroke Michelle's head. She began to purr even louder. Cats liked me, all right. "It's bad for the cat."

The Chocolate Cat

Michael Collins

It was his first visit to Austria, and Paul McGuire spent the three-hour train ride from Innsbruck to the village staring out at the peaks of the Tyrolean Alps, the dark green forests against the snow, and the pristine farmhouses. He marveled at the village itself, like something under a Christmas tree, and the old timbered chalet where he was staying for two weeks.

But nothing made him stare more than the massive white cat that met him just inside the front door like an official greeter. He asked the cat's name as he checked in, and was told it was Schokolade. Since the animal was a vast expanse of pure white, McGuire's former profession as a detective lieutenant made him question the reason for the name.

"Ah," Herr Huber, the proprietor of the ski chalet, laughed, "you will soon find out, Herr McGuire, *ja*."

And so he did.

Recently retired from the Los Angeles Police Department after thirty-five years, McGuire had come to Austria to ski, relax, and think about his future. Since he no longer had to make weight standards, he settled into his second-floor room and went down to indulge in an early afternoon snack in the solarium with its wide view of the slopes and peaks of the Alps. The sun dazzled on the snow and warmed the room to shirtsleeve temperature.

He ordered a Sacher torte and a hot chocolate. Both arrived topped with mounds of whipped cream. This was Austria.

The next thing he knew he had a table companion. The great white cat materialized in front of McGuire's eyes. On the table. An inch from his cup of chocolate and whipped cream. Not the torte and whipped cream. The hot chocolate and whipped cream.

"Okay, Schokolade, I get the message, but not my chocolate."

He set the cat firmly on the floor. Schokolade's big eyes were shocked, betrayed, even suicidal, but McGuire was firm and the cat seemed to sigh in defeat. Sigh, but not leave. McGuire ate and drank and enjoyed the view of mountains and valleys deep with snow. Schokolade sat and stared at every sip he took. Until it was McGuire who sighed and set his cup on the floor with fully a quarter of the chocolate and whipped cream still in it.

In an instant the inch of chocolate and whipped cream was gone, and the white cat looked up for more, chocolate and thick cream clotted on its whiskers.

"And they say we Americans are insensitive," the woman at the next table said.

She was a big woman with a mane of strawberry blonde hair. A long face of regular features, pale skin, and hard eyes. Not young and not old, late thirties with too much makeup and an ultra-chic, ultra-expensive chalet outfit that looked brand-new.

"You met Schokolade and lost the battle too?" he said.

She laughed. An open laugh a lot more natural than her appearance. "Another soft touch. Marian Ransome, San Francisco."

"Paul McGuire, Los Angeles."

"Thank God," Marian Ransome said. "I don't speak German, or any other damn language, and the English here are too stuck-up."

"Glad to be of service. Are you going to be here long?"

"Weeks and weeks. I always wanted to ski the Tyrol but couldn't afford it. So when we got married I made Eddie come to Austria on our honeymoon, and here we are. It's really sweet of Eddie to do it for me, he's a terrible skier."

"I'm sure the gentleman doesn't want to know how bad I am."

A short, balding man stood over Marian Ransome's table and stared at McGuire.

"Oh, there you are, Eddie. This is Paul McGuire from L.A. I just told Paul how sweet you were to come over here for me."

The small man managed a thin smile. "Sweet, maybe, but bruised." Eddie Ransome held his hand out to McGuire. "Ed Ransome, investment and management consulting. What do you do in L.A., Paul?"

"I'm retired," McGuire said. "Always wanted to know more about investing. Must be exciting."

He always avoided mentioning his former work; it tended to either excite people or kill the conversation. He changed the subject to keep anyone from asking what he'd retired from. Focusing the talk on what the other person did usually worked. With Ed Ransome he needn't have worried. As soon as McGuire said he was retired, Ransome lost all interest in him.

"It can be," Ransome said, looked at his watch. "We better go get ready, Marian. It's an hour over to Innsbruck."

"You don't want some hot chocolate?"

"You know I hate chocolate. Come on, I don't want to be late."

Left alone, McGuire ordered another cup of hot chocolate. He was still coming to grips with retirement, felt strangely suspended out of time and place, and seemed to need to be alone. Perhaps to let his life slide into this new world it was going to have to live in.

The hot chocolate came, and he was no longer alone.

Schokolade on the table. Nose to nose.

McGuire laughed.

Over the next few days, McGuire kept busy exploring the village and countryside. He polished his once-a-year technique on the slopes into something resembling true skiing. The Ransomes had the room across the hall from his, but he never saw them except at a distance in the dining room or on the beginner's runs where Eddie tried to learn. Herr Huber told him the woman, Marian, was one of the experts who went out at dawn every morning to ski the top of the mountain.

On the fourth day he met Grace Neville and forgot all about the Ransomes or anyone else.

"You really mustn't allow the cat to bully you."

Schokolade was in his accustomed position at McGuire's feet, watching every sip of hot chocolate, when the tall woman with no-nonsense eyes stood over his table. Her short blonde hair looked hacked off with a knife, and her slim outfit had put a lot of time in on the slopes. An oval face with the long features and peaches-and-cream complexion of the Anglo-Norman patrician glowed ruddy from the cold wind, and showed all of her forty-plus years.

"How do you do that, Ms.—?"

"Grace Neville. You do it by drinking all your chocolate to the dregs. Schokolade won't touch less than an inch with cream. I should think a Los Angeles police detective could handle that."

McGuire was annoyed. "The proprietor talks too much."

"Herr Huber is an old friend. I come here every year."

"I suppose the whole chalet knows?"

"Only me."

"Oh? Why you?"

"I asked."

She sat down at the table and smiled at McGuire. It was a smile that stirred feelings McGuire hadn't known he still had since Sally, his wife of thirty years, had died three years earlier. A smile from a good face. Honest, open, and strong. Grace Neville knew what she wanted and when. McGuire wondered what he wanted, and suddenly realized he was going to enjoy finding out.

"Then the proprietor talks just enough. Are you having dinner with anyone?"

"I'm having it with you, Mr. McGuire. Didn't you know?"

"Paul," he said, "and what are we going to do until dinner?"

"There's a brauhaus at the edge of town you're taking me to so we can tell each other about ourselves."

And that was what they did.

Her father had been Scotland Yard, and she was a barrister. She liked police work. She had been married to an army hero and a judge.

"Both twits," she said.

She was also a Lady, with a capital 'L.'

"It gets me into scads of the best places, especially in your country. Italy and Russia, too. Only France doesn't seem impressed. Nothing impresses the French except themselves. Father found it even worked on criminals. Send in Superintendent Lord Neville and they cracked every time."

"Do I have to bow?"

"Only in bed."

She was fascinated by all his stories, and he was fascinated by her. Her combination of almost brutal directness, power, and naked sensuality was a heady brew he'd never encountered before.

"We'll spend all our time together," she announced after the first hour, "except on the mountain, and decide the rest later."

"Why not on the slopes?"

"I've watched you ski."

"That bad?"

"No, I'm that good. British Olympic team and all that. Years ago, of course. But not to worry, I go out at the crack of dawn. Only way to have the space on the slopes."

When he told her about his wife, she reached and held his hand. She didn't speak, but he knew she was telling him she would have liked a marriage as good as his. When he finished, she gave his hand a hard squeeze. Once. In life, one moved on. McGuire could almost hear Sally saying the same thing and smiling at Grace.

"Oh, God," she groaned suddenly.

Marian Ransome was weaving her way through the tables to them, and flopped into the third chair. "Lady Neville! I didn't know you knew each other. Do either of you know German? What a dumb language. All those stupid endings on words, verbs at the end. Jesus, I gave up. Eddie's still trying. He's smart and a bulldog. That's how he got rich."

"And buys you all those grand outfits," Grace Neville said.

"Not Eddie. I bought everything myself."

"I never doubted it for a second," Grace said.

"Want to borrow anything? We're about the same size."

"What a smashing idea, but I'd really better pass. Too much glamor for me. And I think that's your husband looking for you now, my dear."

Marian Ransome glanced toward where her husband stood inside the brauhaus door. "He can be a real pain. We're going over to Innsbruck again tonight. He loves that damned French restaurant. I guess I better get ready. I'll see you on top of the mountain tomorrow morning, right, Lady Neville?"

"I can't wait, Marian." She watched the strawberry blonde amble toward the impatient Eddie, displaying her wildly chic and expensive outfit to the whole brauhaus. "Insufferable woman. But she can ski."

McGuire laughed. "She likes being rich."

"I don't know which of them is worse. He was surly as a tout until he heard I was Lady Neville. Then he became totally sycophantic, the smarmy little rodent."

"He must have something," McGuire grinned. "She's twenty-five years younger and attractive."

Grace shook her head. "There's something odd there. She's too pleased with herself, and he's too detached."

"That is simple dislike talking. What would your dad say?"

"No, there's something wrong. Why pick a ski resort for a honeymoon when you can't ski worth a tot?"

"Because she wanted to."

"He's not that kind of man. They're probably international jewel thieves planning a heist."

"Their manners aren't good enough."

She laughed, and finished her chocolate to the dregs, much to the disgust of Schokolade. "Well, shall we go upstairs and prove how simple it is to bridge twenty years' age difference?"

They did that, too.

In the morning she was up before dawn. "Only way I can avoid that Ransome woman. Lunch in the dining room. Be there."

Alone, McGuire tried to go back to sleep, but the irregular hours of thirty-five years took over. He was wide awake and decided on an early breakfast. Showered and shaved, he opened his door to retrieve his shined shoes.

Marian Ransome hurried out of the room across the hall in full ski regalia. A black balaclava framed her eyes and mouth, and tried vainly to cover her mass of strawberry blonde hair.

She gave him a wave and a smile, "Late again!" and vanished down the stairs in a bustle of ultra-sleek black-and-red Spandex as tight as skin. She passed Herr Huber at the desk, calling out, "Your marvelous chocolate made me oversleep again, damn it," and was gone with the slam of the outer door.

In the corridor, McGuire picked up his shoes and saw the white cat. It sidled along the hall as stealthily as a twenty-pound animal can. In her haste, Marian Ransome had left the room door ajar. The heavy cat sniffed at the door and in a flash was inside. McGuire laughed to himself and saw an image of Ransome waking up with twenty pounds of white fur on his chest and a vision of blue eyes and long whiskers staring into his face.

When McGuire finished dressing and came out of his room again, he heard violent swearing in the Ransomes' room. Seconds later Schokolade came sauntering out without unseemly haste, its tongue licking thick chocolate and traces of cream from mouth and whiskers with slow enjoyment and regal dignity. Moments later the door slammed shut.

McGuire smiled and went on down to breakfast, wishing Grace Neville were with him, and yet welcoming the time alone to gather his thoughts about yesterday and last night.

*   *   *

After breakfast, McGuire took a walk through the sleeping town and out into the countryside. The snow was packed solid along the narrow roads, and the mountains shined in the early morning sun. The only people out were a few ski bums heading for the lifts, and the farmers feeding their cows and horses in the barns, the steam of animal heat rising from the open barn doors.

The uniformed postman passed him with a friendly wave.

The steep roofs of the houses steamed in the dawn.

In the distance, a magnificent old castle stood on its high ridge above the small houses.

He walked far out away from tourists and the bustle of the town and ski slopes, thinking of Grace Neville and himself. He'd known her only one day, but already she had made him forget Sally. Almost forget. He would never quite forget Sally, and somehow he knew Grace knew that and it made no difference. But where could it go? A retired cop from L.A., and *Lady* Grace Neville, barrister, from Old England? Then he smiled. He could almost hear her voice: *"Any bloody where we want to take it, Yank."*

He went into the solarium for a hot chocolate to warm his bones after the long walk. Eddie Ransome sat alone at a table in his town clothes eating breakfast, his overcoat draped over the chair back, staring out and up toward the high slopes of the ski mountain. He saw McGuire and waved.

"Join me, Paul."

McGuire had no interest in sitting with anyone but Grace Neville this morning, but he had no polite reason to refuse. He sat down and signaled the waiter.

"Guess we're sharing the same boat," Ransome said. "I've been waiting for Marian to come down from her morning runs all week. If I drink much more coffee and this damned whipped cream, I'll need a whole new wardrobe when we get home."

The waiter brought McGuire's chocolate. Could Schokolade be far behind? Eddie Ransome glared at the giant white cat.

"Damned cat is underfoot more than the rug." Then he smiled at McGuire. "Marian told me about you and Lady Neville being an item. That's one powerful woman. You'll have your hands full."

"We met only yesterday, Ransome. I don't think we're an 'item' yet."

"Of course, sorry," Ransome nodded, looked out at the mountain again. "I don't really mind waiting. Better than freezing at dawn out on that mountain. Marian really loves her skiing. I scored a lot of points with this honeymoon idea. I'm even getting to ski pretty well."

McGuire put the cup down for Schokolade. In an instant the big white cat had its face and whiskers stained brown and thick white.

"Well," he said, "I better get out and try to improve my skiing too. Nice talking to you, Ransome."

Eddie Ransome nodded, glanced at his watch, and turned to look out at the mountain again.

McGuire had graduated to the intermediate slopes, and as he swung to a stop at the base of the mountain after his fourth and final run before going back to the chalet to meet Grace for lunch, an agitated group of people crowded around the terminal of the cable car to the top of the mountain. He saw police and security, a ski patrol team loading equipment aboard the cable cars, and the security chief talking earnestly to a distraught Eddie Ransome.

Ransome gripped McGuire's arm with an iron hand. "Have you seen Lady Neville? Has she come down? They're always down by this time! Something's happened to Marian, I know it!"

The ski patrol left on the cable car, and the security chief tried to calm the balding little man. "She probably stayed up longer, conditions were perfect this morning at the top. Now the cars are crowded and she's been delayed, that's all. I'm sure there's nothing to be concerned about."

"Lady Neville?" McGuire asked. "Has she come down?"

"Of course. An hour ago, at least."

The police and security continued to calm Eddie Ransome.

McGuire rode the chalet's van back to town, and went directly into the dining room to meet Grace. When he saw she wasn't there, he took a window table and ordered a beer. He finished the stein, and she still hadn't arrived. He asked the waiter to see if she had left a message for him at the desk.

"Yes, Herr McGuire," the waiter reported. "She requests you go to her room as soon as you return. The message is marked urgent."

McGuire knocked again.

There was still no answer. He listened at the door, heard neither sound nor movement inside Grace's room. Retired, he had none of his tools, not even his gun, but the seventeenth-century locks on the room doors had been replaced with simple spring locks. He checked the empty corridor and used his credit card.

The room was empty. And a mess. Two dresses flung on the bed. The ski outfit she'd worn this morning lying on the floor. Drawers open but not empty. Clothes missing from the closets, but not all. Two suitcases from a set. Not the mess of violence or a search, it was the mess of a hasty departure with the intention of returning.

At the desk, Herr Huber hurried from his office. "Ah, Herr McGuire! Lady Neville wished me to give you her regrets, she was unexpectedly called home. She will phone as soon as the occasion permits, and plans to return shortly. Some family problem, I'm afraid, alas. I apologize for not being here when you received the earlier message. An emergency in the kitchen, *ja*?"

McGuire sat alone in the saloon lounge, a single-malt scotch neat in his hand. At midday, with a brilliant winter sun outside on the snow and mountains, no one came to the bar. And his mind wasn't on the scotch or the sun or the mountains.

He had a violent urge, even need, to be with Grace. Share her joy, or comfort her in tragedy. He hoped it was joy rather than tragedy. His experience of emergencies had been almost all tragedy,

and he found himself wondering if her abrupt departure was connected to what she had wanted to talk about in her room.

Brooding, he only vaguely heard the voices and heavy feet out in
the lobby. Herr Huber's agitated voice. Eddie Ransome. That caught
his attention, and he went out into the lobby with his scotch unfinished behind him.

Two uniformed policemen were inside the front door. Guests
milled about, whispering. Eddie Ransome sat in a high-backed chair,
his head in his hands. A short, stocky man, also in uniform but
wearing a loden coat, talked to him softly but firmly.

In front of the registration desk, Herr Huber stood in the center
of a knot of employees. All watched Eddie Ransome and the man
in loden. As McGuire approached, the proprietor came to meet him,
literally wringing his hands.

"*Ach Gott*, Herr McGuire, a terrible tragedy. Never to my guests
has such a thing happened, *nein, nein*." Herr Huber's tenuous com-
mand of English failed entirely. "Off the mountain, *ja*. All the way
to rocks down. Terrible. One hour ago less they find. It is terrible.
Such good she is. No one can they understand. One of my guests
she could not ever happen to . . ."

The alarms honed by thirty-five years of police work clanged all
through McGuire's head.

"Mrs. Ransome?"

Herr Huber nodded miserably. "So young she is. On the honeymoon. *Ach* . . ."

McGuire realized he would get nothing more definite from the
proprietor. The short man in the loden coat was patting Eddie Ransome's knee and standing up. Two more men had arrived, both in
civilian clothes, and both obviously local officials. The loden man
turned Ransome over to them and walked toward the door, mo-
tioning the two policemen out ahead of him.

McGuire caught up with him at his car parked in front of the
chalet. "Is it Captain or Lieutenant?"

The man bowed to the importance of the tourist. "Inspector
Klammer, sir. To you, Sergeant, I think. You are?"

"Paul McGuire, a friend of Marian Ransome's from Los Angeles.

Can you tell me what happened? I don't want to bother Mr. Ransome."

Klammer looked solemn. "All we know at the moment is that Mrs. Ransome went up on the second cable car this morning. When she failed to come down at her normal time, her husband grew concerned, and the ski patrol went up to look for her. They did not find her at the terminal or on the slopes, so instituted a complete search that, sadly, resulted in the location of her body in a remote ravine near the summit. I'm sorry, Mr. McGuire."

"She was alone?"

"That is what I have been told. A single ski track to the edge of the ravine."

"When did it happen?"

"She had been dead for some hours. I'd say soon after she arrived at the top this morning, alas."

While McGuire had been out walking, and Eddie Ransome was having breakfast far from the top of the mountain. So much for the alarms of thirty-five years of police work. Good thing he *had* retired.

Without Grace Neville, McGuire felt caught in a vast expanse of empty time. He went back on the slopes for the rest of the day. He had his dinner alone in the dining room. He took a long walk through the village in the snow. Finally tired, he went into the solarium to what was becoming his regular table and had a hot chocolate nightcap he hoped would help him sleep.

The hot chocolate was insidious. Soon he'd be as fat as the mound of white instantly sitting on his table and staring at him from immobile blue eyes.

Nothing stopped Schokolade from its quest.

If Grace didn't call in the morning, he'd call her.

It filled the dark room all around McGuire's bed.

A question, a picture. There behind his eyes, buried deep in the shadows of the room and inside his sleeping mind.

A moving picture. Like a dream, in two or three places at the same time. Faceless pictures and soundless words. An old silent film in black and white.

He woke up every few hours, lay looking up at the ceiling where the chalet light reflected from the snow below his windows. Restless, waiting for the faces to clear, the words to take on meaning. But whatever was trying to enter his mind remained silent and murky, an empty charade behind a thick fog.

A charade that slowly faded, and toward dawn he finally fell into a deep sleep.

The sun was high outside his windows when he awakened again, aching in every bone and hungry. He got up, shaved, showered, dressed, and went out to have a late breakfast or early lunch, half his mind still trying to penetrate the faceless silent film hovering somewhere behind his eyes.

The door to the Ransomes' room was open. Someone moved briskly about inside. Drawers opened and closed. McGuire looked in. Eddie Ransome was packing. The balding man turned and saw McGuire. He smiled wanly, shook his head.

"Who can believe it, you know? One minute I'm having coffee and breakfast, enjoying the sun and mountains on my honeymoon and waiting for my bride, and the next minute she's dead. An instant on a mountain, and everything's over."

"You're going home so soon?"

"No reason to stay." He shrugged and looked around at his open suitcases. And hers. "The terrible part is packing her stuff too. But . . . what else can I do with it? Someone back home can use the stuff, I suppose." The small man brushed hard at his eyes. "I can't just leave it! As if she never existed!"

"You're taking her home?"

"You expect me to leave her here, abandon her to strangers?"

"I'm just surprised the police are releasing the body so soon."

"The . . . autopsy is over. Why do they need her? We're both out of here today, tomorrow at the latest. I never want to see this place, this country, or a ski again!"

"You arranged to ship the body that fast?"

He snapped a bag closed, moved to the next. "Fortunately, I fly my own jet."

"Really? All the way from the States?"

He shook his head, almost smiled. "Of course not. I don't fly a Seven-forty-seven. From Paris. I leased it. My reps are arranging a commercial flight from there." The faint smile vanished, and the balding little man stared around the room littered with two weeks of worn and unworn clothes. "Who could have known we'd be flying home this way?" He sat down hard on the bed, held his head in his hands. "Marian was worried. She thought it was dangerous to fly through the mountains."

McGuire looked down at him sympathetically, but his face and eyes frowned. Eddie Ransome was wasting no time leaving Austria.

In late afternoon sunlight, Sergeant Klammer stood to the left of an elegant mahogany desk carved with the imperial eagles of the Habsburg Empire. McGuire didn't know the tall, slender man behind the desk, but the man seemed to know him.

"Mr. McGuire. Please sit down. Sergeant Klammer has spoken about you. I am Examining Magistrate Berger. How can I help?"

McGuire tried to put on his most innocent and ingratiating smile. A concerned friend, nothing more. "I was wondering what the autopsy on Marian Ransome showed, if you'd found anything unusual on top of the mountain when you went up."

Berger wasn't buying the act. "You failed to inform Sergeant Klammer you are a policeman. In California, I believe. A detective lieutenant? You have some suspicions the tragedy was not an accident?"

"A retired detective lieutenant, Magistrate," McGuire said. "And I have a feeling."

"Ah, yes. A feeling." Berger nodded, as if ex-detectives came into his office with a feeling about a death every day. "And on what is this feeling based?"

"It's too easy. Open and shut. An expert skier made a really stupid mistake."

"They do make them. Especially overconfident experts. She was far off the standard runs in an unmarked area, and the ravine is quite hidden."

McGuire groped for the elusive thoughts rolling in the mist of his mind. "It's a funny honeymoon for a man who can barely ski. They were . . . odd. They didn't really *seem* to be on a honeymoon. They . . ."

McGuire stopped. It was like catching shadows. He wasn't even sure how his doubts had started. Something in that silent, faceless movie in his mind all last night.

Berger was gentle. "I'm sure you needed more, ah, solid, suspicions when you investigated, Mr. McGuire."

"Sure, of course," McGuire acknowledged, thought for a moment. "What about the autopsy? Anything unusual?"

"There is always something unusual," Berger said. "In this case, Mrs. Ransome died of a massive head injury consistent with the fall into the ravine. She had in addition a broken arm and other small injuries, none in any way fatal. The time frame fits the condition of the body, the medical examination puts the time between dawn and approximately zero eight hundred hours. The unusual finding in this case is that the smaller injuries are far fewer than we would have expected."

"As if she had been relaxed when she fell? No fear?"

Berger nodded. "The medical examiner has no idea why, or what it could mean, and neither do we."

But it bothered the magistrate. He hadn't opened a folder. He knew the autopsy results by heart, had thought about them.

"She was wearing her skis?" McGuire asked.

"Of course," Sergeant Klammer said. "One had released, the other had broken but was still on."

"Her injuries came from the fall?"

"As far as we can tell," Magistrate Berger said.

"You found nothing unusual at the top?"

Klammer shook his head. "Nothing. A single track to the edge." He shrugged. He had seen too many skiing deaths.

"But she was relaxed when she went over. Could she have been dead or unconscious *before* she went over?"

"She could have hit her head first and then gone over the edge, but her tracks do not indicate that. There is no sign of anyone else that far off the trail. Not within over two hundred meters of her tracks and the ravine."

"Two hundred meters? You mean there were other tracks?"

"Yes. One more set. Another solitary skier. Perhaps two hundred and twenty meters from her track and easily that far from the ravine."

"Could whoever it was have seen her go over?"

Berger said, "No one has come forward. We cannot be sure exactly when the second tracks were made except that it was some time yesterday morning."

McGuire nodded, and stood up. "Thanks for talking to me."

"Not at all. Such a tragic accident is always disturbing."

McGuire walked back to the chalet in the sudden winter twilight, and thought about those other tracks. No one had come forward, so it was probably nothing, the tracks not even made at the same time. Still—

"Of course I have Lady Neville's telephone number in England," Herr Huber said. "I shall ring it?"

"Please," McGuire said. "I'll wait in my room."

Upstairs he sat on the edge of the bed. He hoped he would hear her voice angry at him for calling instead of waiting for her to call him. The minutes seemed to stretch as darkly as the full night outside now. When the phone rang, he snatched the receiver so fast he nearly dropped it.

"McGuire!"

Herr Huber's puzzled voice said, "They say she is not there. They do not understand. They say she is here since two weeks."

"Let me talk to them."

"You wish the call to be put through?"

"Yes."

An equally puzzled female voice came on the line. "Mr. McGuire? I am sorry, but I know of no plans for Madame to come home until the month is up. She isn't there at the chalet?"

"There's no family emergency in England? Some problem?"

"Certainly not."

"And she hasn't contacted you in any way?"

"She has not."

McGuire thanked her and hung up. There on the edge of his bed his stomach did a flip-flop. He couldn't remember when he'd last felt such a sudden fear. The time the psycho had used Sally as a shield? He still didn't like to think of that long day, how close he had come to killing his wife instead of the poor psycho.

Magistrate Berger was leaving his office but greeted McGuire with typical Austrian courtesy, only a slight stiffness in his voice to show he wasn't totally pleased.

"Ah, Mr. McGuire. What can I help you with this time?"

McGuire might have caught a hint of sarcasm in the emphasis on *this time*, and smiled because he had done the same thing to interfering civilians, but not tonight. All he could think about was Grace Neville and Eddie Ransome.

"I think Eddie Ransome killed his wife, and now he's done something to a woman named Grace Neville."

Berger stared at him. "Lady Neville? Explain, please."

McGuire told him of Grace's urgent message to meet her in her room instead of at lunch, her sudden departure before he could get there, and the phone call to England. "She had no reason to make up a lie, Magistrate. And what did she want to tell me so urgently and privately it couldn't wait for lunch?"

Berger studied McGuire for a moment, then sat down and waved him to a chair. "I will admit Mr. Ransome's haste to take his wife's body out of Austria makes me uneasy. But look at the facts, Mr.

McGuire. You yourself saw Mrs. Ransome leave her room alone that morning to go to the top of the mountain. Her death occurred at a time when Ransome could not have killed her. Even if there were some clever plan, how would her body have been found where it was with no trace in the snow of anyone having been in that ravine or anywhere closer than two hundred meters?"

"Someone carried the body to the edge, tossed her over, back-tracked in the same set of ski tracks."

"Please, Lieutenant, give us a shade of credit. You think we did not consider that? With double weight the tracks would have been much deeper, and skiing over an existing track can never be perfect, will leave obvious signs. There were none."

"And Lady Neville? Why is she missing?"

"Ah, yes, Lady Neville." Berger hesitated. "Perhaps her apparent lie was intended only for you? I'm sorry, but resort romances are quite common. I expect Lady Neville has merely gone elsewhere, alas."

The magistrate was embarrassed. McGuire felt his face redden and his stomach turn over. He had never even thought of that. But his thirty-five years as a cop told him it was a far more plausible explanation, that he had been another old fool reading romance into a casual fling at a ski chalet.

McGuire barely recalled leaving Berger's office and stumbling through the dark, snowy streets to the chalet and the bar where he sat brooding over another single-malt. She had dumped him, nothing more. Why was he surprised? Why hadn't he even thought of that possibility? Was he that much in need? Why should he have thought it was anything more than a brief romance?

"There you are, McGuire," Eddie Ransome said, his hand held out. "I wanted to say goodbye. If you're ever in San Francisco and need some investment help, look me up. Here's my card."

McGuire stared at the extended card. "Thought you'd already gone, Ransome."

"Damn red tape. Kept me an extra day, special tests on the body.

Bullshit. They just wanted an extra day's money from the rich American. But I'm off now, first thing in the morning."

Ransome's period of mourning seemed to have lasted one day, his dead wife no more now than *the body.* McGuire took the business card. "You're holding up pretty well."

"Life goes on, right? Got to get back to work. Don't forget, you need to make extra money, look me up." Then he shook his head sadly. "Hope you and Lady Neville have better luck here than we did."

McGuire stared into his scotch after Ransome had gone. Why didn't he trust the man? Why was he sure Ransome had murdered his wife and was going to get away with it? Then again, he'd been sure he and Grace Neville were starting something big, too. No fool like an old fool. That seemed to apply to old cops as well as to widowers who couldn't tell a casual affair from true love.

He was the last one in the bar, alone with his expensive single-malt, when they finally had to politely throw him out.

He came awake in the dark bedroom. His head throbbed, and his mouth was dry as a desert. As he lay unmoving, he became aware of faint light behind the rectangles of the windows. Dawn. Was that what had awakened him?

No, something else. And he realized what it had been—footsteps out in the corridor. Hurrying footsteps exactly the same as the morning Marian Ransome died. A woman's footsteps in boots. He jumped up, dressed, and picked up his shoes on the way out.

The corridor was empty, all the doors closed except one—Grace Neville's door!

He took the stairs down two at a time, his shoes still in his hand. Behind the registration desk the proprietor waved to him, smiling from ear to ear.

"She has returned. It was not such bad trouble after all, *ja?* She tells me to tell you, lunch in the dining room, this time she will be there."

"Returned? Grace? Lady Neville?"

"*Ja, ja.* She is now on the mountain already." Herr Huber beamed, glad to have a favorite client back.

McGuire felt a surge of joy—and then a sudden giant fear.

"You're sure?" he said. "You're sure it was Lady Neville?"

Huber frowned. "How could I not be sure, Herr McGuire? To me herself she spoke. *Ja.*" McGuire saw the faint flicker in the proprietor's eyes. A flicker of doubt. A sudden uneasiness to reinforce a question he didn't even know he had. "She has the same clothes, voice . . ." the old man trailed off, his eyes almost scared.

"Clothes? Voice?" McGuire's eyes bored through the proprietor. "Where did she speak to you from? Where were you?"

Huber licked his lips. "I am in my office. The door it is open as always. I see her pass the desk, get up to go to her, but she speaks the message for you and is gone away."

McGuire stared at the man. "You're not sure, are you? Now that I've made you question what you saw, you're not sure it really was Lady Neville. You saw her twenty feet away, moving past the desk. Did you see her face at all?"

Huber blinked, confused and a little afraid. "I see her face, Herr McGuire, but not much. She wears, how do you say it in your language, the thing that covers around the face, and the ears, and the neck and . . ."

"A balaclava?"

"Yes, that is it. A balaclava."

McGuire had never seen Grace wear a balaclava to ski or at any other time, but Marian Ransome had worn one the morning she died. He thought of the extra tracks on top of the mountain more than two hundred meters from the fatal trail of Marian Ransome's skis.

"Where's Ransome?"

Herr Huber said, "He leaves before dawn to fly home."

"Where's the airport?"

"Innsbruck, Herr McGuire."

"No, I mean here."

"We do not have airport. We are much too small."

"But . . ."

In his mind McGuire heard Eddie Ransome's voice that first time in the solarium after Marian Ransome had spoken to him about Schokolade: "We better go get ready, Marian. It's an hour to Innsbruck." How did you get from the village to Innsbruck in an hour? By train or road it was three or four hours.

Then the silent movie of two nights ago suddenly had sound, and color, and faces. McGuire saw the corridor outside his room, and Schokolade, and Marian Ransome. He heard the dead woman's voice, and he knew.

Magistrate Berger was no happier at being rousted from bed than he had been to have a last-minute visitor the night before. In his living room, unshaven, Sergeant Klammer, who had brought McGuire to him, standing nervously in a corner, Berger listened to McGuire with a scowl.

"It was the cat, the hot chocolate," McGuire said. "When Marian Ransome left their room that morning, she didn't close the door. The cat slipped in and came out with chocolate and cream on its whiskers. But I heard Marian tell Herr Huber his marvelous hot chocolate had made her oversleep again."

Berger sighed. "People don't always drink the whole cup."

"Schokolade wouldn't touch dregs, and there wouldn't be a layer of cream left on top to get on its whiskers. Besides, I talked to the room maid. She said Marian Ransome's cup had still been full that morning. She hadn't touched it."

"Maids can confuse days," Berger said, but he didn't sigh and his scowl had turned thoughtful.

"Not that day," McGuire said.

"Mrs. Ransome was trying to be nice to the proprietor."

"Huber and the maid say she always drank her chocolate, it helped her sleep."

"Something happened the night before to make her forget to drink her hot chocolate."

McGuire was grim. "Yeah, something happened. What happened

was that Marian Ransome was killed. In the room, or somewhere else. It wasn't Mrs. Ransome who left the room that morning. It was someone who looked a lot like her, with a balaclava to hide part of her face, and a strawberry blonde wig. Someone skilled enough to imitate her voice and movement, who'd been coached by Ransome. Someone who came back from Innsbruck with Ransome the night before disguised as his wife, went out early that morning to ski, but didn't like hot chocolate."

Berger was listening now.

McGuire went on, "It wasn't Lady Neville who returned this morning and went right out to ski the same high slopes. And soon the real Lady Neville is going to have an accident on the mountain too. If it isn't already too late."

"How did Mrs. Ransome's body get into the ravine?"

"How do you get from here to Innsbruck in an hour?"

Berger looked at Sergeant Klammer. "Call Innsbruck, tell Hartmann."

The magistrate headed for the door, with McGuire right behind him.

The tiny heliport was between the village and the ski slopes.

"Sure, Mr. Ransome come in from Innsbruck in a rented 'copter. Used it a lot."

The heliport manager was a relocated Austrian-American with an Austrian wife.

"Three nights ago?"

"Sure. He likes some restaurant over in Innsbruck."

"Mrs. Ransome went with him?"

"Like always. Honeymoon and all. Too bad what happened."

"When did they get back?"

"Maybe one A.M. Last chopper in before I closed up."

"Both of them?"

"You think she walked?" He laughed, but his heart wasn't in it. "The accident, right? He could have tossed her out? Well, he didn't.

She got out of the chopper and damn near ran to their car. I mean, it was cold. He came in, signed off on the flight, and they drove off. Hell, you couldn't never miss that hair."

"No," McGuire said. "You couldn't miss that hair. When did he take off again the next morning?"

"He didn't, mister. Not that morning, or any other time after she got killed. Until he took the body out this morning."

Berger snapped, "When this morning?"

"Maybe twenty minutes ago. He was late, red tape for the body, I guess."

"Was anyone else with him?" McGuire said.

"Just him and the coffin."

"You're sure? Think!" Berger cried.

"Sure I'm sure. I took out the back seats so the coffin'd fit, and there wasn't no one in the front with Mr. Ransome."

McGuire said, "He must have Grace hidden somewhere, plans to pick her up."

Berger ran for his car and radio. Five minutes later, two Christoperus rescue helicopters thundered low above the heliport and settled slowly to the ground.

It was a police chopper from Innsbruck that found them.

A helicopter on the ground, almost hidden in the morning shadow of an isolated farmhouse.

A second helicopter out in the open, Eddie Ransome gassing it up, and the woman watching him. They were on their way into the farmhouse when the police and rescue choppers swooped down on them from out of the morning sun.

McGuire was the first to jump clear, stumbling toward the farmhouse.

Ransome tried to run, was floundering in the deep snow like a dying elk when the police surrounded him.

The woman never moved. She waited with her hands high until the police reached her. Her name was Carla Fuller, and she started talking before they even handcuffed her.

McGuire found Grace in the farmhouse, tied to a chair and furious at him for taking so long to arrive. "Father would have had me out of here and into the nearest pub two days ago."

"Better late than never," McGuire grinned.

"Clichés on top of it! Untie me, you clown, and fly me to a hot bath and a dry martini."

Kommissar Hartmann from Innsbruck cabled San Francisco. The SFPD knew Eddie Ransome only too well. In other states he'd served time for embezzlement and fraud, and they'd been watching his new operation for a year but hadn't been able to find anything wrong.

Carla Fuller told the rest of the story. A professional actress with plastic features and a gift for voices, she'd known Ransome for years, in more ways than one. "Marian was a nothing file clerk, but she spotted Eddie's operation as a pyramid scam and threatened to go to the cops if he didn't marry her. She wanted to come here for the honeymoon, and that's when Eddie came to me. I always liked Eddie, and she was a two-bit blackmailer, so I said okay." Then she began to cry. "I must have been crazy."

Ransome leased a jet to fly to Innsbruck, and a helicopter from Innsbruck to the village. The night before the accident, he landed at the farmhouse on the way back from Innsbruck, killed Marian, dressed her for skiing, and dropped her body into the ravine from the helicopter. He and Carla Fuller returned to the village, waited until dawn, and Carla did her act.

Eddie had leased a second helicopter, had it waiting at the farmhouse. He slipped out of the chalet soon after Carla Fuller, drove to the farmhouse, flew the second chopper to the ravine and picked up Carla waiting at the edge minutes after dawn!

That far off the main ski areas, at that hour, Ransome was sure no one would see the chopper hovering low for less than a minute. But Grace Neville had sensed something strange about the Ransomes.

"When I saw her leave the main areas, I followed," Grace told them all in the warmth of the chalet bar. "I saw him do the pickup. I wasn't sure what was going on, didn't know the real Marian was dead in the ravine, but I knew something was wrong. Unfortunately, Ransome saw me out there. When I got back to my room they were waiting. You know the rest."

"Another planned accident on the slopes," McGuire said.

"The slopes," Berger said, "that was the key. It had to be a ski resort. To make an accident believable, and for the cold and snow to hide the real time of death. If Mrs. Ransome had been a swimmer instead of a skier, she might still be alive."

After the officials left to take Ransome and Carla Fuller to Innsbruck, Grace ordered her third martini.

"You know," she said, "I think I've had enough snow for now. Perhaps Cannes. Or Majorca. Do you swim better than you ski?"

"Like a porpoise."

"Then what are we waiting for?"

"Cannes or Majorca?"

"Let's make it both."

And that's what they did.

The Envelopes, Please

Gary A. Braunbeck

"You want to *what?*"

"You heard me," said my brother. "I want to make a movie about what happened."

"Oh come on! What kind of a movie could you—"

"I'm thinking along the lines of a Woody Allenish *Take the Money and Run* type of thing, only with more emotional resonance and meaningful irony."

"I don't recall feeling there was anything meaningfully ironic when that gun was shoved into my back."

"You're missing the point. I want to head into the same territory Altman did with *The Player*, only not as dark. More self-satiric. I need to know if you'll grant me the rights to your side of the story."

"How in hell would you start something like that?"

"Follow me. We open on a scene that's taking place well after the events have unfolded—you know, the two protagonists seeing and talking to each other about what happened to them, only the conversation is a little vague. Compelling enough to hold the viewer's interest but not specific enough that we play all our cards too soon.

We cut back and forth from one protagonist to the other, finally
ending in a slow cross-fade to the real start of the story."

"And that would be . . . ?"

"A medium shot of a guy reaching for the phone as it rings, right?
And as he picks up the handset we have this voice-over narra-
tion . . ."

Closing day of the Cannes Film Festival, my younger brother Douglas called my hotel room to ask if I could do a couple of favors—
one for him, one for the jury.

"I thought the jury was sequestered until the awards ceremony
tonight," I said.

"*Sequestered?* No, no, no—the Manson jury was sequestered; we
are under armed guard."

He'd told me about this at dinner last night. On the morning of
the awards ceremony, the members of the jury, their luggage fully
packed, were picked up at their hotel and taken to an "undisclosed"
location where they were locked in a room and weren't allowed to
leave until they had agreed on the disbursement of the film
awards—a prospect Doug had not been looking forward to.

"Stretching the truth a bit, aren't you?" I asked.

"No, Pete, I'm not. I knew that this place was supposed to be kept
secret; what I didn't know is that the house is gated, the gate is
locked, and the grounds are patroled by armed guards and attack
dogs."

I couldn't help but smile. "Well, you *did* jump right on the invitation."

"And you thought picking a best film would be easy. Try doing it
with nine other grumpy people when you're locked up like the
Rosenbergs."

Having won the Palme d'Or the previous year for his movie
Searching for Survivors (which he co-wrote, produced, and directed),
Doug had been asked to head the jury this time around, a duty he
took, as he did everything connected to filmmaking, with more than
a *soupçon* of seriousness.

"What do you need me to do?"

"Did you happen to, uh . . . bring along a couple of my extra insulin kits?"

"If I say yes, are you going to chew me a new one for acting like a mother hen? I only—wait a minute."

"Took you long enough."

"Jesus, Doug, when's your next shot due?"

"About half an hour ago. I'm sorry, I just now discovered that I'd run out."

Our late father had been just as careless with his medication, and wound up slipping into a diabetic coma from which he never emerged.

"Ah, *Doug*," I said, wanting to be angry at him but feeling only concern.

"I promise that you can lecture me all you want later. Get the kits and be waiting by the pool. Someone will be there to pick you up in about fifteen minutes."

"How long can you hold out?"

He swallowed. Twice. It sounded painful. "Another forty, forty-five minutes. Thanks, Pete. I love you, Bigbro."

"What's the other favor?"

"Not over the phone. You'll find out soon enough."

I replaced the handset in its cradle, took the insulin kits from my luggage, and started to make my way toward the pool. Passing through the lobby, even as worried as I was, I couldn't help but look out one of the massive front windows facing the edge of the cliffs and admire the stunning beauty of the Mediterranean, a sea "as mysteriously coloured as agates and carnelians of childhood, green as green milk, blue as laundry water, wine dark," as F. Scott Fitzgerald had described it so many years ago. This time of day the distant image of chaotic Cannes, some five miles away but clearly visible from several places on the grounds, was little more than a sparkling pink-and-cream ripple whose seeming tranquility was as deceptive as it was compelling.

Deciding I needed an equalizer for my nerves, I stopped at the bar long enough to order a Lerina—a wonderful sweet green liqueur manufactured by the monks at nearby St. Honorat in Les Iles de Lérins. Besides tasting wonderful, it had a remarkably soothing (as opposed to depressing) effect on me. As I stood waiting for the bartender to get to me, I once again found myself admiring the understated grandeur of the hotel in which I was staying.

The Hotêl du Cap, tucked safely away on a grassy hillside from the madness of Cannes, was the most exclusive and expensive in the Côte d'Azur. Doug had made my reservation last year promptly following his triumph at the festival, and though I was at first disappointed not to be staying at the Majestic or one of the other hotels near the Palais des Festivals, I was quickly taken by the air of hard-earned elitism exuded by everyone at the hotel, staff as well as guests.

"Not bad for a guy who used to deliver pizzas in Cedar Hill," I whispered to myself as my drink was handed to me. Taking a sip, I nodded my approval and began carefully moving past the German tycoons and flashy American showbiz types who were scurrying about. The clientele might not have been as grand or glitzy or glamorous as it had been in the days when the likes of Fred Astaire, Betty Grable, Haile Selassie, and Picasso could be found lounging in the lobby, but I enjoyed walking out the back doors and down through the stately park to the Eden Roc restaurant with its swimming pool by the sea. I loved standing there and imagining the days when Fitzgerald, champagne glass in his hand, would watch poor, mad Zelda dive from the rocks. The rich were, indeed, different.

I found an empty chaise near the edge of the pool, set my drink on the small attached table, and took a seat, donning my sunglasses and leaning back to enjoy the sun and the crisp, salty smell of the air.

Two women sitting nearby began talking in the decidedly bored but somehow deliciously sexy manner that seemed unique to women in this area of the world. One of them had that Lauren Bacall/Kathleen Turner purr thing going, so I oh-so-slowly turned my head to get a look at her.

Both of them wore string bikinis that were just one good breeze away from nonexistence. The one with the Bacall/Turner purr was a little heavier than her friend, but that suited me just fine; I'd seen more than my share of anorexic beauty queens since arriving here fifteen days ago. A woman with some actual physical density (i.e., a *shape*) was a welcome—not to mention exciting—relief.

She leaned toward her friend and said, in a voice so low and breathy I knew I'd be hearing it in my dreams for weeks to come, something like, *"Avez-vous la crème de mamelon?"* and her friend nodded and handed her a tube and the next thing I know my breathy-voiced goddess whips off her top to expose a perfect pair of breasts and starts rubbing cream on her nipples.

Listen to my silence as she did this.

Then her friend whips off her top and starts creaming *her* nipples.

Only then did I notice that every woman around the pool was sunbathing topless. All those firm, bronzed bodies. All that heat beaming down from the sky. All the breath that wasn't entering my lungs. All the thoughts that *were* entering my mind.

I understood now why Doug loved showbiz.

Then something purred on my other side and I turned back to face the dumbest-looking cat I had ever seen.

"Hello, Tasha," I said, reaching into my pocket for the small pouch of kitty treats I'd taken to carrying with me at all times.

"Meep," replied the cat, rubbing her face against my hand, then snatching the treat from between my fingers. I picked her up and began petting her. Tasha was the hotel's mascot, a gorgeous (but, as I said, stupid-looking) Siamese that had been (so the story goes) abandoned here a few years ago and was quickly adopted by the staff and management, who watched over her with the same concern and affection most people save for their children. One of the eccentricities I'd noticed about Cannes and its surrounding hamlets was that most business establishments had some type of animal always hanging around the premises; cats were the most popular (hence my always carrying a pouch of kitty treats—I like cats; sue me), followed a close second by various exotic birds, then by dogs, and, in one case, a llama. Locals said it was superstition handed down since 1834, when Lord Broughman and Vaux were turned away from the port at Var and had to wait out the French cholera epidemic in a then-sparsely populated little fishing village called—drumroll, please—Cannes. It was said that the first living thing to greet Broughman when he set foot on the island was a cat, and so friendly was the animal—as were the people who followed it—that he decided to settle here and build the famous Villa Eléonore Louise on the Fréjus Road, just west of Le Suquet—a stunning structure that remains a popular tourist attraction to this day.

"Have you any idea how much history rides on your fuzzy little back?" I asked Tasha, stroking her neck.

"Mwraugh," she said, then purred loud enough to attract the attention of the two topless wonders to my left; both women smiled at me and I felt as if they were undressing me with their eyes.

Wishful thinking on my part, I know, but it was the French Riviera at the height of its glamor, and if a guy can't shift his id into overdrive under such circumstances, then he might as well stay in Ohio and spend his vacation watching paint dry—one of the more exciting things to do in that state, by the way.

"Mr. Ely?" said a voice from behind me. One of the nipple goddesses looked over when she heard my last name; images of finding an enticing note waiting in my message box when I returned danced briefly through my head.

I turned around and saw a tall, sinewy man dressed in a traditional black chauffeur's uniform standing behind me.

"Yes?"

The guy actually clicked the heels of his shoes and bowed. Then he caught sight of Tasha, wrinkled his nose in apparent disgust, and took a step back, pointing toward the hotel parking lot. "My name is Philippe and I will be your driver. I do not mean to seem rude, but we should—"

I was already on my feet, and without thinking about it handed Tasha to the woman who had been the first to display her breasts to me (how often does a guy get the chance to say that?). It might have been my id in overdrive again, but I swear she pressed her . . . her*self* against me when she took the cat. I know that she kept staring at me as Philippe and I made our way back toward the lobby. (All right; I fully admit she might have been making eyes at Philippe, but I'd rather not believe it. The id may be strong but the ego is rice pudding.)

The limo was one of those seemingly half-mile-long monstrosities that has everything inside but a toilet.

Except this one did have a toilet.

It also had, much to my surprise, my brother waiting in the back seat.

Looking wrung-out, pale, and shaking.

"I sure hope you've got something for me," he said. At least he was munching on a chocolate bar and drinking a glass of orange juice. I climbed in and gave him the insulin kit, then a quick hug. Philippe closed the door behind me, then grabbed a taxi to take him up to the driver's door where he climbed in, started the car, and drove away.

"Why didn't you tell me you were coming?" I asked after Doug had finished with his medicine.

"The paranoia of the festival organizers is infectious. They worry that people might be monitoring cellular phone transmissions. If it were known one of the jury members was out and about, it might start some nasty rumors about the awards ceremony. There are evil forces about—or so they tell us. Don't ask me to explain the logic behind that to you because it'd give us both a massive brain hemorrhage."

I put a hand on his shoulder. "You okay now?"

"Bigbro comes to my rescue once again."

"Whenever you need it, Doug, you know that."

He smiled at me, and I at him.

"We're having a moment, aren't we?" he asked.

"Yeah, I guess so."

"I've heard about these." Silence. "Is it over yet?"

"We've got to do something about this sentimental streak of yours."

"This coming from the man who cried at the end of all five *Rocky* movies."

"Yeah, well."

He could tease me all he wanted to. I owed Doug a lot; *Searching for Survivors* had been based on a somewhat self-indulgent novella I'd written back in my college days. It had been published in the campus literary journal, where it was met by almost universal indifference save for Doug, who browbeat me into submitting a revised, streamlined version of the piece to The Paris Review. They asked for a revision, bought it, and published it the spring of the following year. Much to my shock, it was reprinted in three *Year's Best* anthologies, was nominated for an O. Henry Award, and won a Pushcart Prize—which, according to my agent, was what enabled her to sell my first novel for a respectable five-figure advance. The novel was well-received (I have the New York *Times* review in a frame on the wall of my office) and sold enough copies to go into a second, then third printing. It wound up selling nearly a hundred thousand copies, turning a decent profit for everyone concerned, which was enough to convince the publisher to offer a six-figure advance on a three-book contract. To top it all off, the film rights to my first novel had sold for nearly two hundred thousand dollars— which was why I could afford the trip to Cannes.

None of which, I still say, would have happened had not my smartass little brother pestered me into fixing the story and submitting it.

Sitting in the back seat of the obscenely luxurious limo with him that day, I felt a pang of regret that Dad hadn't lived to see our success; Mom couldn't have been more tickled for us, and both Doug and I had made sure that she would not be wanting for anything for the rest of her life, but there was still a palpable sense of loss among all of us; a silent space where once there had been a voice, and that silence reminded us that there was no sin or disgrace in enjoying the fruits of your labors, so long as you remembered that none of us are here for very long so it'd be nice if you shared your happiness with those you love.

Which puts things in their proper perspective when you find yourself schmoozing with the rich and famous in one of the most glamorous spots in the world. The French Riviera was a sybaritic heaven for those who believed that original sin had something to do with the absence of a tan or the accumulation of more than two percent body fat.

Or when your brother starts talking about spies.

"It started in the early 1950s because of McCarthy's objections to 'un-American sentiments' in *Stalag 17* when it competed here. McCarthy got the idea in his head that it wasn't enough to stamp out the Red Threat in Hollywood alone—he wanted to attack 'Communist-friendly' filmmakers whose movies came from outside the U.S. It wasn't hard for him to bully some people into coming over to his side. Am I boring you? You seem bored."

I shrugged. "Just a little confused, that's all."

"Be patient and all shall be revealed. Where was I?"

"Tailgunner Joe."

"Ah, yes. He sent spies over here—bogus film critics, a few legitimate producers, and several of his own team. The idea was to screen as many films as possible and report any 'dangerous' or 'questionable' material to him. If the films were in competition, they were supposed to somehow undermine the filmmaker's credibility. Barring that, they were to try to sabotage the festival in any way possible."

I shook my head and looked out at the yachts docked at the pier by the closed winter casino. "Jesus. Did he manage to do much damage?"

"When *Stalag 17* played here, someone broke into the theater the night before its premiere screening and tried to destroy the actual film. Jury members reported bribe attempts, death threats, people following them, the theater got bomb threats . . . it was a hot time in the old town."

"But McCarthy didn't last long."

"No, but there were thousands of other unscrupulous types not involved in the witch hunts who had good reason to pick up on McCarthy's cue—reporters, studio heads, and distributors not least among them."

"Okay, here's the twenty-five-cent question: Why?"

"Think about it: From a purely business standpoint, what's the one interest reporters, studio heads, and film distributors would have in common?"

I puzzled over that one for a minute, came up with a few ideas, discarded them, then a few more, and finally decided on what was, to me, one of the most obvious. "They would all want to know what films win the most awards."

"Right. Now, take it a step further. If you were a reporter sent here to cover the festival, it'd be quite a coup if you could find out what films won the awards before anyone else did. If you were a studio head or distributor, knowing the winners ahead of time—especially if those winners were independent productions, as many of the films competing here are—would enable you to seek out the necessary parties to strike up a solid deal for yourself and your company."

"But no one ever knows the winners ahead of time."

Doug shook his head. "Not true. If the jury can decide early on what performers will be given awards—actor, actress, supporting players—then it gives the festival organizers time to find if those performers are here. If not, they can contact them and have them flown in in time for the ceremony. And it's not just been restricted to performers in the past. Rumor has it that the year *Taxi Driver* won, the jury had decided on all the awards halfway through the festival.

"That's the preamble; here's where you need to pay attention: Just like McCarthy's spies tried to bribe judges to sabotage the festival, there are certain unscrupulous types who will pay a great deal of money to get a look at the announcement cards before the ceremony."

"I thought those were heavily guarded."

"They are, but as I'm sure you know, if someone wants to get at something bad enough, they'll find a way to do it. And anyone who comes here has the money to secure the means. You saw the card that they gave to me with the award last year, right? You even commented on how exquisite the calligraphy was.

"All of the announcement cards are handcrafted by a calligrapher who lives in Mougins—it's a little village not far from here. She's seventy and lives alone. During the festival her house is closely watched by private security—round-the-clock surveillance, electronic sweeps for bugs, her phone is replaced every day as a safeguard against any undetected wiretaps."

I laughed. "Lord, you'd think we were talking about nuclear secrets."

"I told you they were paranoid."

I reached into my pocket for some chewing gum and pulled out the pouch of kitty treats by mistake. Slipping that into my side pants pocket, I located the gum, popped a stick into my mouth, and said, "What is it the jury wants me to do?"

He reached under the seat and pulled out a stack of off-white envelopes whose flaps were edged in gold trim. They were tied together with two thin, golden ribbons, one stretched horizontally, one vertically, both meeting in the middle where they were tied into the shape of a butterfly's wings. He grinned and handed them to me.

"These look like the announcements."

"That's the whole idea. This is a phony set, made by the same calligrapher. They do it this way every year in case any of the aforementioned unscrupulous types resort to theft."

"Why do I not like where I think this is going?"

"It's not that bad. All you have to do is take these envelopes back to the Majestic and make a little production number out of giving them to the festival rep who'll be waiting there for you. If you could flash them on your way in so that the paparazzi get a good look and maybe follow you, that'd be just peachy."

"That's it? I don't have to mutter any code words or look for someone in a fedora and trench coat or listen for the theme from *The Third Man* being whistled ominously from the shadows?"

He stared at me, expressionless. "Have I ever told you that sometimes the only way I can differentiate one end of you from the other is because of the teeth? *Yes*, that's all you have to do. In exchange, you get a VIP pass to all festivities tonight *and* you can sit at the jury's table."

"Did you see me shudder there? That was the thrill zapping through me."

The car turned onto a dirt road lined on both sides with palm trees and heavy foliage and began slowing down. Doug rolled down one of the tinted windows and took a deep breath of the damp, air. "Almost time for me to get out, Bigbro." He offered the envelopes once again. "Would it help if I said please?"

I took them from his hand. "You never had to ask, you know that."

"I don't like acting on assumptions when it comes to anyone outside of the movie industry. I don't know a lot of trustworthy people, and I'd rather have ground glass rubbed in my eyes than do anything to offend you."

"That's a good line. You should write it down and use it somewhere."

"I'm sure you'll beat me to it," he said as an armed guard who looked like one of Che Guevara's rebels came up to the limo and opened the door for him.

"I don't see any house," I said, looking out.

"That's the whole idea. Miguel here will blindfold me after you leave and guide me back to the compound on foot. That way no one but the guards and festival officials will ever know the location."

"You're a better man than I am, Gunga Din."

"Great movie. I cried when Sam Jaffe died."

"No, you didn't. I did."

"Ah, well. Chin up; maybe Stallone'll do *Rocky VI*."

Miguel closed the door and Philippe drove away. I leaned back in the seat and looked at the envelopes, then closed my eyes and enjoyed the ride.

We stopped about fifteen minutes later, and when Philippe opened the door I was immediately overpowered by the smell of the sea. I climbed out, blinking against the late-afternoon sun, and found myself looking at an old and decaying port where only one boat was docked.

"Where are we?"

"The west end of the island," said Philippe. "This port is rumored to have been used by Jean Lafitte and his pirates. They say some of his treasure may be buried in the hills behind us."

"What are we doing here?"

"Advancing my career."

I started to turn around but was stopped by a sound.

There are three sounds that cannot be mistaken for any other noise; water dripping from a leaky faucet, someone blowing their nose, and the metallic click of a hammer being cocked back on a gun.

Philippe jammed the gun in my back and pulled one of my arms behind my back. "I don't wish to hurt you, Mr. Ely, but I will if I have to. Be very quiet and get into the boat."

I held out my free hand—the one holding the envelopes. "You want these, is that it?"

"I could care less about what's in those, but my employer does not share my feelings."

"What did they do, bribe you?"

"I have a screenplay. My employer knows people who can get it made into a film."

"But what you really want to do is direct, right?"

He jammed the barrel deeper into my ribs. It hurt. A lot.

I got into the boat and sat down as Philippe fired up the outboard motor; it choked once, then sputtered to life. We rode out of the port and made a left, heading toward what looked to be open sea. My heart was somewhere up around my nasal passages because I just knew this creep was going to take me out to the middle of the sea, take the envelopes away, then make me jump overboard and swim back.

I can't swim. Hence my concern.

But true to his word, Philippe didn't hurt me.

Twenty minutes or so after we'd left the port, a small island came into view. It looked oddly familiar for some reason, and as we pulled up alongside a dilapidated dock it hit me.

"This is where American International filmed *The Island of Dr. Moreau.*" I looked up at my captor. "The remake, the one with Burt Lancaster. It was a lot better than the one with Charles Laughton."

Philippe said nothing, only waved the gun to the side, which I took to be his way of suggesting I get out of the boat. I did, he came up behind me and shoved the gun into my back—the same spot as before, which was going to have a hell of a bruise if I lived through this—and we set off toward a heavily pebbled path that snaked through the trees and bushes and past something that looked like a small swamp to emerge near the entrance to a large stone structure.

"An abandoned fortress from the time of Lord Broughman and Vaux," said Philippe. "It used to be a major drop-off point for drug smugglers in the nineteen seventies."

"What the hell are you, some kind of tour guide?"

"As a matter of fact, yes. Now please move."

We entered the fortress, making our way over stone and dead vegetation, until we reached what appeared to be some kind of lookout room at the far end. Philippe put his free hand on my shoulder and shoved me through the doorway.

A woman with her back to us stood looking out through a large hole in the crumbling wall. "This island could be such a lovely place if one were to invest the time and money into its development, don't you think, Mr. Ely?"

Then she turned around.

It took a moment for me to recognize her, what with her breasts being covered and all.

Even if I hadn't recognized her by her face, I would've realized she was the first Nipple Goddess from the pool by what she was holding.

Tasha.

The cat looked up at me and said, "Meep."

"I never could resist a cute kitty," said the woman.

I knew then that she and Philippe *had* been exchanging looks at the hotel earlier, but not for the reasons my ego had feared.

"I don't get it," I said.

She came toward me, stroking Tasha's neck. "It's not all that complicated, Mr. Ely. My father and I have a decided stake in the outcome of the festival. It would be auspicious if we knew the Palme d'Or winner before tonight's award ceremony."

"Mind if I ask why?"

"Yes, I do."

"Then at least tell me how you knew I'd have the envelopes in my possession."

"One of my employees is on the room service staff at the Majestic. They overheard your brother mentioning your name in reference to some kind of delivery. It didn't take a genius to realize he'd planned to have you deliver the names of the winners to the festival representative at the hotel. Now may I have the envelopes, please?"

I wanted to laugh but the thought of the gun pointed at my back drained the humor from the moment. I held out the envelopes and she took them from my hand, dropping Tasha.

Somewhere between the cat hitting the ground and the woman opening the top envelope, I noticed that Philippe was breathing funny. I turned and saw that not only were his eyes red and puffy but his face was slightly swollen and very sweaty.

"You're allergic to cats, aren't you?" I asked.

He coughed, then sneezed, then tried kicking Tasha away from him. The cat hissed at him and made its way over onto a ledge about head-level with Philippe and myself.

I looked over and saw that Nipple Goddess was reading the card she'd taken from the Palme d'Or envelope. She squinted her eyes, shook her head, and said, "What in God's name is *The Corpse Grinders*?"

I burst out laughing. That movie had to have been Doug's idea. (To fully appreciate the irony, look it up in the *Creature Features Movie Guide* or ask any horror movie fanatic to summarize the plot for you; you'll understand then why I found it funny.)

The woman's face grew tight and angry. "Stop laughing, Mr. Ely."

"Sorry," I said, reaching into my pants pocket.

Philippe, his eyes swollen and tearing, shook the gun as if to say, *Keep your hands where I can see them,* then started hacking away as a new series of coughs wracked through him.

I took out the pouch of kitty treats and heaved its contents at his face.

Tasha, getting a good whiff of the treats, leapt from her perch and landed on Philippe's shoulder. He cried out, pulled in a phlegm-filled breath, and staggered back, hands flailing wildly at the cat.

Did I forget to mention that he also dropped his gun?

I lunged forward, kneed him in the groin, snatched up the gun, grabbed Tasha, and ran as fast as I could, the sound of coughing, wheezing, and groaning fading sweetly away behind me.

The boat was a little tricky—no one will ever accuse me of being a closet navigator—but I finally managed to get back to Cannes.

I guess I looked a lot worse for the experience than I thought, because upon setting foot on the north dock (the only place I could find a space between the yachts) I was immediately accosted by no fewer than six security guards.

You should've seen the looks on their faces when I told them my story. . . .

"There's the problem," I said to Doug. "You don't have a big, action-packed ending."

"I don't *want* a big, action-packed ending."

"I know, I know, emotional resonance—a term you use way too much, by the way—and meaningful irony."

"You make it all sound kind of lame."

"Well, you have to admit, in dramatic terms it doesn't so much end as just . . . stop."

"So what? You have any idea how many so-called literary works have no definite resolution? You should know, you've written enough stories like that."

"That's the key to success as a serious author. You write a smooth, linear story, then lop off the beginning and the end and publish only the middle. People think you're a genius."

He sighed. "I suppose you're right. I mean, we never found out the woman's identity or what her stake in all of this was, did we?"

"She and Philippe were long gone by the time the authorities got to the island."

"And it didn't really damage the festival in any way."

"Nope."

"So what's left?"

"Maybe I'll turn it into a short story."

"Yeah, right. And start it how?"

"Maybe with this conversation—you know, me saying, 'You want to *what*?' and taking it from there."

A small "meep" behind me reminded me it was time for Tasha to be fed. How could I have forgotten about her? I went through a lot of trouble to buy her from the hotel and bring her back to America.

"I gotta go, Doug. Tasha's hungry."

"You and that darn cat."

"She saved my life."

"Any chance the two of you will come to next year's festival with me?"

I reached over and stroked her neck. "I don't think so. Too much intrigue for my taste."

"So you get a short story out of this and I get squat, is that how it works?"

"Yeah—a classic turnabout resolution. First-rate literary fodder."

"Who do you suppose is going to buy a story like that?"

"I don't know, maybe a mystery magazine or anthology. We'll see."

"A hundred bucks says no way."

"You're on. See you at Mom's for dinner tomorrow night."

I hung up, then turned to Tasha. "So tell me, if I can't offer an explanation of the criminal's identity or her intentions, how would you suggest I end the story?"

She cocked her head to the side and stared at me.

"Maybe with something enigmatic?"

She licked her lips, blinked her eyes, and meowed.

"Good idea," I said, and began making my notes, wondering if there'd be an audience for this type of thing.

But a Sleep and a Forgetting . . .

Daniel B. Brawner

Inspector Dijon smirked through his neatly trimmed goatee. He poured himself a cup of strong coffee and settled back in the old wooden office chair.

"You have me most curious," he said. "Do you expect to convince me that you resisted the offer to murder your employer in exchange for four hundred thousand francs and the favors of his beautiful wife . . . Monsieur Pinocchio?" the inspector added, hooting with laughter.

I resisted a sudden impulse to scratch my nose and continued with my story. Six months ago, I explained, the ink still wet on my poetry MFA from Iowa, Elizabeth Calhoun hired me off a bar stool in Omaha to be her family's chauffeur. It was only later that my duties were expanded to include murder and adultery. And to take care of her husband's cat.

Inspector Dijon gasped. "You, a poet, had to baby-sit a cat? The indignity! For this you killed him, yes?"

Mr. C. used to say I was nothing but a stray cat myself. Sometimes I'd be gone for two or three days, prowling the alleys in Chicago or

Kansas City and come dragging in, as he said, "Full of burrs and bad breath, looking for a bowl of milk."

Elizabeth offered me $100,000 and the pink slip to the Mercedes if I would accompany them on a tour of *château* country and kill her husband. I saw it as a chance, as Wordsworth would say, to "drink in" the splendors of the Loire Valley, home of Robert the Strong who died fighting the Vikings; the last resting place of Henry II and Leonardo da Vinci; the birthplace of Annette Vallon, who had Wordsworth's child and broke his heart. How could I say no?

Mr. C. was a good sport about it. He gave me a job when nobody else would. He paid me too much money and treated me like one of the family. I couldn't stand the idea of killing him without knowing him better, so we had some good, long talks.

I learned that my employer was a rodeo clown, a self-taught engineer, and a self-made millionaire. He was the 1948 welterweight Golden Gloves champion of Nebraska and would have turned professional, except he could hardly see his hand in front of his face (let alone his opponents' hands) without his glasses.

He made his fortune in the fastener business. Mr. C. never learned to drive, but in 1968 he bought a new Mercedes 300 SEL convertible because Road and Track called it the best sedan in the world. He told me he hadn't looked at another car since, and I believe him. In 1978, after a disastrous first marriage, he proposed to and married the model Elizabeth Stratton because Glamour magazine called her the most beautiful woman on earth and because she laughed at his jokes. She called him Mr. Magoo.

Mr. C. retired last month, leaving Calhoun Fasteners in the hands of his son-in-law, the weak-kneed Wendell Winsome. He agreed to take his first vacation in thirty years because, after a few weeks of rattling about in their ten-bedroom colonial, he would have agreed to go anywhere. He was moping around like Alexander the Great with no more worlds to conquer. It was sad, really. Elizabeth set up the whole thing with this agency that caters to wealthy retired people—a kind of elder hostel for the rich and feeble.

We picked up the Mercedes at the airport in Paris and took the Autoroute south to Orléans. Near Blois, we turned off to the magnificent Château de Chambord. Mr. C. absolutely loved the place. Oh, he didn't care that it's 475 years old or even that it took 1,800 workmen twelve years to complete. But he was enchanted that François I thought of the 440–room mansion as just his hunting lodge and that if Leonardo da Vinci hadn't talked him out it, he would have actually diverted the Loire River to form the moat!

For several minutes, Mr. C. stood staring up at that monument to excess with its alligator bas-reliefs and conch shell alcoves. He took my arm, and in a kind of husky voice he said, "It takes a lot to amuse some people."

Several of the other guests had already arrived. A Rolls-Royce Silver Shadow rested picturesquely in the driveway. A stately woman in her seventies, wearing a full-length, white sable coat, stepped gracefully from an ancient Citroen.

"That's a bit much for June, don't you think?" Elizabeth said, referring to the sable. She herself looked stunning in a forest green wool riding jacket over a white silk shirt with black stretch riding pants. She insisted the outfit was a designer original but her husband said he assumed she got it, along with the rest of her wardrobe, from the Victoria's Secret catalog. Not that he minded. He still thought she was the most beautiful woman on earth. "Mr. Magoo!" she muttered, once his back was turned.

A stretch Lincoln pulled up and two thickly muscled men in ill-fitting suits emerged. Houdini jerked and tried to escape, but I held him tight. Houdini, Mr. C.'s cat, got his name from his ability to get out of or into any locked room. Although he never seemed to like Elizabeth, Houdini would sometimes slip into her room, disregarding the closed door, and sleep on her bed just for spite. But Houdini loved Mr. C. When he slept on Mr. C.'s bed, he usually brought a dead mouse. A stoop-shouldered figure dressed for dinner got out of the far side of the Lincoln and disappeared into the crowd.

"Richard," Elizabeth inquired casually, "wasn't that your old enemy—what's his name?"

"McCoy?" Mr. C. whipped around to get a look but his heavy, horn-rimmed glasses flew off his face and landed in the moat with a plunk. If he had been able to see that far, Mr. C. could have watched the black earpieces of his glasses being dragged to the bottom of the deep, gray water supplied by the River Cosson.

"Oh, dear," Elizabeth said, shaking her head. Elizabeth once took classes in elementary education and maintained that she would have been a kindergarten teacher if her career as a supermodel hadn't interfered. She never got as far as doing her student teaching. But sometimes she practiced on Mr. C. "Look what you've done. You've gone and lost your glasses!"

Mr. C. was essentially blind without his glasses. "I didn't lose them, honey. I just put them in a safe place."

While Elizabeth used her considerable charms to convince one of the gardeners to get a long-handled net and fish for Mr. C.'s glasses, I decided to check in.

"Monsieur?" The porter tapped me a little severely on the shoulder. He surveyed me disdainfully with beady little eyes that straddled his long, hooked nose. He looked like a buzzard with a pedigree. "Cats are not allowed in the château," he announced.

Houdini, a massive Maine Coon mix, lay across my shoulders in a half snooze.

"I beg your pardon, sir," I replied, stuffing a fifty-dollar bill in his coat pocket, "but this is not a cat. It is a mink collar." I stroked Houdini and he purred loudly.

The porter's buzzard eyes followed the route of the bribe and he flared his considerable nostrils in a sneer. "Perhaps in his haste to obtain a bargain, Monsieur neglected to thoroughly examine his fur. It seems there is a cat inside."

I squared my shoulders and attempted to look offended as I deposited $100 in the porter's pocket. "I can see you are a gentleman of refinement and discrimination," I said. "But I believe if you look again, you will find that you are mistaken." Just then, Houdini yawned and stretched, collapsing again on my shoulders.

The porter seemed unmoved. "Your collar has just twitched its tail, Monsieur," he observed.

I opened my wallet and withdrew the remaining $300 and stuffed it into the porter's bulging pocket. "It is a very lively collar," I agreed.

"A very lively collar indeed, sir," the porter conceded and handed me our keys.

Our rooms were on the second floor, and I had begun to look around for the elevator when suddenly I found myself staring at Chambord's colossal double-helix staircase. Although it appears to be a single set of stairs, opposing armies could charge—one up, the other down—their respective spirals and never cross the battle line. When I arrived at Elizabeth's suite, she was already there, leaning languidly against the door, waiting for me.

"You and I have some unfinished business," she said, unbuttoning just the top button of her silk shirt.

Houdini glared at her and hissed.

"Get that filthy animal away from me!" she spat back.

I rubbed Houdini between his ears and he seemed to settle down. "He'll behave himself if you will," I said, unlocking her door.

Elizabeth slunk inside and tossed her jacket onto the canopied Queen Anne bed. "Then you'd better put him in a cage!" She bared her perfect, pearly white fangs and kicked off her patent leather riding boots. Houdini leapt off my back and curled up on the sumptuous bed. Elizabeth pretended not to notice and slipped out of her stretch pants and shirt. She stood, framed against the large Italianate window, backlit with the warm reddening glow of the evening sun. She was wearing a short gold satin chemise that clung to her lovingly at the top and, below the waist, swayed loosely around her like a melting church bell.

"Ask not for whom the bell tolls," I warned myself. "We were about to get down to business," I reminded her.

Her cover girl lips parted slightly in a sly smile. Her gray eyes shone black in the dim light. "Tomorrow we do it!" she said, gliding toward me as if her feet were wheels and crushed my only tie in her small fist. "Tomorrow you kill the bastard. Even if his daughter does inherit his fortune, I'll still get the two million dollar key-man insurance money the company has on him. I've arranged for us all to take a hot-air balloon ride from Blois. There will be an unfortunate accident. Afterwards we'll come back up here to mourn my dear husband, and the next morning they'll have to burn our sheets.

I will tell you that you are brave and handsome." She licked her lips. "And what will you say about me?"

I permitted myself the liberty of touching her lightly around her sinuous waist—more for support than seduction.

> *She was a phantom of delight*
> *When first she gleamed upon my sight,*
> *A lovely apparition, sent*
> *To be a moment's ornament . . .*

Elizabeth appeared to be simultaneously charmed and confused. "You say the sweetest things," she said tentatively.

"Wordsworth," I corrected. "Wordsworth says the sweetest things. For my part, I couldn't care less."

She released my wrinkled tie and shoved me back a step. "Just do it!" she menaced. "All I have to do is pick up the phone, and twenty-four hours later you'll be just so much raw hamburger left out on the counter to spoil. How's that for poetic justice?" she added, probably imagining she had said something terribly clever.

"Let's go," I said. "Or we'll be late for dinner."

By the time we had changed for dinner and located Mr. C., Houdini had already escaped from the room where I was trying to hide him from the manager and was sitting at the table in his master's lap. Mr. C., still without his Coke-bottle glasses, had cornered the chef.

"The name's Richard C. Calhoun, Calhoun Fasteners. Nuts, bolts, washers, and screws."

"*Enchanté*, Monsieur Calhoun," he said with a stiff little bow.

"Call me Nuts!" Mr. C. offered brightly. "What's your name, son?"

The chef was an astonished-looking little man with wild black eyebrows and a pinched face like a mole's. "I am called Henri Le Fait," he enunciated with great dignity, dropping the *H* and taking particular care with the uvular *r* in his first name.

"Pleased to meet you!" said Mr. C. "So what's for supper, Ornery?"

Elizabeth leaned over to me and whispered, "Can't we kill him tonight?"

I shushed her and we stayed out of range of Mr. C.'s limited eyesight.

Henri was already off and running, twittering on about sauces and spices. "And our special entrée this evening is *matelot d'anguilles.*"

Mr. C. snorted. "Why, that ain't nothing but eel stew."

Henri looked stricken, as if someone had said something untoward about his mother. He quickly regained his composure. "*Oui,* Monsieur Nuts. But such a stew!" And in a display of quivering ecstasy, the chef simultaneously kissed all the fingertips on his right hand three times.

This performance seemed to have a subduing effect on Mr. C. "I can see you like it real well, Ornery. We'll try and save you some."

"I got something to tell you two," Mr. C. said gravely after Henri had left. "I don't know how to say this, but I can't put it off any longer." Elizabeth turned pale and shot a guilty look in my direction. I swallowed hard and waited. "We're all having eel stew tonight!" he said, laughing so loudly that every head in the dining hall turned our way. "I'm sorry, really I am." He wiped the tears of laughter away with his sleeve. "But you should have seen that little guy. It would've broke his heart if I'd ordered steak. Maybe it's a good thing I can't see what I'm eating tonight."

The next morning, Mr. C. seemed a little uneasy.

"I've got a queasy feeling about this balloon ride," he said. "Much as I like to get my money's worth, I'd just as soon not ever see that eel stew again. And besides, Houdini's disappeared. I hate to go anywhere without him."

"Oh, Richard," Elizabeth chided, "don't be such a baby! A hot-air balloon ride is as gentle as a porch swing. You'll have the time of your life."

Mr. C. reluctantly stepped into the wicker basket of one of the azure blue balloons, decorated with enormous pictures of spring flowers. "I don't know what I'm going to do in this contraption," he grumbled. "I can't see as far as my feet, let alone anything on the ground."

Elizabeth said something about there being no more room in our basket and slipped off to join the group in the next balloon. The pilot in our craft pulled a cord and a surprisingly loud blast of flame from the burner shot upwards into an opening at the base of the vehicle and the earth began to fall away from us. We were accompanied by a prosperous-looking elderly couple from the château. The gray-haired gentleman jumped when the burner fired off again and gripped the edge of the basket with his back to the open sky.

Mr. C. turned to him and said, "You know, Bill, sometimes I just don't understand that woman."

"Pardon me," said the gray-haired man, "but are you addressing me?"

Mr. C. laughed. "Shucks, I'm sorry. I lost my glasses and I can't see a thing. My name is Richard C. Calhoun, Calhoun Fasteners. Nuts, bolts, washers, and screws."

The old gentleman reluctantly let go of the basket with his right hand and offered it to Mr. C. "I'm Donald Carlyle and this," he said, indicating the severely elegant dowager next to him, "is my wife Cynthia."

Cynthia raised a limp-wristed hand in Mr. C's direction. "Pleased to meet you, Mr. Calhoun."

"Call me Nuts," Mr. C. said, and as he reached for her hand, the balloon passed over the Loire River and hit an air pocket, sending the craft plummeting ten feet with a jerk. Mr. C. stumbled into Cynthia, sending her screaming into the suspension ropes with him right on top of her. For a split second, I saw my window of opportunity. The pilot was distracted, trying to steady the balloon, Mr. C. and Cynthia were blocking each other's fields of vision, and Donald had his eyes shut tight. It would have been a cinch to grab Mr. C.'s pant leg and flip him out of the basket like a pancake off the griddle.

"For the next few minutes, we may be experiencing some minor turbulence," our pilot droned. "Please remain seated during this time. Air-sickness bags are available in the side compartments for your convenience."

Donald was turning green by now and was beginning to gulp air.

"Excuse me all to pieces, Mrs. Carlyle," Mr. C. said, backing away from Cynthia, who stood staring blindly into space with her mouth open. "Tell me, Donald, what line of work are you in?"

Donald fumbled in the side compartment for one of the bags. "I'm in the business," he said, taking short breaths, "of manufacturing aircraft . . . and lightweight aluminum engines."

Mr. C. slapped Donald on the shoulder, sending a shock wave visibly through his entire body. "And you're looking for a better price on rivets and stainless steel screws—am I right?"

Donald looked as if he might actually jump out of the gondola. "I, uh, I don't know," he stammered.

I happened to look over at the other balloon which sailed about a hundred meters to the south of us. Elizabeth was talking to the two burly men who had gotten out of the limousine at the chateau. A gust of wind blew open the coat of the man nearest to me. I could see the outline of a leather strap across his chest and a flash of metal.

"I'm going to be honest with you, Don," said Mr. C. "I've got a whole carload of stainless steel sheet metal screws collecting dust in a warehouse in Atlanta. The whole kit and caboodle was manufactured to military specs, earmarked for the B–1 bomber—and I guess you know what happened to *that* whole business."

Donald had given up searching for the air-sickness bag and was looking wistfully over the side of the gondola. There was a muffled burst, as if from a pneumatic stapler as a phosphorous ball from a flare gun burned two gaping holes in the balloon's hot-air envelope.

"I'm supposed to be on vacation," Mr. C. continued. "Hell!" he chucked, "I'm supposed to be retired! My son-in-law Wendell is in charge now and he's just sick about those screws. He's probably in his office right now, crying his little heart out over it."

"There is no cause for alarm, but we appear to be losing altitude," the pilot announced in his usual monotone. "Please remain in your seats while we make our descent. I am radioing ahead for transportation. We should be on the ground shortly."

Donald was in the early stages of a panic attack. He was also wheezing a little and clutching at his left arm. Cynthia was still staring blankly into the open sky.

"So what do you say, Don?" Mr. C. said, wrapping up his pitch. "Let's make Wendell a happy man and take some of those screws off his hands." He scribbled something on a piece of paper and shoved it under Donald's nose. "Now does that look like the price you were looking for?"

Our companion balloon was closer now and I could clearly see one of the men had a scoped pistol with a silencer and was aiming it in our direction. Elizabeth was watching the whole thing from her corner of the gondola.

Donald gaped at the paper and seemed to come back to life a little. "Yes, it is," he managed to say.

Mr. C. beamed. "Fine! That's just fine." He whipped out a cellular telephone, punched two buttons on the speed dialer, and handed it to Donald. "When you get a connection, just give the lady your purchase order number and tell her Nuts sent you."

In the other balloon, while one of the men distracted the pilot, the other trained his gun on Mr. C. I had turned to warn my boss when suddenly I heard a scream coming from the other balloon. I looked back in time to see the gunman drop his weapon over the side. He was struggling with something on his face. It was Houdini. The man cried out again and stumbled over the edge of the basket, cat and all.

By now we were descending at a brisk rate. However, Donald seemed to be getting some color back in his face and he and Mr. C. were chatting about the price of steel. The pilot threw the last of the sandbags over the side and had the burner going wide-open to try and keep us from plunging into the earth like a dart.

The pilot's valiant efforts proved successful. Our rather abrupt landing concluded without incident, except that our pilot bit his tongue, preventing him from making any more heartening remarks as we stepped out of the balloon. Donald and Mr. C. shook hands warmly and Cynthia was led away to the awaiting ambulance for observation. Two police cars had arrived and were already scouring Chambord's 13,000–acre forest for the sky-diving assassin.

Back at the château, we sipped a little vintage brandy to help us subdue the day's excitement before dinner. Oblivious to the earlier attempt on his life and to the thread from which his life now dangled, Mr. C. appeared to be in fine spirits.

"I tell you, Betty, if I'd known hot-air balloons were this much fun, I'd have gone up in one years ago!"

Elizabeth was wearing a long, off-the-shoulder velvet dress so black that any light rays around her plunged to their death in a fit of jealous despair. She was working on her third brandy and was beginning to speak freely.

"Well, it wasn't so much fun for that poor bastard who did a jackknife into the Loire," she said, challenging her husband's good mood.

Mr. C. sighed. "Did you know? That was Larry 'the Lock Washer' Wallace. One of McCoy's goons. I don't know what the hell he was doing here. But they've been following me around for five years, trying to skim off some of my business. And they're always a day late and a dollar short. The poor, confused kid hitched up with the wrong team. McCoy always wanted to be number one in the fastener business." He shook his head sadly. "Just didn't have the nuts for it."

Hamlet's speech came to mind and I quoted, " 'How weary, stale, flat, and unprofitable / Seem to me all the uses of this world.' "

Mr. C. set down his drink. "Oh, that's silly, Bill," he protested. "This is only my second day of vacation and already I've made forty-six thousand dollars."

"That's just it, Richard," Elizabeth said, exasperated. "We used to have such good times together. Now whenever we try to do something, you're off making another deal. You're supposed to relax on your vacation!"

"I am relaxed, honey," he said cheerfully. "I find making money very restful."

Elizabeth propped one silky leg up on the black lacquer coffee table. "What are you planning to do with all that money? You can't take it with you."

Mr. C. chuckled. "Darling, that practical side of yours is going to keep you from having any fun at all. I remember my Uncle Nestor. He was a hardworking man. When I was a little kid, I used to go over to his house and help him chop wood. Every summer we'd put up four or five cords of firewood and every spring it would be gone. Then one day I saw somebody hauling away a pickup full of wood from the big stack behind my uncle's house. I came running up and shouted, 'Uncle Nestor! Uncle Nestor! Somebody's stealing your wood!' He just smiled at me and said, 'Son,' he said, 'they ain't stealing my wood. I'm giving it to them.' I said, 'But if you run out of firewood this winter, you'll freeze!' He said, 'I reckon I'll stay warm enough as long as my fuel oil holds out.' My uncle never had a woodstove. But the old coot surely did love to chop firewood. Honey, I don't have the slightest idea what to do with the money. Just thinking about how to spend all that loot sounds like a job to me. And as you know, I'm retired. And by the way," he said, interrupting himself, "where in the hell's Houdini?"

"Richard, dear, there's something I need to tell you about your cat," Elizabeth began gingerly.

A shadow passed over Mr. C.'s jovial countenance. "And what would that be, Betty?"

Behind us, somebody cleared his throat. Mr. C. turned around to find the porter holding a large, rumpled cat. "Monsieur," he said, addressing my boss. "We found your driver's mink collar in the kitchen, eating the chicken Alsacienne." The cat leapt into his master's arms.

"Houdini, you big lunk!" Mr. C. cried. "Where have you been?" He gave the porter a wad of bills to cover damages to the chicken Alsacienne and headed back to his room to comb out the burrs in the cat's coat. "Oh, and Bill," he called over his shoulder. "Have Ornery send up a corned beef sandwich for me and something nice for Houdini—some kind of pronounceable fish or something."

Elizabeth's gray eyes burned black. "You see how he thinks more of that mongrel cat than he does of me." She stifled a sniffle. "I bet he's even made a provision for that thing in his will."

"Forget about that," I said. "Just what was going on with those thugs in the balloon today?"

"What, don't you believe in a free market economy?" she said coyly. "You've got competition, Shakespeare! McCoy is planning a hostile takeover and Richard is still the majority stockholder of Calhoun Fasteners. When he signs that new will his daughter gets half his shares, and she'd never sell to McCoy."

"What kind of deal is that snake offering you?" I demanded.

She scraped her long red nails across the leather armrest. "It's business. Don't worry your pretty head about it, lover. Let's just say that if you get him first, our partnership still stands. Just don't wait too long." She licked her lips. "Or that position could be filled."

I loosened my tie to let out some of the steam. "Let's say, for the sake of argument, that I am interested . . ."

Elizabeth snorted. "You're interested, all right."

"When would there be another opportunity?"

"I made another little deal with the gardener," she said, gloating. "Tomorrow, we drive to Saumur and the Musée du Champignon—that is the Mushroom Museum to you. You know that oaf will eat anything, especially when they're giving out free samples. All you have to do is make the switch." She withdrew a plastic bag from her purse containing what looked like stewed toadstools. "Hell, I might even sue the museum!" She cackled at the thought.

"Are you sure you want to go ahead with this?" I asked.

She sneered. "Now that Richard is retired, what is there for him to look forward to but death?"

" '. . . is but a sleep and a forgetting,' " I said, quoting Wordsworth's *Intimations of Immortality.*

> *"The soul that rises with us, our life's star,*
> *Hath had elsewhere it setting,*
> *And cometh from afar."*

* * *

La Musée du Champignon seemed a likely place to die. For eighteen francs, we were given a tour of the famous subterranean gardens where edible fungi are grown. The rock-walled caverns were lined with the lithified remains of prehistoric sea creatures. The damp, stale air hung heavy with the smell of death and decay.

"Whoever thought of this place was one brilliant son of a gun!" enthused Mr. C. "They started out with nothing but a hole in the ground and turned it into one of the most productive farms in the Loire Valley."

"And wait until you taste the truffles!" Elizabeth said, surreptitiously stuffing the sautéed "Death Cup" Amanita mushrooms in my coat pocket.

"I understand pigs like them," Mr. C. chuckled. "Do you think Houdini would want to try some?"

"Oh, I'm sure he would!" Elizabeth was clearly supportive of the idea.

Mr. C. stuck his little finger through Houdini's carrying cage. "I'm sorry we have to keep you boxed up, old boy," he said, consoling the cat. "But we can't have you off hiding in these caves like a bat." Houdini rubbed luxuriously against the extended finger and purred.

I leaned over to Elizabeth and whispered, "Where's McCoy?" She nodded in the direction of the one remaining henchman and McCoy himself, whom I overheard complaining to his employee.

"Whose idea was it to do him in this place?" McCoy grumbled. "As blind as he is, you could walk up and hit him with a shovel." He leaned over with his hands on his knees and groaned. "I'm the one being killed here. My arthritis will do me in long before that spineless driver ever gets around to poisoning him. Eddie, as soon as Calhoun separates from the crowd, you walk up and inject him with that syringe full of adrenaline. They'll think the old horse thief died of a heart attack."

Eddie stuck his hands in his coat pockets. "I'll kill him. But not while that cat's around. You saw what it done to Larry."

McCoy raised his cane and stumbled back against the cave wall.

"You idiot!" he seethed. "You belong in a mushroom museum! Don't you see, they have that stinking ratcatcher in a cage? What am I paying you for? Give me that syringe and get out of here before somebody mistakes you for a big mushroom."

Elizabeth had also overheard some of their conversation. "This is your last chance, Shakespeare."

I passed her back the bag of toadstools. "Forget it," I said. "I'm not doing it."

She looked at me with disgust. "Coward! All right, I'd rather do it myself than split my share with that vulture McCoy."

"Mr. C. loves you, you know," I whispered. "He told me. He's told you many times, but you don't pay any attention."

"He has a fine way of showing it," she said, "giving all his money to his daughter. What about me? Doesn't he ever think of what it will be like for me when I'm old and ugly and I don't know how to do anything but take care of an old man and his stupid cat?" She started to sob.

I looked up in time to see McCoy limping toward Mr. C. with the hypodermic needle in his hand.

"Look out, Mr. C.!" I shouted.

Houdini had evidently been working at the cage door latch with his teeth because the moment I called out, he sprang from the cage and leapt upon McCoy's arthritic knee, flailing away with his teeth and claws. McCoy dropped the syringe, which skidded harmlessly across the floor. Screaming at the top of his lungs, he toppled to the ground, trying in vain to free himself from the Cuisinart slashes of Houdini. McCoy drew out a revolver and fired, striking himself in the foot.

Elizabeth grabbed Mr. C. and was dragging him away when I turned and raced toward McCoy, who was shrieking and shooting in all directions. I saw movement out of the corner of my eye and glanced up in time to see the policeman's fist.

"And that's the last thing I remember."

Inspector Dijon shook his head. *"C'est plus qu'un crime, c'est une faute!"* he said.

"Translation, please?"

The inspector looked up from his reverie. "It is more than a crime. It is a blunder."

"You must believe I am not a murderer," I pleaded. "I've been given no payment and nobody has been killed."

"Perhaps, Monsieur, you can be thankful that incompetence is not a crime. But as to the killing, we now have two dead bodies."

I gasped. "That assassin, Monsieur Wallace, and his employer." He yawned and stretched. "Yes, it seems all the excitement proved too much for McCoy, and in addition to the bullet in his foot, he had an attack of the heart and died. Fortunately, no innocent people were injured."

"But what about Mr. C. and Eliz . . . uh, his wife?"

"Pardon me," Mr. C. strode in, wearing the glasses that had landed in the moat. "But I think we can straighten all this out."

"It was all a big misunderstanding." Elizabeth was holding the purring Houdini and was making an effort to keep from grinning. "We would have come sooner, but we were having a little . . . second honeymoon." She actually blushed.

Dijon was flabbergasted. "Where on earth have you been?" he demanded.

Mr. C. was also fighting to keep a smile off his face. "There's this real nice little place about ten miles southeast of here, Fontevraud— am I pronouncing that right?"

"The medieval abbey," Dijon suggested, "for repentant female sinners?"

"It seemed as good a place as any," Elizabeth said.

The inspector tossed his pencil on the desk in disgust. "Am I to understand that no charges will be filed?"

"Well, she did give my glasses back," Mr. C. said.

Elizabeth stroked Houdini's ears. "It turns out I was all wrong about that stupid will—not that it would matter to me now. His daughter and I were each getting half the estate all along. Richard's attorney had pulled the file on the former Mrs. McCoy by mistake."

"What will you folks do now?" I asked Mr. C.

"We'll be taking a slow tour of the wine country and then the white beaches in the south. You might as well keep these," he said, tossing me the extra set of keys to the Mercedes. "We both are going to have better things to do than watch the road."

"And what about you?" Elizabeth asked me.

> *"Trading echoes with the bluff,*
> *the sound is sweet, but not enough*
> *to make the source seem more sublime.*
> *But in the end, at least . . . it's mine."*

"Wordsworth?" Elizabeth asked.

"Bill Brown," I said.

The Cat, the Watch and the Deep Blue Sea

Bruce Holland Rogers

"It's my life too, David!" Emily said from the door. "The store is my business as much as yours! Why do you keep forgetting that?"

David Merriam leaned awkwardly against the diminutive dressing table. He and his wife stood as far apart as they could in the cramped space, but it wasn't far enough. Emily's arms were folded, her fists balled tight. Her anger needed much more room than the cruise ship cabin afforded.

"And now . . . you just don't ask Grandad for money! I thought you knew him better than that. How long do you think he's going to be mad at us? I could have *told* you this was exactly the wrong thing to do. And in front of the others! Did you stop to think that maybe I didn't want my brothers to know we're going bankrupt? Did you stop to think that maybe I didn't want to wave that bit of private business under my cousin's nose? David, you could have *asked* me first!"

"I'm sorry. I just thought—"

"No, you didn't. You didn't think. There are some things you just don't bring up with Grandad. Now we're going to be the black sheep this year. You made things *worse.*"

"Grandad might change his mind, Em." David knew this wasn't likely. Aldrich Spence had grown very quiet and very cold when David had started talking about how bad business was lately. "I didn't ask him to just throw some cash our way and bail us out. I only suggested that a loan—"

"You just don't ask Grandad for anything. If he wants to, he gives, but you don't ask. You know how he is!"

"I'm sorry. I lost my head and we're out ten thousand dollars. I was stupid. Okay?"

"It's not the money! David, it has never been the money!"

"What do you want me to say?" It came out sounding much more like a challenge than he intended.

Emily stood glaring at him for a moment. "This is getting us exactly nowhere." She opened the door.

Emily was gone before David could say, "Em, don't—"

For a moment he considered going after her, but what would be the point? They needed to have a fight, he needed to let her take his head off because she was right, right, right. But the cabin was impossibly cramped, and the rest of the ship was too public.

David pulled down the cabin's folded bed and sat on the edge of it. He looked at the porthole. It was a fake. Theirs was an interior cabin, and the little round window above the bed looked out on nothing but a panel of steel six inches away. It seemed appropriate. Six inches was about how much breathing room David felt he still had in his life.

It was his own fault that Emily was so angry. He had always *said* that they were co-managers of their store, Merriam Games, but it was true that he'd done too many things without asking her. Impulsive things.

Some of his decisions had turned out to be good ones. He had bought a huge shipment of a trading card game called Castles Fantastic. The cards featured colorful artwork, and the game that went with them was fast-paced and fun. Better still, from a retailer's perspective, the game was easier to win if a player owned many, many cards. David knew, as soon as the distributor showed it to him, that Castles Fantastic would be an enormous hit.

To Emily, it didn't matter that he'd turned out to be right. He had tied up the store's capital in Castles Fantastic without asking her. Then, still making decisions without her, he had ordered a huge lot of the game's second edition just about the time the fad was dying. He neglected to restock the store's usual steady sellers—backgammon boards and Monopoly and mystery games. Merriam Games ended up with a storeroom filled with trading cards they could hardly give away.

And it wasn't just this one time.

The store was deep in debt now. That was how he preferred to think of it. The store owed a lot of money, though of course the signatures at the bottom of the loan agreements were his and Emily's.

There was a sharp rap at the door.

"Em?" he said. "Emily?" But the rap just sounded again, hard and quick.

David opened the door to meet the icy glare of Emily's grandfather. In a voice too loud for the carpeted corridor, Aldrich Spence said, "I believe you have something that belongs to me."

"Something that belongs to you?"

"My watch, damnation!" The old man leaned forward on his silver-headed cane. "You know just what I mean. There were just the seven of us in the lounge when I had my watch out on the table!"

"The hunting watch? Weren't you wearing it?"

"Don't play with me! You were there! You watched what I was doing!"

David remembered. Sanford, Emily's younger brother, had asked to see the antique. Spence had removed the watch from its fob and put it on the table for him. Spence had handed it back, and then David remembered seeing the watch lying on the table as Spence turned to ask Emily to get another Rusty Nail from the bar.

"It was on the table," David said.

"I forgot it. I do forget things. But I'm not quite the old dotard you apparently think I am."

"Grandad, if I had your watch—"

Spence waved him off. "No, don't start with that." He scowl softened. "David, I lived through the Depression. I know what need is. I know it far better than you. And I also know how it can drive a man . . . some men to do things that are unreasoned. But that's not an excuse. When you're desperate, that's the very time to find the best in yourself." He stepped into the cabin and peered about. "Where is it? Not many places to hide it in here. If you weren't relying entirely on my generosity for this cruise, you could have a real stateroom like Ramsay."

"You're wrong. I didn't take the watch."

Aldrich Spence shook his head. "I'd have never thought you capable of such a thing. But neither did I ever expect you to come begging for money."

"That's enough," David said. "I wasn't begging, and I didn't take your watch."

"You find my generosity insufficient, do you?"

David had seen this kind of bluster aimed before at Emily's brothers, Ramsay and Sanford, and at her cousin, Candace. It was all part of being designated the black sheep for the year. And he'd brought it on himself, just as Emily said.

He worked to control his voice as he said, "You've been quite generous with us, and I appreciate that."

"You think I'll forgive something like this, I imagine. You think that next year maybe you'll be standing with your hand out again and be rewarded, eh?"

David clenched his jaw. Now he was getting a taste of Aldrich Spence's game from the losing side. Well, there was some justice to that. David had stood by and watched as Em's brothers and cousin drifted in and out of favor over seven years of these family reunions. And he'd never spoken up about how unfair the old man was.

But that had been of necessity. The truth was that Merriam Games would have failed years ago if not for the annual favored grandchild gifts from Em's Grandad. Every year the favored grandchildren received a gift of ten thousand dollars. And the grandchild who wasn't measuring up, usually Candace or Ramsay, got the free vacation but no cash bonus at the end.

Until now, David and Emily had never had to deal with being out of favor.

"I didn't take the watch," David said, "but I'll find it."

The old man snorted. "You do that. Make a miraculous discovery. Save face. All that matters to me is that I—have—it—back!" In time with his last four words, he rapped his cane on the floor.

"Everybody takes a turn," said Ramsay Spence. He was propped in a deck chair beside the pool but facing away from it. "God knows I've done my share of service as the wayward grandson." He didn't look at David or Emily, but kept staring at the clouds beyond the ship's rail as he sipped his drink. His eyes were glazed.

"It's one thing to be on the outs with Grandad for not living up to his expectations, whatever they happen to be this year," Emily said. "It's far worse to be accused of something we didn't do."

Something *we* didn't do. David was grateful that she put it that way.

In the pool behind Ramsay, his wife was trying to settle a dispute between their four- and five-year-old sons while balancing the toddler on her hip. The boys clutched either end of a toy boat.

"Is it possible," David suggested, "that one of the kids grabbed the watch while it was there on the table?"

The five-year-old pulled the boat out of his brother's hands. The younger boy socked him, and then they both started to howl.

Ramsay still stared at the clouds. "Sure, it's possible. It's possible that the old man dropped the watch into a different pocket. It's possible that Sandy pocketed the watch—he was the one who asked to see it in the first place, right? But it doesn't matter."

Ramsay's wife set her daughter down to better deal with the boys, but then the toddler started to cry too, and the boys wailed all the louder.

"What matters," Ramsay continued, a little louder than before, "is that Grandad's decided that you're the rotten apples this year. That won't change if the watch turns up." He turned his head slightly. "Lynn, can't you get them to shut up?"

Lynn Spence grabbed the squalling toddler under the arms, swung her up, and brought her to Ramsay. "She's all yours. The boys and I are going back to the cabin."

"Jeez," Ramsay said. He drained his glass, then set it down and started to bounce his daughter on his knee. It only made her cry louder, but he didn't seem to notice. He looked at Emily and smirked. "The economic urge. This is what I get for trying to be good."

On their way to find Candace, David said, "The economic urge? What was that about?"

"You haven't heard Grandad's story about the economic urge?"

David shook his head.

"Grandad graduated with his engineering degree during the Depression. My Dad was a year old, and my Gram was pregnant with my uncle. When Grandad asked for work at a construction company in Denver, they told him they didn't have any engineering openings, but he could have a job as a hod carrier."

"What's a hod carrier?"

"The bottom man at a construction site. He carries bricks and mortar all day. Backbreaking work. Grandad took the job because he had mouths to feed. The site foreman just about worked him into the ground. Then the company called him back into the office and said that they did, in fact, need an engineer. But they wanted to find one who was willing to work."

"Hell of an interview technique."

"It affected Grandad. It made him very loyal, and he stayed with the company through hard times. Sometimes he had to take half his pay in nearly worthless company stock. By the time World War Two produced a construction boom, he owned a decent chunk of the company."

"What's this got to do with your brother?"

"Ramsay make the mistake of telling Grandad years and years

ago that he didn't plan on having kids. Grandad gave him a speech about how raising a family during the Depression had given him the economic urge. He said Ramsay would never amount to anything without a wife and kids to make him hungry. Ramsay was on the outs that year."

Emily started up the stairway to the casino. "Of course, being on the outs wasn't so costly then. This was before Grandad had started handing out checks at the end of these reunions. But Ramsay got the point."

"Ramsay started a family to make Grandad happy?"

Emily shrugged. "I'm sure it's not that simple. In any case, having kids didn't keep Ramsay from being on the outs again later."

They stepped into the casino. At this time of day, only one blackjack table was active, and the craps tables were covered. There were two women at the slot machines, but neither of them was Candace.

"Well, this is a first," David said.

They tried her cabin.

Surveying Candace's cabin, the shoes tossed against the bathroom door, the bed down in the middle of the day, the clutter of open cosmetics cases on the dressing table, and the pink and blue pawprints on the sheets, David said, "You brought a cat on board?"

"Where did it say no pets?" Candace said. She scratched Pumpkin behind his ears with long red fingernails. "It's not like I tried to hide him. He was in the carrier when I brought him onto the ship."

The sequined cat carrier on the floor looked much more like a fancy hatbox. Next to it were four paper cups from the casino. Three were empty, but one was half-full of dimes.

On one corner of the bed, jammed against the wall, was a balled-up white sweater. Like the sheets, it was marked with pink and blue smears. Pumpkin had apparently investigated the open cases of eye shadow before walking across the bed.

"We have to clear customs when we get back to Miami," David said. "The cat will have to be quarantined."

"For ninety days. I know, I know. The purser told me all of that."
Candace gave the whole issue a dismissive wave, and Pumpkin
jumped from her lap to the floor. "What's the point? It's not as if
I'd take him off the ship in Mexico and let him get some disease or
something. Stay away from Emily, Pumpkin."

"Anyway," Emily said, edging away from the cat, "do you remember seeing Grandad show Sandy the watch?"

"Yes, and I was there when Grandad realized it was missing. I
looked under the table for him. And I kept asking him to look in
his pockets again to make sure, but he wouldn't. I kind of thought
he might have put it back in the wrong pocket."

David scooped Pumpkin up before the cat could rub against Emily's legs. "If somebody took it," David said, "it had to be one of us,
right? Or one of Ramsay's kids?"

"What about the waitress?" Candace suggested.

"No," Emily said. "The barmaid was just mixing. We were getting
the drinks from the bar and bringing them over ourselves, remember?"

"This really stinks for you guys," Candace said.

"Yeah," David said. "It does." He stroked Pumpkin, then handed
him back to Candace.

"To tell you the truth, though, I don't mind having the heat off
for once. Grandad isn't exactly thrilled that I'm in the entertainment
business. As far as he's concerned, it's a thin line between nightclub
singer and fallen woman. He'd be so much happier if I were Mrs.
Wife and Mother. He'd be *delighted*."

Pumpkin jumped from Candace's lap to the dressing table. "No,
you don't!" Candace grabbed him. "You are a very bad cat! You're
going to kitty jail for ninety days!" Then she snuggled him. "Poor
Pumpkin."

In the corridor, David waited until they were a safe distance from
Candace's door, then said, "How could she not know that a cat on
a cruise ship was a dumb idea?"

"She loves cats," Emily said.

"I like cats."

"And I married you anyway."

* * *

Sanford, Emily's younger brother, was a little harder to track down. He wasn't in his cabin, in any of the lounges, or walking the promenade deck. They finally found him in the exercise room, furiously pedaling a stationary bike.

"Yeah," he said, wiping his forehead with his sleeve. "I remember looking at the watch."

David said, "And then?"

Sandy shrugged. "I can't say for sure. I don't remember him putting it away. I don't remember him *not* doing it either. He lost it, huh?"

"He says David stole it," Emily said.

Sandy laughed. "So you're in for it this year, is that it?"

"You think it's funny?"

"I do," Sandy said. He pedaled faster. "I hate this ship," he said. "All we do is eat, except for when Grandad rounds us all up to sit in the lounge. I'm getting fat. I can feel it."

He slowed his pedaling a bit, chewing his lip. "What would happen if next year we all said we weren't coming? If we went on strike? Would he disinherit us all?"

Emily frowned. She didn't like talk of inheritance.

"Not that we could pull it off," Sandy continued. "Candace would cave in at the last minute. You know, the only loyal grandchild. Or Ramsay would." Sandy grinned. "Or you would, Em."

"You wouldn't?" David said.

Sandy laughed. "I might. I just might. This year I swore I wasn't coming. But school's expensive. I could really use a ten-thousand-dollar loyalty dividend. All it costs me is a week of mind-numbing boredom."

"You don't have to be bored," Emily said. "There's a lot to do."

"Right. I can shoot skeet for five bucks a pop, or knock overpriced golf balls into the ocean from the fantail. Oh, and there are the cheesy lounge acts at night. Or I could be like Candace and dump a year's worth of car payments into the slot machines, one dime at a time."

"There are shore excursions. We'll be in Cozumel tomorrow."

"Em, dear," Sandy said, "you're defending this? You'd go for a hokey vacation like this if you were spending your own money? Don't answer. Don't ruin my opinion of my big sister."

"What would you rather do?" David asked.

"Got an hour? I'll make you a list." Sandy picked up the pace of his pedaling. "We could all tell Grandad that we stole the watch together. We could say we pounded it to bits with a hammer, just for spite. He *would* disinherit us, but then we'd be free."

"At least we get to see each other once a year," Emily said. "It's not that bad."

"It's not that good," Sandy said.

"So," Emily said, staring out over the darkening sea. "What do we know that we didn't know already?"

David folded his hands over the rail. "I know that I wish we hadn't come this year. We could be at home negotiating with bankers instead of solving the case of the missing pocket watch."

"When else do I get to see my family?"

"It's not like you're seeing them at their best, Em. Vacationing with Grandad is like touring a minefield."

Her mouth was tight.

"I'm sorry. He *is* your grandfather."

"He means well."

"Does he, Em? Does he really?"

"What do you mean?"

David shrugged. "Maybe I've been selling games too long. It just seems so . . . artful. Even after he started having kids, Ramsay was on the outs when his business was in trouble. Candace was the black sheep right after she left school and started her nightclub singing, and she was barely scraping by. Now it's our turn. Is it really because I offended your grandfather, or is it because we're the ones in trouble this year, the ones most in need of a cushion?"

They watched the sea in silence.

"Anyway, we can forget all of this tomorrow," David said. "I signed us up for a snorkeling tour. Sound fun?"

Emily's voice was cold. "What kind of tour?"

"On a boat. They take you out to look at the reef."

"An all-day tour?"

"Well, until the afternoon. The ship isn't in Cozumel all that long."

Emily shook her head. "You did it again, David."

"What? I did what?"

"You decided without me. Did you ask what I wanted to do on the island?"

"I thought I'd surprise you."

She was silent for a long time.

"Maybe I can get a refund," he said.

"That's not the point."

Something scraped the deck behind them. Aldrich Spence's cane. "Well?" he said.

"Grandad," said Emily, turning. "We haven't found your watch. But we have been looking."

"That watch didn't grow legs. It didn't just get up and walk away, you know," Spence said. Then, more softly, he said, "I understand. Far better than you realize, I understand."

David opened his mouth, then let it close.

Spence stepped up to the rail, between David and Emily. "When you're young, it's so much easier to make mistakes. You don't really have . . . perspective. Children make all the difference. You don't really grow up until you have little ones relying on you. When I was a young man—"

Emily said, "Grandad, please. We've been over this."

"Not often enough," Spence said.

"We'll start a family," Emily said. "When we're ready."

"David, in your best year, how much has your little toy store made you?"

"It's not a toy store, it's a game store," Emily said. "And it's not just David's business. We run it together. And whether we do well in business or not has nothing to do with whether or not we have children.''

''Emily, dear, please. I'm talking to your husband.''

''I won't play,'' David said, shaking his head. ''Sorry, Em. I've had it with this.''

He turned and walked away from the rail, but not so quickly that he didn't hear Aldrich Spence say to Emily, ''What does he mean, he won't play? What in heaven's name is he talking about?''

David found Sandy standing in line for dinner.

''I thought you were sick of eating.''

''I am, but like I say, what else is there? When in Rome . . . I'll work it off on the island tomorrow. Think I can rent a bicycle?''

''I guess. Probably.''

''Care to join me for dinner?''

Ramsay, Lynn, and their children were at the front of the line. Two of the kids were crying.

''I don't think I can handle the dining room just now,'' David said. ''Thanks just the same.''

He took the stairs to the casino. He found Candace in front of her favorite slot machine. There was a paper coin cup next to her, but it was empty. ''Lost everything yet?'' he said.

Candace fed five dimes into the slot, then pulled the handle. Two bars. The machine lit up, rang its bell, and spat a modest payout into the nearly empty tray.

''Not quite everything,'' she said. She was wearing a white sweater, the one that had been balled up on the bed. It was still marked with faint eye-shadow pawprints in pink and blue.

''Your cat really made a mess while you were out.''

''He's mad that I leave him alone so much.''

''That your only sweater, Candace?''

''It's my lucky sweater. I was wearing it on the first night, when I was winning.''

''They might have changed the rules since then, you know.''

''What do you mean?'' She pulled the handle again.

''I mean you weren't the only one winning big on the first night. But the casinos on cruise ships aren't regulated. You weren't the only one cleaning up on slots the first night. After the first night, after you've done pretty well and tell all your friends at breakfast, they come in while the casino's closed and fix the machines. They re-balance the wheels."

"They can do that?" She fed in another five dimes and pulled the lever.

"They can."

"That's rotten. You could have told me."

"Didn't know you needed to be told," he said.

Candace scraped the last coins up out of the tray, fed them in, and pulled the handle one last time. Nothing.

"Done," she said.

"Win a few, lose a few."

"Live and learn," said Candace.

David thought of his pending bankruptcy, his *faux pas* with Grandad, his excursion plans made without consulting Emily. "Some of us are slow learners," he said.

The next day, Grandad Spence stayed on the cruise ship because, he said at breakfast, he didn't care for Mexicans and he'd already been robbed once this trip. Nobody spoke up to insist that he come ashore. Nobody volunteered to stay on board with him.

Candace took a taxi into San Miguel for a day of shopping, Sandy rented his bicycle near the passenger terminal at the dock. What Ramsay, Lynn, and the children were doing, David didn't ask and he didn't care.

To David's relief, Emily enjoyed the snorkeling excursion to Palancar Reef. At first he didn't think she would. They were on a boat with five other couples, and Emily spent the trip out to the reef pointedly meeting other people and not talking to her husband.

But in the water, things improved. Emily took David's hand when he offered it.

Their guide taught them how to surface-dive. David discovered he had a knack for it. He showed off a little by diving deep enough to look under the coral heads where the guide pointed out a moray eel. He was the only tourist who got a good look. Emily was content to take his word that the eel really was down there. In open water, they saw stingrays cruising near the pale blue sandy bottom.

By the time the boat was heading back toward the island, Emily was laughing at the guide's bad jokes and winking at David. David caught himself thinking, *See? This wasn't such a bad idea.*

He kept his mouth shut.

"What do you want to do now? Still want to shop?"

"We don't have much time," Emily said.

"Time enough to browse a little. Then we'll get a taxi and grab something to eat near the passenger terminal. Okay?"

He left her browsing in a gift shop on the Avenida Rafael Melgar. Then he went out to the curb to ask a taxi driver about pawnshops.

"So where'd you run off to while I was shopping?" Emily asked. They sat in Ernesto's, an open-air restaurant within sight of the cruise ship.

"I had an errand to run."

"Buy me something?"

"No." David pushed back from the table a little and watched the restaurant's two cats as they prowled from table to table, looking for scraps.

Emily followed his gaze and said, "They're so skinny."

"I doubt they get fed."

Emily tore a piece of grouper from the fajitas she hadn't been able to finish. "Here. Give them this."

"You're feeling sorry for a cat?"

"I'm allergic, not mean," Emily said. Then she called, "Hey, cat! Chow time. Come here."

"You've got to use a higher pitch to get their attention," David told her. And he clicked his tongue: "Tch tch tch!"

Both cats turned at once.

"High sounds. Little mousy sounds. That's what they hear best." And he smiled.

* * *

They stood on the fantail, watching the lights of San Miguel fade in the distance. The ship's wake was gray in the moonlight.

Sandy found them. "Grandad summons," he said. "He's in the piano lounge."

"What happens if we don't show?" David said.

"You reveal the blackness of your hearts," Sandy said. "All previous sins are compounded by disobedience."

"We'll be there," Emily said.

"But we'll take our time," David added. "Did you have a good bike ride?"

"It was great, once I got away from the tourists. How was your excursion?"

"Terrific," David said. "We had a wonderful day. Hold the fort for us in the piano bar, will you?"

Sandy saluted. "Don't make me hold out alone forever," he said, and he left.

"So what was it you wanted to show me?" Emily said.

"You do believe me about the watch, right? That I didn't steal it?"

"Of course."

He took the watch from his pocket. "I did steal it."

She looked incredulous. "David?"

"I'm glad you find that hard to believe. What I should say is that I bought it, and it was a steal."

"Where?"

"I found it in a pawnshop in San Miguel. The man who sold it to me gave me a story about how it was a valuable antique, which I refused to believe. He let me have it for less than it's worth, which means he didn't believe it either."

Emily took the watch from him and flipped it open. "*Is* it Grandad's?"

"Of course it's his." David took it back. "What, you think I'd just be lucky and find the spitting image in a Mexican pawnshop?"

"But who? How'd you know to even look?"

"A cat told me. Pumpkin. You know those pawprints he made all over Candace's sheets?"

"Pink and blue."

"Right. Now, it was no surprise to see his pawprints on the dressing table or on the bed. Pumpkin was just prowling around. But Candace's sweater was rolled up in a ball and crammed into a corner, not exactly an interesting prowling surface. And it was too small to take a catnap on. What attracted him?"

Emily thought about it. "You've already told me, haven't you? At the fajita place." And she clicked her tongue. "Tch tch tch tch tch."

"A high-pitched ticking, just the sort of thing a cat's ears are tuned to." David held the watch to his ear. "Candace didn't get much for it, selling it outright."

Emily took a breath. "Why'd she do it?"

"Well, she's gambled away her vacation money, I'm pretty sure of that. But maybe she's as fed up with Grandad as Sandy is. She just isn't as willing to admit it." David unfolded a bill of sale. "We could take this to Grandad. He might believe my story. Then again, he's so convinced of my guilt that he might insist that I paid off the pawnbroker for a fake receipt. When Grandad decides who the villain is for the year, it's hard to change his mind. Anyway, that's option one."

"Poor Candace."

"Poor Candace indeed. She was certainly willing to let us fry in her place, wasn't she? Although, to be fair, we haven't had a turn as the goat. Maybe it really *is* our turn, in which case we could just return the watch to Grandad, claim that we found it somewhere, and let the chips fall where they may."

Then David looked out over the black water. "And then there's option three."

"Which is?"

David closed his fist around the watch. "Emily, when we do finally have children, I want it to be our decision completely. I don't want even a trace of suspicion that we'd make a decision that important for the sake of Aldrich Spence's money." Then, more quietly, he said, "Your grandfather is playing a game. I used to be able to stand on the sidelines and watch him play. Now it really bothers me."

"We've never lost Grandad's game before now. Not in the five years we've been married."

"Exactly. Makes me feel small, but there it is."

"What's option three?"

David opened his hand again. Again he looked out at the ship's wake.

He could see in her eyes that she understood.

"He'd never know," David said. "He might go on thinking that I stole the watch and stay angry forever. I doubt that, but we should think about what we're risking. You might lose your inheritance. He's never actually threatened that, but he might do it. But would that be so bad? We'd be free. We could go bankrupt on our own, we could decide how to live our lives, we could come on these vacations or decide not to."

"Because we made the gesture," Emily said. "Because we decided to resign from the game."

"Exactly. And Em, I wanted to just do it. When I brought the watch back onto the ship, I came back here while you were changing, and watched the water. I could have done it then, but I didn't. Do you see what I'm saying?"

Emily took the watch from him. "Thank you, David. It's an important decision. It's a good one to share."

Then she threw the watch. It flashed briefly in her hand, but then it was out of the ship's lights and invisible in the night sky. There was no splash that they could see.

They stood together a long time, watching the wake.

The Past-Life Alien Abduction Workshop Murder

Tracy A. Knight

The fresh, warm breeze flowed inland from the Bahia de Banderas, playfully tousling Dr. Eric Avery's hair. He was glad he'd decided to take a two-hour beach break before preparing tomorrow's presentation on hypnosis. Setting aside the journal he'd been reading, he closed his eyes and entered a light trance state (which, in a less professional setting, he referred to as dozing), letting himself be enveloped by the temperate December day.

Puerto Vallarta. For a man who'd been raised in the rural Midwest, the city was magically exotic. From its cobblestone streets to its quaint shops, from its beaches to the sparkling blue ocean, from its palm-covered hills to its red tile roofs, Puerto Vallarta was a healthy diversion from Eric's psychological practice.

Feeling a sharp pinch on his left thigh, Eric at first thought he'd been stung by a scorpion or whatever deadly denizens populated the beaches of Puerto Vallarta. Opening his eyes, he saw that a tiny kitten stood next to him, trembling on its breadstick legs, large green eyes looking at him as if he might be the newly descended God of the Tiny Tigers. Its left paw was raised. Apparently the kitten had noticed the drowsing human and decided that semiconsciousness might be conducive to a charitable attitude.

"Hi there," Eric said, reaching down and patting the yellow tiger-striped kitten. "Fancy seeing you here. What's the idea of clawing me?"

Without a moment's hesitation, the kitten jumped up onto Eric's shoulder, then took another short leap to the top of Eric's head. There it sat. Eric couldn't do anything but remain unmoving and puzzled.

"Honey?"

Eric turned his head slowly so as not to toss off the kitten. His wife Rebecca stood there clad in her bikini, a beach towel draped over her arm.

She smiled broadly. "Eric, when you said you wanted to come to Puerto Vallarta to take in facets of life you'd never experienced, I didn't realize it'd include having cats sit on your head."

"We've only been married three months. I have many dark secrets of desire I've been afraid to share with you. Having small felines crouch on my crown is only one. Imagine what is to come, I dare you."

"Ooooo," Rebecca said breathily, straightening the beach towel next to Eric and sitting down. She cocked her head, regarding the placid kitten. "Well, I guess the cat was looking for the highest, pointiest place on the beach."

"Funny." Eric felt the kitten shifting its weight. "Rebecca, would you mind telling me what the kitten is doing right now?"

"Sure, honey. It's grooming itself, licking its front paw to be exact."

"Fine. If you see it lift its tail, could you give me a signal?"

"Finger-spelling to indicate uninvited urination, you mean?"

"Spoken like a true attorney. Yes, please."

The kitten, apparently tiring of its holy vantage point, stood up on Eric's head, deploying it claws to get a good hold.

"Ouch!"

"It's okay, Eric. It's just getting ready to jump down. Your head wasn't quite flat enough for it, I guess."

The kitten jumped from Eric's head into his lap, immediately coiling up and closing its eyes.

Lying back on his towel, breathing in the aromatic breeze, Eric said, "There, that's better. Ahhh. This is the life, huh, Rebecca?"

"Can't be beat," she said. "Although I'm not sure giving a presentation at the New Tomorrows World Conference is going to enhance your professional status. I saw a schedule of events: 'Crystal Healing: From Hemorrhoids to Brain Stem Tumors'; 'Channeling Yesterday's Tyrants to Solve Today's Problems: The Really New Conservatism'; 'Hypnotic Regression to Uncover Past-Life Alien Abductions.' "

"You're kidding, right?"

"Nope. I picked up a program on my way out of the hotel."

Eric sighed. "Oh well. Since our honeymoon consisted of attending a Nastic Bonespoor concert in Chicago, I figured I owed you something a bit more exotic. Getting the gig here meant a free trip, room and board in beautiful Puerto Vallarta. And who knows? Maybe my presentation on the uses and misuses of hypnosis in research will enlighten those who accidentally attend."

"Nice spin."

Eric sat up. As if this represented the reappearance of a mystical mountain, the kitten awoke from its nap and again leapt to the top of Eric's head, this time without even an intermediate stop on the human's shoulder-plateau.

High-pitched laughter came from behind them.

Eric turned, feeling the kitten shift its weight like a surfer. A young Mexican boy stood there, pointing toward Eric. Stranger still, the boy held a rope leash, at the end of which stood a middling-sized iguana.

"*Aqui! Aqui!*" the boy shouted. "*Gato comico! Cuidado!*"

The boy's eyes widened at the exact moment Eric felt something warm streaming down his back.

"Honey?"

"Yes, Eric?"

"Can you take this cat while I go shower off? This wonderful animal just relieved itself on me."

Rebecca laughed her hearty laugh, then reached over and took hold of the kitten. "Aw, what a nice baby," she said, cradling it. "Did da liddo boy fwighten you? Or da man and his big wumpy head?"

Eric stood up and shook the sand from his beach towel. "Please, Rebecca, baby talk has a bad effect on me. As soon as I shower, let's go back to the room."

"Okay, but the kitten goes with us. It's too small to be alone."

Eric huffed, only half-joking, as he headed for the small collection of beachside showers. Passing the boy, Eric said, "I'm not sure what you said, *amigo*, but I'm certain you were making fun of me. That's a bit ironic for someone who has an iguana on a leash, don't you think?"

The iguana tickled the air with its tongue.

The boy, obviously not understanding Eric, slapped his hand over his mouth and laughed again.

Walking to their room in the Krystal Hotel, Eric and Rebecca passed several of the conference rooms where this afternoon's presentations were in progress.

"Stop a second, I have to read this," Eric said, standing in front of a large door festooned with ribbons hanging across a bright orange poster. "Geez, you weren't kidding, were you?"

"Hurry up," Rebecca said, tickling the cat's chin. "Our baby needs some milk." She kissed the kitten's head.

"Sheesh. They'll probably kick us out of the hotel for having that cat."

"Nonsense. They wouldn't kick out a hotshot psychologist."

"Right." He peered closely at the poster. It read:

PAST-LIFE ALIEN ABDUCTION ABREACTION THERAPY (PLAAAT)

WE KNOW THAT CURRENT PSYCHOLOGICAL PROBLEMS ARE OFTEN CAUSED BY PAST-LIFE TRAUMA. WE ALSO KNOW THAT ALIEN ABDUCTIONS ARE AN INCREASING CAUSE OF CURRENT POST-TRAUMATIC STRESS. IN THIS PARTICIPATORY WORKSHOP, ELVIN MCGARFNEY, CERTIFIED HYPNO-THERAPIST, WILL REGRESS PARTICIPANTS TO PAST LIVES. MANY WILL FIND THEIR PAST LIVES INCLUDE EXPERIENCES OF ALIEN ABDUCTION. BY UN-COVERING THESE TRAUMAS, PARTICIPANTS CAN LEARN TO SHED THE DAUNTING CLOAKS OF PAST LIVES AND PAST ALIEN ABDUCTIONS.

"Unbelievable," Eric muttered to himself. "*Certified hypnotherapist*: probably means he attended one day's training at Goober's Hypnosis Training Spa and Shoe Repair."

At that moment the conference room door burst open, knocking Eric to the floor.

A bald, overweight man came stumbling from the room like an extra in a zombie movie, sweat pouring down his pasty face. "Murder," the man croaked. "Murder."

More impressively, this man was followed out by a skeletal fellow wearing cutoffs and a Rolling Stones T-shirt bounding from the room on all fours. Seeing Eric crumpled on the floor next to him, the man stopped, raised one arm like an arthritic Bela Lugosi, and hissed.

The kitten leapt from Rebecca's arms, scrambled across the carpeted hallway and jumped toward the cat-man, swiping its claw in a glancing blow across the man's forehead, leaving a thin red scratch. The kitten then jumped onto Eric's chest.

The cat-man shook his head. "What happened?" he said, rising to his feet, rubbing his scratched forehead. "What am I doing here?"

"Murder!" the overweight man bellowed again.

Eric grabbed the kitten, stood up and handed the feline back to Rebecca, who stood frozen in place, shocked by the drama playing out before her.

Walking into the large conference room, Eric saw four partici-pants lying on the floor, face down.

One workshopper had a knife embedded in the center of his back.

Kneeling next to the body, Eric saw that the knife's handle sported a pattern of hand-painted red roses.

He felt for a pulse. Nothing.

The other three workshoppers—an elderly man and two middle-aged women—slowly emerged from their collective haze. They looked at their fallen workshop brother, at each other, then at Eric. "What happened here?" one of the women asked.

Eric said, "Looks to me like someone killed this man. Any of you see what happened?"

"No," the older man said. "I was back in the eighteen hundreds. I didn't know anything happened back here."

One of the women, who looked like a peroxided parochial-school teacher, said, "And I was on the planet of Yrterrablot, eating a feast with the High Crowned Heads."

The other woman, an attractive redhead, said, "My husband was acting like he wanted to strangle me . . ."

"This was in a past life too?" Eric said.

"No, I was just flashing back to when I told him I wanted to come to this conference."

The pasty, overweight man shambled back into the room, holding the arm of a local police officer. "This is where it happened. See? There's the man."

"An ambulance is on the way," said the young officer.

Eric was surprised that the officer spoke such clear English, but even more surprised when he recognized the young man.

"Danny? Danny Ortez?"

The policeman looked at Eric for a second before a gleam of recognition spread across his face. "Dr. Avery? My goodness, I never thought I'd see you again."

As they shook hands, Rebecca, kitten in tow, walked up behind Eric. The cat-man followed her in.

"Rebecca, this is Danny Ortez. He was in my Theories of Personality course the year I taught at Iowa State."

Rebecca untangled her right arm from the kitten's embrace and shook Officer Ortez's hand.

"Did you two see anything?" Ortez asked.

"No," Eric answered. "We were just walking by when this man burst out of the room, followed by the fellow on all fours."

"Allow me to introduce myself," the overweight man said, extending his hand. "Elvin McGarfney."

"Eric Avery. Pleased."

"If you'll excuse me," said Officer Ortez, "I need to get to work."

Eric said, "That's fine, Danny. We need to get up to our room. If we can help in any way, please let us know."

Walking down the corridor toward the elevator, Eric said, "Nice conference."

"Just lovely," Rebecca said, snuggling the kitten. "You know, Eric, this kitten was ready to lay down its life for you back there. We have an obligation to take care of it for the rest of its life. That's a Puerto Vallartan custom, is it not?"

"Right."

The kitten, whom the couple had dubbed Purrcy, lapped milk from the small bowl on the floor.

"Just think, honey," Rebecca said, sitting next to Eric on the bed and leaning her head against his shoulder. "Our first child is having his—or her—first room service."

"It's a him. I picked him up and saw his tiny ornaments," Eric said. "Not to downplay the kitten's importance, but that murder downstairs is still bugging me. I suspect one of the participants had a long-standing grudge against the victim and during the regression, laid him out like a lake trout."

"Honey?"

"Yes."

"When you try to sound like Sherlock Holmes, you sound like Forrest Gump."

Assuming a slow drawl, Eric said, "Mah wife is like a box of chocklits: Yah never know what blemish she's gonna bring up."

A knock on the door interrupted their moment.

Opening the door, Eric was surprised to see Officer Danny Cortez standing there.

"Danny. Nice to see you again."

"If I didn't know you, I wouldn't ask you," Danny said.

"Ask me what?"

"Whether or not you'd help me with this investigation."

"I'll help any way I can, but I don't see how . . ."

"Look, Dr. Avery, I've just spent ninety minutes with McGarfney and his workshop participants. I'm not getting anywhere. McGarfney had turned off the lights during this regression thing he was doing. When he turned the lights back on, the man was dead. He didn't hear a thing. Neither did any of the participants. They were all in their own little la-la lands, I guess."

"Who was the victim?"

Danny pulled a notepad from his front pocket and flipped it open. "His name was Hollis Markey. Ironworker from Rockford, Illinois. I called his wife this afternoon. The trip to this conference was a birthday present from her, so you can imagine how she feels. There seems to be no motive here, Dr. Avery. The group members were complete strangers before the workshop this afternoon. I can't find a motive."

"Could someone have come into the room?"

Danny shook his head. "Don't think so. McGarfney locked the doors when the regression started so they wouldn't be disturbed."

"So where do I fit in?"

"I'd like you to interview everybody who was in that room, see what you can find out, see what you think. This is your field, after all."

"Regressions to alien abduction experiences in past lives is a bit on the far fringe of my field . . . but I'll give it a try if you like. It'd be interesting just to talk to these folks. I might learn something. If it's helpful to you, so much the better."

Elvin McGarfney had changed into a suit. His red checkered tie hung only to the center of his chest. After Eric sat down in the conference room, McGarfney pulled up a chair uncomfortably close to Eric.

"This is terrible," McGarfney said, wiping a hand over his brow and the shiny top of his head, eyes remaining intently focused on Eric's.

"I understand you didn't hear anything."

McGarfney shook his head. "Not a thing."

"I noticed a video camera in the corner of the room. Were you recording the workshop?"

"You bet. I was hoping to market the tape as a training aid."

"Can I have a look?"

McGarfney wheeled the stand holding the television set and VCR close to them. He pulled a pair of eyeglasses from his front pocket and put them on, then leaned close to the VCR's blinking time display.

After watching McGarfney fiddle with various buttons for nearly a minute, Eric asked, "Need some help there?"

McGarfney didn't respond, just leaned closer to the video recorder.

Finally, Eric stood up and leaned down next to the man. "So do you need any help?"

McGarfney shot Eric a startled look, then said, "No, that's all right, Doctor. I think I've got it now."

Sure enough, with a rigid index finger, McGarfney pressed the Play button.

The television screen momentarily glowed silver-gray, then the videotape commenced.

On the screen, the five workshop members were lying on their backs in a circle, heads toward the center. As he strode in measured steps around the group, McGarfney intoned simple relaxation directives, instructing the group to let each major muscle group relax in succession until they felt a sense of utter calm caressing them.

Not bad for someone with only weekend training, Eric thought.

McGarfney then told the group to picture themselves rising out of their bodies, out through the ceiling, and into the sky so high that the nearby Sierra Madre mountains would look like a tabletop model. The group then was instructed to sail even higher, out of the world's grasp until they saw the Earth as a glittering shard of blue-green crystal.

"Now," McGarfney told the group, "you will gently but quickly fall back toward the Earth, down to a time and place when you have had contact with alien entities."

Wow, he threw me off the back of the truck on that turn, Eric thought.

Each of the workshop participants began moving ever so slightly. A few (the cat-man included) slowly turned their heads left to right repeatedly as if trying to cast off the opening scene of a bad dream.

McGarfney knelt over the group members, one by one, nose to nose, giving them individual suggestions.

At one point, Eric noticed that the red-haired female had begun thrashing and moaning. Still, McGarfney remained over the cat-man, calmly giving suggestions, only an inch away from the man's face.

"What's happening with her?" Eric asked, pointing at the screen. "She looks agitated. Why didn't you go over and work with her?"

McGarfney's eyes remained locked on Eric's. He waited a few moments, then said, bristles in his voice, "Perhaps you're more adept at this than I am, *Dr.* Avery, but I give my full concentration to only one subject at a time."

"Fine, fine," Eric said. *Sheesh, thin-skinned therapist, this one.*

After McGarfney had made the rounds, he walked to one wall and used the dimmer switch to douse the lights.

Less than a minute passed before the lights came back up.

All the workshop participants were face-down on the floor. One—Hollis Markey—had a knife sticking out of his back.

Pointing to the television set, Eric asked, "Why are they all on their stomachs? When you turned the lights off, they were all on their backs."

"Once the lights were out, I told them as a group that when they'd made contact with their abduction experience, they would roll onto their stomachs. With their faces pressed against the floor, the suffocating feelings we want them to abreact are increased."

"I see," Eric said. He didn't.

"One more thing, Dr. Avery. I do think I have one angle on this murder that might prove valuable. I spent a day in training at a Dissociative Disorders and Satanic Ritual Abuse Treatment Center in Chicago. The head psychiatrist there showed me a book he kept of all the symbols of satanism he'd uncovered through his work with therapy patients."

"And?"

"And one of the satanic signs is a cluster of roses . . . just like on the shaft of the knife."

"So you're saying . . . what? This was, like, a satanic hit?"

McGarfney shrugged. "Could be. Just trying to help."

"You think this conference would draw a lot of satanists?"

"What better way to dim the light than invade the light bulb?"

"I see." Eric didn't.

Luckily the conversation didn't have to continue. The four surviving members of McGarfney's group strode into the room.

Eric pulled five chairs into a circle, excused McGarfney from the room, and opened the floor for discussion.

The cat-man introduced himself as Melvin Sanders, thirty-five years old, a community-college English instructor when he wasn't reliving past feline lives or projecting himself astrally. Eric found him to be a polite, intelligent man, even when Melvin said, "I *was* a cat, you know. In Egyptian times. I was worshiped. In fact, it was my role in that society that brought me to the aliens' attention."

"You're a luckier man than I," Eric said, trying to remain empathic. "I was probably one of the lugs that had to drag those stones for the pyramids, minimum-wage work. You said during the trance you had no awareness of what was going on during the murder. In your state, could you have murdered Hollis Markey?"

Melvin looked at Eric as if he were a retarded insurance salesman. "Dr. Avery, cats don't use weapons."

"Of course." Eric turned next to the elderly gentleman, who introduced himself as Jonathan White. A retired police officer, Mr. White had come to the conference for some personal exploration, nothing more. "I'm not one of those kooks," he said, much to the consternation of Melvin the cat-man. "I figured I'd lived through so much, I just wanted to see what all of this New Age stuff was about. It was kind of fun . . . until this."

Eric leaned toward Mr. White. "You were a police officer. What do *you* think happened? Who could've killed Hollis Markey?"

"Can't imagine," Mr. White said, shaking his head. "I was back in the eighteen hundreds fighting off some aliens who'd abducted me and an Indian squaw for . . . well, for some experimentation."

"I see." Unfortunately, Eric *did*.

"Anyway, no matter what you think of this regression therapy, I was zonked out. I couldn't have got to my feet and found Hollis in the dark, much less kill the guy."

"Good point," Eric conceded. "What about you ladies?"

Amanda Ponts and Shirley Fagan were both schoolteachers (which explained why Amanda looked like a peroxided parochial-school teacher; she was). They'd come as part of a tour from Texas, though they were on separate buses and thus hadn't met each other. "We were out of it, too, Dr. Avery," Amanda said. "I was on another planet . . . or at least that's what I thought at the time. Now I'm not so sure . . ."

Shirley pushed red bangs away from her forehead and gave Eric a shy smile. "And I was barely hypnotized. I couldn't stop thinking of how my husband berated me so for signing up for this trip."

While part of him wanted to stay for an extended session with this colorful group of humans, Eric decided to call it a night. He had to take Rebecca to dinner, then go over his notes for tomorrow morning's presentation. Most importantly, however, he had the distinct feeling he wasn't getting anyplace. No suspects. No motive. Just four regression adventurers and their overanxious tour guide.

"I'll tell you what," Eric said, "if I need you for anything else, how can I get in contact with you?"

The four happily supplied their room numbers.

After a duck-with-pears dinner at La Perla, Eric and Rebecca returned to their hotel room. Eric unwrapped the table scraps he'd brought for Purrcy and set them on the floor.

Judging from Purrcy's flattened ears and freight train rumbles, the kitten assumed he'd traversed the cosmic membrane into kitty heaven.

"I knew you'd fall in love with Purrcy," Rebecca said.

"Yeah, well, I was just giving you a hard time. I love cats. They live life nobly, unlike us humans."

"So we can take him home with us?"

"If Purrcy agrees, which I'm sure he will."

Rebecca smiled, then narrowed her eyebrows and said, "So no further insights on the Hollis Markey murder?"

"Not really. Maybe a satanic spirit from the past appeared in the room just long enough to commit the murder, then dissolved into the ether."

"From what you said, I think maybe the schoolteachers did it. A conspiracy. Shirley Fagan was taking out her frustration with her husband on a poor ironworker."

"At least that's a motive of some kind. I even wonder whether the retired policeman, Jonathan White, might have had some kind of flashback to his days on the force and struck out at the nearest guy. Still, that's a pretty thin theory. None of it makes sense. None of it."

"I hear you," Rebecca said.

Rebecca's statement came at the exact instant Purrcy caught Eric's eye. Every time either Eric or Rebecca said something, Purrcy turned his ears like tiny radar dishes, allowing him to follow the conversation without interrupting his dinner.

"Wait a minute," Eric said. "I've got it!" He kissed Rebecca firmly on the lips then walked over and patted Purrcy, who stopped eating long enough to shoot Eric a dirty look: *Get outta here, Lumpy. I'm eatin' a duck.*

"What do you mean, Eric?"

Picking up the telephone, Eric said, "Just come with me tomorrow morning. I'll either look like a genius or an idiot. Either way, I'd like you there with me."

When Officer Ortez answered the phone, Eric asked him to come to the hotel tomorrow and wait in the lounge while Eric assembled

McGarfney and the four workshoppers in the conference room. He promised Danny Ortez he'd leave the hotel with the murderer.

Eric asked Elvin McGarfney to take a seat in the corner of the conference room. McGarfney kept Eric locked in his gaze as Eric explained. "With your permission, I'm going to take these folks through a brief regression. If what I think is true, the murderer will be revealed." He pointed to the four workshoppers who were lying face-up on the floor, small mattresses beneath them. "A satanic force won't be able to resist the opportunity."

McGarfney nodded, but with concern on his face. "You don't think there's a chance someone will be hurt . . . or killed?"

"Not a chance," Eric said with confidence.

Rebecca gave him a puzzled look.

After taking the four through a standard relaxation protocol, Eric intoned, "And now, with the ease that you experienced before, you'll go back to that time when you were abducted by aliens. Only this time, you'll view the abduction like a movie, you'll live through it vicariously, absorbing all there is to be learned from the experience."

Then, just as he'd seen McGarfney do, Eric knelt over the group members, one by one, and whispered into their ears.

"Now, as I turn the lights off, you'll find the abduction experience deepening, and you'll find yourself following all of my suggestions. All of them."

Eric winked at the frowning Rebecca as he strode across the room and dimmed the lights until the room was shrouded in darkness.

A few moments of uncomfortable silence passed.

Then sounds of scuffling.

Then a loud thump, followed by a series of quieter thumps.

Eric turned on the lights.

The four workshop members had rolled across the room and lay against a far wall.

Elvin McGarfney knelt in the center of the room, a rose-handled dagger in his hand. He was stabbing one of the mattresses (Melvin the cat-man's, to be exact) over and over again.

Room fully lit, McGarfney saw what it was he was doing, looked up sheepishly at Eric, and dropped the dagger.

Rebecca opened the conference-room door. Danny Ortez walked in, handcuffs at the ready.

"There's your man, Danny," Eric said, pointing toward Mc-Garfney, who now stood up and faced Eric, his pasty face gone a whiter shade of pale.

As he cuffed McGarfney, Danny asked Eric, "How did you figure it out?"

"I didn't, not at first. Not until I watched our cat listening carefully to us at the same time Rebecca said the word *hear*. Yeah, sounds strange. Synchronicity? Dumb luck? Who knows? But that's the first time it occurred to me that McGarfney always kept his eyes on me, that he didn't notice I was speaking if I was behind his back, that he gave his individual suggestions one by one, not even noticing when another group member was in distress. At first I thought he was just concentrating fully. Then it hit me."

"You mean . . . ?"

"Right. Elvin McGarfney is deaf. Reads lips like a champ, but deaf. I wasn't one hundred percent sure; that's why I whispered to all the group members that they were to roll off their mattresses and to the side of the room. He wouldn't see or hear me give the suggestion, and in the dark, he wouldn't notice the group members rolling away from him. I was banking on the fact he'd try to kill again."

Danny scratched his head. "Why would he try again?"

"Two reasons. He was defensive when I questioned him about his techniques, and I took pains to sound like there wasn't a chance anyone'd be hurt. I was assuming he'd want to show me up, and would want me to be responsible for another dead workshopper. Secondly, he assured me the murder was part of a satanic conspiracy. Folks like that, folks who are strongly invested in their conspiracy beliefs, they want other people to believe them . . . sometimes no matter the cost."

"A deaf therapist?" Danny said as he looked at McGarfney, who stared back helplessly.

McGarfney nodded. "He's right."

"There're a lot of wonderful therapists who happen to be deaf," Eric said. "The problem these days is that a lot of therapists are deaf . . . *figuratively*. More concerned with proving their personal biases than with helping their clients. McGarfney just happened to be deaf in both senses of the word."

It wasn't until that moment that Eric noticed the other group members lying still at the room's perimeter.

Turning to them, Eric said, "And now, whenever you're ready, you can relax and slowly come back to the room, feeling refreshed, feeling better than before."

Before returning to full consciousness, Melvin scampered over on all fours and rubbed against Eric's leg, purring.

After his presentation, Eric walked down to Playa d'Oro, where he found Rebecca and Purrcy sunning themselves on the beach.

He sat down on the edge of Rebecca's beach towel. Purrcy promptly jumped onto Eric's head and began his grooming ritual.

"So how many people came to your presentation?" Rebecca asked.

"Three. One picked his nose through the entire thing. One went to sleep. The other asked me if I could regress him far enough to where he could find his mother's womb again."

"What did you tell him?"

"I told him if he wanted to find his mother's womb he'd have to ask at the wegistration desk."

Rebecca burst into laughter. Eric joined her, which unfortunately joggled Purrcy's perch and caused the kitten to do a quick claw-grip on Eric's scalp.

"Ouch!"

"Relax, honey, Purrcy just wants to be close to you."

"He will be. I bought a cat carrier in the hotel gift shop. Soon he'll be setting up shop in our home."

"You're quite a guy, Eric Avery."

"Thanks, Rebecca. Say, next time how about we go to a New Age lawyer's convention? You can give a presentation on the Karmic

Defense—you know, killing someone because they killed you in a previous life."

"Nice idea, but there aren't any New Age lawyer conventions—not yet anyway."

Reaching up to his head and patting Purrcy, Eric said, "It'll be good for us to have this cat around. It'll remind us about how nicely life can be lived. Unlike people, unlike the people at this conference, maybe there's no need to muckrake our own lives, finding things to explain our pain, finding things to worry about. You'll never see a squirrel leaning against a tree, head in hand, obssessing over the coming winter . . ."

". . . or a cat getting an ulcer over where he might get his next meal."

"Right," Eric said. "I wish we were all like Purrcy. Compassionate, gentle, nonjudgmental."

The three beings were silent beneath the sapphire sky, the warm sun: Rebecca lying down, one arm draped across her eyes, a smile on her face; Eric sitting up straight, eyes closed, a smile on his face; Purrcy, sitting atop his new pet's head, curiously watching the passing parade of silly humans and wishing he could laugh.

Here Today, Dead To Maui

Catherine Dain

"A millionaire found me changing planes for Maui! Why is he short and ugly, Lord, when you know I like them tall?" Michael sang as he emerged from the bathroom wearing the hibiscus print shirt he had bought the day before.

"That's gross," Faith said. "Materialistic. Midlife Mick Jagger. And nobody came near you on the airplane. Or in the Hilo airport. Except for the fat woman who put the orchids around your neck."

"Because I was traveling with you and Elizabeth. Everyone was looking at her. If I'd been alone, who knows? Besides, if you're so ascetically inclined, why did you accept the offer of a first-class airplane ticket and a week in a suite at the Lahaina Hilton?" Michael leaned against the central post marking the open french doors to the deck and stretched out his arms. "White sand! Ocean! Clean air!"

"Elizabeth's contract specified two tickets. No point in letting one go to waste when you didn't have anybody else to ask." Faith poured herself a second cup of coffee. She didn't particularly like the Kona blend, but it was all room service had to offer.

"Can't you just enjoy the vacation?" Michael turned back and sighed.

"Elizabeth has one more day of shooting. You're not on vacation until tomorrow."

"To Maui, and to Maui, and to Maui. Life creeps in its petty pace, especially when one is not quite on vacation." He knelt down in front of one of the flowered chintz armchairs so that he was level with Elizabeth. "Say *Maui.*"

"Mrowr," she replied, blue eyes focusing intently on his dark ones.

"Maui."

"Mrowr."

"See how smart she is?"

"You didn't feed her this morning. She's actually saying she's annoyed."

Michael straightened up. "When did you become an expert on my cat?"

"I've been part of her environment since you adopted her. She thinks of me as extended family. I felt obliged to return the compliment by paying attention to her behavior. Since I've spent my life—or two careers anyway, the dead one as an actress and the live one as a therapist—studying human behavior, and the cat thinks she's human, it wasn't hard. Trust me. She's hungry."

"So am I." He picked a cheese danish out of the basket on the coffee table. "But she's supposed to be hungry. Otherwise, she might not eat on cue."

"You'd better hurry with that. Elizabeth's call is in half an hour. Eddie will be here any minute with the car."

"They have to set up a shot on the deck of an old whaler. No way are they going to be ready on time." Michael poured himself a cup of coffee and settled in the other chintz armchair.

"Then I think you ought to feed her."

"She only has to be hungry and annoyed for the next couple of hours. She'll be fine."

Faith shrugged. "Suit yourself. But if we're going to be here for a while, could you move to another chair? That one clashes with your shirt."

"All the furniture clashes with my shirt. This is Hawaii—the shirt is supposed to clash. Buy a muumuu and get in the spirit."

"Hawaiian clothes are the best thing that could have happened to the tourist industry. You can't tell you've gained fifteen pounds until you're home and it's too late. If I start to gain, I'll think about the muumuu."

"How can anyone gain on a diet of fish, rice, and fruit? If you're really going to stick to that. Get a muumuu or not. Put orchids in your hair. Drink mai-tais by the pool."

"Maybe when we've finished the shoot." Faith picked a blueberry muffin out of the basket. Blueberries counted as fruit. "I may even search for romance."

"You won't have to search far. Eddie Inouye has made it clear he's available."

"Yes, and he doesn't care who takes him up on the offer. No thanks."

"Well, one of us has to be nice to him if we want him to drive us to the sacred pools of Hana tomorrow. The road through the rain forest is supposed to be challenging, and I don't want Elizabeth's life at risk."

"I'll drive," Faith said. "You can hold Elizabeth and look at the scenery."

"I'll have to think about that," Michael replied. He finished his danish and started on a pecan bun.

"Eddie," they chorused as the phone rang.

Michael stuffed the bun into his mouth and scooped Elizabeth into her carrier. Faith assured Eddie they would be right down.

The elevator took them to the lobby, where Eddie—a short, eager twenty-year-old wearing a shirt that clashed with everything—was waiting.

"*Aloha*," he said, grinning. "Phil said to tell you they're on time. We have to hurry."

"That has to be a lie. Can I go back for the basket of pastries?" Michael asked.

"I told you we should have fed her," Faith snapped.

"No, no," Eddie said. "He means it. Phil promised he'll have her finished before lunch. Okay?"

"Three hours," Michael said to Faith. "We can handle that."

"Elizabeth is on L.A. time, remember. I've never known you to be this callous."

"Oh, for God's sake, Faith. One morning. For two days' deprivation every six months, she gets to eat shrimp, salmon, and chicken the rest of the year!" Michael turned hastily to Eddie. "Only for snacks, of course. Three meals a day she eats Pretty Kitty cat food."

"Don't worry, Eddie isn't going to turn you in," Faith said. "Are you?"

"No way, *wahine*," Eddie answered, still grinning. "Driving is my main livelihood. If I talk, nobody wants to ride with me anymore."

Faith nodded. "Let's go."

Eddie had parked his Honda right in front of the hotel, in the taxi loading zone. Two taxi drivers glared as Faith and Michael got into the back seat.

Eddie whisked the car away from the cluster of tall white hotels, over the causeway, and down the narrow road the short distance to the Lahaina harbor. The day was so beautiful that Faith almost began to enjoy herself.

"What's it like living here?" Michael asked.

"Like this," Eddie answered. "Like every morning when I wake up, it's the first day of vacation."

"It must rain," Faith said. "There's a rain forest on the island."

"Yeah, but it only rains for five minutes at a time. Most of the time. Except for hurricanes, and this isn't the season."

"Stop it, Faith," Michael snapped. "No disasters. I am not anticipating a disaster on Maui."

Faith glared back.

"This is as close as I can get," Eddie said cheerfully. He had maneuvered through the jaywalking tourists to the pier, but there was no place to pull over. Two large silver trucks were taking up three parking spaces apiece. Several horns began to beep the second the

Honda's brake lights went on. "I'll find a place to park and meet you on the set. Just yell if you want to make a quick getaway."

"Thanks," Michael said. "I was optimistic enough to schedule a tennis lesson for three and a massage for four."

"No problem." Eddie grinned at him.

The beeps became steady as Faith got out and took Elizabeth's carrier so that Michael could join her. They slipped between the trucks to the wooden walkway.

The whalers were smaller and newer than Faith had expected, but then her idea of a whaler was based on John Huston's *Moby Dick*. She suspected that these had been used since the nineteenth century.

"I don't understand why they're shooting a cat food commercial on a whaler," Faith said.

"Cats love fish," Michael explained, in a tone that let her know any idiot could figure it out. "Pretty Kitty is for cats with a whale of an appetite."

"Yes, but whalers kill whales. When this commercial airs, they're going to lose all the New Agers and Trekkers and Greens who own cats. Maybe half the cat owners in the country." Faith picked her way carefully over heavy cables that snaked from the trucks to a ship halfway down the pier.

"Maybe half the cat owners in L.A., tops. Besides, it's a tax deductible week in Maui for anyone from Pretty Kitty, the ad agency, or the production company who wants to visit the shoot. Although the L.A. ad business is so bad I don't think anyone from the agency came." Michael waved at the deck. "*Aloha*, we're here."

"Oh, good." A young woman in tank top and jeans leaned over the railing. Two days in Maui had given her Southern California tan a bronze glow and turned the peroxide streaks in her stringy brown hair almost white. She waved a clipboard at them. "Phil is setting up for the shot of Elizabeth now. He's lighting her stand-in."

Michael had one foot on the wooden ladder. He stopped so suddenly that Faith hit him with the carrier.

"What stand-in?" he asked.

The woman held a finger to her lips, then beckoned him aboard.

"What stand-in?" Michael asked again, after reaching the deck in two bounds.

Faith clambered up after him, bracing the carrier awkwardly on each rung.

"Mrowr," Elizabeth said.

"Sorry," Faith murmured to the carrier.

"Faith, Jennifer," Michael said as he belatedly reached for the handle.

"Hi, Faith. Hi, Sweetums," Jennifer added to the carrier.

"Mrowr."

Faith nodded assent.

"Where's Eddie?" Jennifer asked.

"Parking the car. What stand-in?" Michael's voice shot up an octave, and Jennifer shushed him again.

"One of the Pretty Kitty executives is here with his wife, daughter, and cat," she whispered. "The daughter really wants to see her cat in a commercial. I hope Elizabeth is in fine form."

"Of course she is! What an outrage!" Michael snapped.

"Okay, okay," Jennifer said, holding up her hand. "I'm just telling you what's going on."

"We have a contract!" Michael lowered his voice.

"I know. But Pretty Kitty hired the ad agency, and the ad agency hired the production company."

"What does that mean?"

"It means that everyone is being very, very nice. Especially Phil. This is his first network job, you know. I think he'd do anything to get more."

"All right." Michael sighed and turned to Faith. "You see why I didn't feed her. One lousy shot and I'd have to get a job."

"Jennifer! Let's go!" a male voice called.

Faith, Michael, and Elizabeth followed Jennifer aft, stepping between cables when possible.

Cameras, lights, and reflectors were all focused on a very fluffy cat the color of an underripe cantaloupe, wearing a cubic zirconium collar. Her amber eyes darted nervously around the crowd. A red-haired, freckled girl about ten years old was sitting cross-legged beside her, smiling at anyone who would smile back.

"That's Marlene," Jennifer whispered to Michael, drawing the name out to three syllables. "As in Dietrich. The girl's name is Boots. Good luck."

She took her clipboard over to the camera.

Michael shook his head, gaze still fastened on Marlene. "She's pretty, but she's not an actress. We're fine." He looked around, spotting a youth with a three-day growth of beard, whose knees were sticking out of his Levi's. The young man was wearing the only Hawaiian shirt that might have come out of a suitcase, not a store. "Phil! I hope we're not late. I didn't realize we were shooting on MTV video time."

"Hey, Michael, how ya doing?" Phil trotted the four steps that separated them and clapped Michael on the back. "Glad to see the star has arrived." He cupped his hands around his mouth. "Okay! Get ready for a take." Then he knelt down beside the girl. "Boots, honey, I'm really grateful for your help. And I'm going to remember what a beautiful cat Marlene is, next time we're casting."

Boots looked at him adoringly. She carefully picked up Marlene, then winced when the nervous cat sank bare claws into her naked shoulders.

Michael lifted Elizabeth from the carrier and placed her down on the crossed pieces of silver tape marking the spot Marlene had vacated. Elizabeth stretched, surveyed the assembled group, winked one blue eye at the cameraman, and settled onto her haunches, pearly tail falling naturally into place.

"Here." Someone thrust a crystal dish heaped with Pretty Kitty into Michael's hand. He put it down on another taped mark to Elizabeth's right.

"Roll the tape!" Phil called.

"Rolling!"

"Slate the camera!"

"Slated. Take one."

"Action!"

"Discover the food," Michael whispered.

Elizabeth turned toward the dish. Her eyes widened dramatically. She approached the dish and sniffed, then looked back toward Michael.

"That's right, baby, time to eat," he whispered.

Elizabeth sniffed again. She shook her head. Straightening up, she made a graceful pirouette and overturned the dish with one kick from her left hind leg.

"Cut!" Phil called.

"Oh my God," Michael moaned.

Faith tugged his arm. "There's something wrong with the food."

"What?"

"Something wrong, damn it, *think.*"

"There's something wrong with the food!" Michael yelled.

"What do you mean, son?"

Michael discovered he was standing next to a tall, florid man still decorated with a fading airport lei. Red hair and freckles marked him as Boots's father, even if he wasn't old enough to be Michael's. He was glaring down menacingly.

"I mean sabotage!" Michael gasped. "It can't be Pretty Kitty!"

"Come on, Michael." Phil clapped him on the shoulder again. Michael was starting to feel hemmed in. "We'll try another take. If it'll make you happy, we'll even open a new can."

"Where's Elizabeth?" Faith had squeezed between the men to the overturned dish. Elizabeth was nowhere in sight.

"Elizabeth!" Michael dropped to his knees, to search for her at her own level.

"Hey, guys, anybody seen the cat?" Phil asked.

The murmurs from the crew were all negative.

"Could she have jumped overboard?" The question came from a short, dark-haired woman in a muumuu draped with a fading lei that matched the one Boots's father was wearing.

"Absolutely not!" Michael snapped. Still, he crawled to the edge of the deck and checked the ocean. The gentle blue waves were unbroken. "Elizabeth!"

His stomach churned and he began gasping for breath.

"All right! That's enough!" Faith was standing on Elizabeth's mark. The lights had been turned off, but the reflectors focused enough sunlight to create a glow around her shins. Her arms were upraised, palms out, like an evangelist. Everyone quieted down and stared. She was glad she hadn't worn a muumuu. The way the long sleeves of her white overblouse fell back past her elbows made a more dramatic effect. "I have to ask one question. You!" Her right hand swooped down, index finger pointing to Boots's father. "Are you driving a rental car?"

"Why, yes." His face became even more florid.

"Thank you." Both palms out again, Faith looked at each silent face in front of her. "I know who took Elizabeth. And I know who sprayed the ant poison on the Pretty Kitty." She waited for the gasps to subside. "We will all turn toward the railing, eyes shut, while I count to thirty. During that time, I expect Elizabeth to reappear on her mark. Otherwise, the person responsible will be looking at both civil and criminal charges. Which will not be good for that person's livelihood. Now! Toward the railing. One! Two!"

Faith had reached twenty-seven by the time she heard the soft *Mrowr* and felt Elizabeth rub against her leg.

"Elizabeth!" Michael cried.

"Thank you all," Faith said, bowing, as the crew applauded.

"Let's get ready for the next take!" Phil shouted. "New can of cat food! Clean up the mess from the old one!"

"I'd like to fix the dish," Faith said.

"Down the stairs to the galley." Phil pointed toward the low cabin.

Michael hugged Elizabeth. He even sobbed a little into her fur, which she didn't like at all.

Faith returned a moment later with the crystal dish, piled high. She set it down on the mark.

Michael released Elizabeth in the general area of the other mark. The cat swiftly groomed the spot where Michael's tears had dampened her fur and then settled precisely in the center of the taped cross, tail flaring gracefully.

"Roll the tape!" Phil called. "Let's do it again!"

Take two went without a hitch. Elizabeth approached the food daintily, then attacked it with gusto.

When she was finished, she sat back and cleaned her face, first with her tongue, then with her paw. The camera captured her entire performance.

"Perfect!" Phil said. "Now the high five."

Michael prepared for the signature shot that gave Elizabeth her value. He would kneel, with his right arm raised, and snap his fingers. Elizabeth would leap up and slap his palm with her right paw.

This, too, she did perfectly.

"That's a wrap for the cat," Phil said. "Thanks, Michael. Good job."

"You're welcome." Michael had Elizabeth in his arms as soon as he heard the word *wrap*.

Faith retrieved the carrier from the top of the low cabin, where she had placed it for safekeeping.

"The car's about two blocks away. You want me to get it?" Eddie Inouye materialized next to her.

"I think we can walk back to the hotel," she said. "We want to see a little of Lahaina, and we can do that this afternoon. But tomorrow morning at ten we'd like to leave for some sightseeing, especially the sacred pools of Hana. Do you think you could pick us up then?"

"I'll be there." Eddie grinned at her and took off again.

Michael snapped the carrier shut. Jennifer grabbed his arm before he could pick it up.

"I'm so glad Elizabeth is all right," she said. "Really."

Faith had already started down the ladder by the time Michael caught up. He handed her the carrier, then followed her down.

"All right," he said as they picked their way between cables toward the street. "Which of them was it? Eddie or Jennifer?"

"Both. Eddie sprayed the ant poison, Jennifer grabbed the cat."

"How did you figure it out?"

"Well, I guessed a lot of it. I knew when Eddie said he wouldn't give you away on the cat food that someone else had been talking in his car. It wasn't Marlene's family, because they had a rental. Most members of the crew rode in the trucks with the equipment." She paused until they passed the trucks in question. "And Jennifer pointedly told us that Phil wanted this job to lead to more—not realizing that the best outcome for Phil would be a great commercial, which he wouldn't get if he cast a bad actress in the lead, just to do a favor for the big boss. Favors get more work only at Jennifer's level. Not only that, but from the look on her face when she asked where Eddie was, it occurred to me that he might be a little less available than he was yesterday."

"She enlisted him in the plot?"

"Such as it was. Mostly improvised, I think." They were back on the narrow sidewalk. Faith surveyed the small shops across the street, with their window displays of muumuus. "How about lunch?"

"Tell me the rest first."

"Eddie didn't think we'd suspect ant poison, after you told him that Elizabeth doesn't normally eat Pretty Kitty. He thought you'd suspect simple cat perversity."

Michael raised his eyebrows innocently.

"Mrowr," Elizabeth said.

"I know, dear," Faith said to the carrier. "You're a professional. That's the point."

"But when sabotaging the food didn't work, someone had to grab her, someone who knew her, hence Jennifer."

"Good work," Faith said drily, patting Michael's shoulder.

"How did you know it was ant poison?"

"I didn't. I just thought ants are a problem in tropical climates, so wherever there was food, there had to be ant poison. I checked the galley when I refilled the dish, and I was right."

"I'm awfully glad you're here," Michael said. "I may not always tell you that, but I am grateful for your friendship. I'll buy lunch."

"Here today, dead to Maui," Faith said. "Lunch will do for a start. And did you say you had an appointment for a massage this afternoon?"

"It's yours." Michael sighed.

"Take Elizabeth, run on ahead, and order salmon for three from room service. I'll be there as soon as I've made a quick purchase. Vacation starts now."

"Maui." The word came clearly from the carrier.

"Indeed."

Pudgygate

Kristine Kathryn Rusch

The wind off the Pacific Ocean is cold, even in Malibu. A group of fifteen young men huddle close to the celebratory bonfire they have built on a secluded stretch of beach. A short distance away, the cars wait like obedient children. Inside one, a cellular phone rings for the fifth time in an hour.

The sand is still warm from the day's sun. A tapped keg topples like a drunken soldier, but few of the men are drinking anymore. They have been talking since noon, catching up on the years since they graduated from Cal Tech and went on their separate ways.

The conversation has deteriorated from highly placed and sometimes top secret research, grant applications, and the possibility of full professorships (as opposed to careers in government science labs) to the kinds of conversations they used to have in the dorm lounges late at night.

Desmond brought up his most embarrassing moment—something to do with toilet paper and the girls' locker room when he was in middle school—and Benjamin followed with his, Scott with his, and Michael with his.

But the conversation has stopped, for Reuben has taken the stage. Reuben, who took a mysterious trip to London in his senior year and has refused to talk about it ever since. Reuben is a kind of hero to them all because he crammed two semesters into one that last year and still managed to graduate with honors.

"Toilet paper on your shoes?" he says as he settles in the center of the circle, legs crossed. He looks like the before picture in a body-building ad, but his skin has cleared in the intervening years, giving him a handsomeness he never possessed before. His hair is longer too, just touching the tips of his tiny ears. "Getting caught peeing on your coach's Volvo? Throwing up all over the Homecoming Queen at the dance? Come on, men, that's kid stuff."

"Kid stuff?" says Scott. His tone is a bit defensive. His Homecoming Queen story did get a lot of laughs.

"Yeah," Reuben says. "Kid stuff. My most embarrassing moment happened at a state dinner when I was in England." And then, because the group does not gasp or do anything else to show that it is impressed, he adds, "In front of Princess Di."

"Princess Di?" asks Benjamin. "*The* Princess Di?"

"Man," says a voice in the blackness. "She's hot. Old, but hot."

"You didn't get sick on her, did you?" asks Scott.

"Not quite," says Reuben, "but it might have been better if I did."

When Lester asked me if I wanted to meet Princess Di (Reuben says, settling into the storytelling cadence he is known for within the group), I never thought it through. I knew Lester had connections— his father was an MP (that's Member of Parliament for you non-Anglophiles)—and Lester himself had spent summers with the royal family. So I spent my last thousand bucks and skipped the first semester of my final year at Cal Tech to winter in London.

I had brought a tux and my best hair creme. I even thought of getting my nose pierced, but then a friend told me that Di was not an Xer and might find the entire idea a bit gross. (I was a bit relieved; I am prone to sinus infections.)

That same friend sniffed at me for even imagining that anything would come of my meeting with Di. After all, she was a princess and I was a scrawny physics student who knew his way around quarks and computer languages—not the elegant dining rooms of Europe. But I had watched *Pretty Woman* enough to learn about place settings—

("*Pretty Woman*?" Scott says. "You watched *Pretty Woman* more than once?")

("Leave him alone," says Benjamin. "It was a date movie. You did see it on dates, didn't you?")

—and I figured what I didn't know, Lester would teach me.

And teach me he did. Place settings, Waterford crystal, the order of all seven courses. Seems Di had cut back on her social engagements. Lester's family was one of the few receiving her, and while I stayed at the house, I learned not to answer the phone, which rang incessantly, particularly in the middle of the night.

This was before the press learned that one of Di's quirks was her penchant for phone harassment. Before the world learned that Di slept with her riding instructor and Charles never loved her. But it was after the bulimia stories, Squidgygate, and the public separation.

Di was lonely.

I hoped to take advantage of that.

Until Lester told me the real reason he had asked me to spend September with his family. They had to host a minor state dinner with the head of a state of a small country in the middle of Europe. The head of state, like the rest of us mortals, was fascinated with Shy Di, and refused to meet with John Major unless he could also meet with Diana. A ticklish thing at best, since at that point Di was on the farthest outs she could be with the royals. They refused to socialize with her, and so Lester's father offered in June to host the dinner privately.

No one could have known how difficult *privately* had become.

You see, Di was a darling of the international press, and the center of tabloid attention at home. If she wasn't so frail, she probably would have killed a reporter or two by now. The family learned in July that hiring a catering staff was out of the question. Half the reporters on Fleet Street now moonlighted for the bigger name restaurants in hopes of a story. So the family had to rely on people they trusted, and when they came up one waiter short, Lester thought of me.

And all those posters of Di in my dorm room.

He figured I was an easy mark. He was right.

(Except for the screaming match the morning I found out. I slammed out of the house, stopped on that quiet English street, with its lovely row of trees, and realized that it was my pride or a chance to gaze on Di in person. I, of course, turned around.)

So, on the night in question, when I should have been wearing my silver tux with my grandfather's diamond cuff links, I was instead wearing a borrowed black tux stained with gravy. The tastefully tight cummerbund covered the gravy stain, but not the feeling of shoddiness it imparted to me. And I still couldn't learn when to serve from the left and when to serve from the right.

Lester, in exasperation, finally gave up, told me to watch the other waiters—most of whom were as pimply, scrawny, and underfed as myself—then retired to his own room to dress for dinner.

Lester would get to eat with the family.

The traitor.

The chef was really the gardener, a middle-aged Idahonian named (I kid you not) Bubba. Bubba was big, Bubba was strong, and Bubba could protect a princess. But Bubba had only one seven-course meal in his rather limited repertoire—a traditional Thanksgiving dinner with all the trimmings. The Americans among the waitstaff recognized it and tittered when they realized they were serving a colonial meal to the imperialists. But Bubba took offense at that.

"Them pilgrim guys," he said more than once, "was Brits when they landed on that Rock."

We all agreed but took a vow of silence anyway. To us, a turkey dinner could never be elegant, not even when it was served on the family's highly polished serving set. And all of us worried, in one way or another, what that infatuated head of state would think when faced with drumsticks, yams, and pumpkin pie.

"Not our problem," said Cletus, the blond All-American hunk who had gone to MIT with Lester during his one summer in Boston. If Di noticed anyone on the waitstaff, it would be Cletus.

"Nope. We just gotta make sure we serve this stuff in the best possible way," said Finigan, the tall, skinny redhead who had met Lester during that infamous year at the University of Chicago.

"I hope you guys know what goes left and what goes right," I said. I was so nervous my face had broken out in four different places.

"Pay it no nevermind," said Bobby Ray, the short, square Louisiana boy who had introduced Lester to Bourbon Street during his brief (and no longer recorded on his transcript) stay at Tulane. "If one of us messes up, all of us mess up. It might be an icebreaker."

"Lester's mother said we weren't to speak to the guests," said Percival, the pasty twenty-five-year-old who had yet to reach his adult growth. He had been the class goat and Lester's bunkmate at Eton during the period Lester called "the hell years."

"Lester's mother," said Georgia, the only girl in the group, with a decided sneer. Georgia was a gum-chewing Angelino of Puerto Rican descent whose black hair was so short and body was so thin, she looked better dressed as a man than all of us except Cletus. "Lester's mother's spine is so straight that she can't bend over to save her life."

Did I say that Georgia predates Lester's Cal Tech period by a wild twenty-four hours that ended in a fight outside the Viper Room? And this time, Lester was not the one caught fighting.

"First course," Bubba said.

We all turned and froze in horror. Dozens of deviled eggs stared up from the shiny silver serving trays like glow-in-the-dark eyeballs.

"These are the appetizers?" Percival asked, his voice small.

"You gotta problem with that?" Bubba crossed his thick arms—his wrists alone were the size of Percival's skull—and frowned.

"Absolutely not," Percival said with more pluck than I had given him credit for. He picked up the first tray, balanced it on his shoulder like a good waiter, and backed out of the swinging door.

As he backed out of the door, Lester's neutered tom, Pudge, sauntered in. Pudge was square as a linebacker, white with a touch of red, and had blue eyes from a roaming Siamese in his family's past. He was also the most focused cat on the planet.

None of us thought much about him, though, since he had never focused on any of us.

Until the salad course.

Those of you who know Lester should be aware that this was happening in the London townhouse, not in the eighteenth-century manse in Chiswick or the family estate outside of Kent. For those of you who don't know Lester—well, bear with me a moment while I set the scene.

The brownstone had been remodeled in the recent past by an architect with Vision. The kitchen—which was large enough to seat all of Parliament and still allow someone to cook a meal—was now off the formal dining room. Family dining was down the hall.

"Inconvenience every day of the week except Sunday," Lester liked to say.

Formal dining was in a room as large as the kitchen, filled with heavy mahogany furniture and two chandeliers that looked as if they had once been made for gaslight. A Chinese screen (from some aunt's missionary days) hid the wet bar in the corner. *Objets d'art* lined the shelves on the walls—collectible plates (which Lester assured me were *not* limited editions from the Franklin Mint), antique vases (pronounced vaaaaazes), and chipped, ugly statues from some uncle's Egyptian salad days. (At the other formal meal I attended, the guy from the British Museum drooled over those damaged things and claimed that the family might want to do a public service and donate the statues, particularly the one of Horus which even I knew was worth something because it had rubies instead of eyes. Nothing more was said. Public service, apparently, is not Lester's family's forte.)

The guests mingled in the library, which Lester's parents had settled on after a heated debate ("The front parlor has your family's hideous weapons collection," snapped Lester's mother, "which is not something a young woman in the middle of a marital crisis should see, or have access to, for that matter!"), and sipped expensive liquor while Bubba finished the first course.

We were to put the appetizers on the table, and then the butler would call the family in to dinner. We tried to arrange the serving platters of eggs as far away from the lights as possible, but the butler (who had been with the family nearly fifty years) still blanched. Nonetheless, he went off to perform his duty, and we fled the room.

In the kitchen, Pudge sat in front of the hot stove, staring at the roasting turkey inside. Bubba was preparing the second course— the soup course—for which (it soon became apparent) he had special-ordered a case of Campbell's Chicken Noodle from the States. The sound of the can opener didn't arouse Pudge, who was more intent on the sizzling bird than even the opportunity for cat food.

We had ten minutes to debate the best serving method for soup while Bubba zapped individual bowls in the microwave. ("Are you supposed to do that with fine china?" Georgia asked. "You seen anything else I should use?" Bubba countered.) He topped each boiling bowlful with a sprig of parsley, then sent us on our way.

The soup course allowed us to get our first glimpse of the guests. The foreign head of state (whom we were to refer to as Your Honored and Respected Sir, if we were to refer at all) wore a dark gray tux that accented his silvering hair. His face, unlined thanks to some obvious plastic surgery, had all the warmth of the Tower of London. His wife, wearing a gown covered with tiny diamonds, looked like an aging Barbie doll. Lester's family filled the gaps in the table. And Di, even though she was surrounded by a crowd of people, sat alone.

She wore a tiny tiara in her hair that matched the choker around her neck. Her dress was off the shoulder, revealing the slight rise of her breasts. She smiled as she flirted with the head of state, but the smile never reached her eyes. Her voice had an airy, little-girlish tone that I hadn't noticed in her public speeches. She ate part of an egg, leaving a dainty half-moon on her plate.

I whisked the plate away. Wonder of wonders, miracle of miracles, I had been assigned to Di's chair. Lester winked at me as I whisked with one hand and set with the other.

Di's hair smelled of jasmine, and I bent so close to her I could feel the warmth of her skin.

I managed to place the soup bowl without spilling a drop.

Di didn't even notice.

And then, all too soon, it was over. We carried the dirty dishes back to the kitchen (to be dealt with by the morning's cleaning crew), to await our next task.

Cletus went to the window to count the bodyguards the princess had brought with her. Finigan went to the other window to see if he could tell the princess's guards from those of the foreign heads of state. Georgia kibbitzed from the back, betting they couldn't tell Lester's family guards from the guests' guards.

I sat on a chair near the stove, which put me right next to Pudge. He was still staring at the turkey, his big blue eyes shining with fascination.

He had been at the stare-down over an hour now, and showed no signs of moving.

Bubba, on the other hand, was circling the kitchen like a man possessed. He was finally in his element. The salad course featured greens from his garden, topped with all sorts of veggies great and small. The veggies were nurtured by Bubba's large but capable hands, and he treated them like precious children as he put the finishing touches on the plates.

For once, a dish I would be proud to serve to a princess. The salad looked like something out of a restaurant, with onions sliced so thin they looked like tiny bracelets resting on top of the romaine.

The dressing boats were on the table (I had already checked when I saw Bubba and learned there was going to be a salad course), so we had nothing to worry about.

"Hey, Bubs," Georgia said. "What comes next after the salad?"

Bubba set the plate on a tray and then grabbed potholders. "Not sure," he said. "Been thinking maybe the cranberries can be a course all by themselves."

"You're not certain?" Percival asked, his face going whiter than the butler's had when he saw the eggs. "Good God, man, this is a state dinner!"

"What do you care?" Gently, with a booted foot, Bubba shoved Pudge aside, and opened the oven door. The rich smell of roast turkey filled the kitchen. Pudge stood and approached the open door.

"Why, sir," Percival said, "I care because we, the waitstaff, will have to suffer the displeasure of the guests would the meal not be— how should I say it?—up to snuff."

"He means if they don't like it, we get all the flak," Bobby Ray said.

"I know what he means." Bubba pushed Pudge aside again. Then Bubba bent at the waist and hauled the turkey out of the oven. The bird was huge, golden brown, and the juices dripped from its sides into the pan below. Bubba might not know how to cook soup, but he sure knew his turkey.

He put the turkey on the counter near the sink, then grabbed the pots filled with potatoes, and placed them on the stovetop. Then he opened the refrigerator and pulled out six pies. The fillings were loose, but I recognized them anyway: pumpkin, mincemeat, and apple. He put those in the now-empty oven.

"You can bake them all at the same temperature?" I asked.

"What is everybody, a critic?" Bubba snapped. "You try cooking a meal for the princess a Wales. At least you guys get a look at her."

Georgia left her spot at the window and came into the kitchen. She took a piece of romaine off the nearest salad. "Now, now, Bubba," she said, sounding not at all reassuring. "We simply want this meal to go as well as you do."

"I been working on this for the last week and—dang!" Bubba slapped a meaty hand against his own forehead. "Babe, can you open the cranberries? And kid"— he was looking at me— "I need you ta take the bread outta that fancy warming-pan thing."

It took me a moment to locate the fancy warming-pan thing, which proved a nice distraction so that neither Bubba nor Georgia saw me grin while she harangued him for calling her Babe. I took the bread out and arranged the slices in the wicker baskets that Bubba had left near the warming-pan thing (which looked, in case you're wondering, like a giant metal bread box with a heater).

By the time I turned around, Georgia was opening large cans of imported cranberry jelly (the flat kind that takes the form of the can), Bubba was putting shredded Parmesan on the salad, and Pudge was on the counter beside the turkey, happily nibbling the knobby end of a drumstick.

"Pudge!" I screamed from across the room. Bubba whirled, but Percival beat him to the cat's side. Pudge got tossed halfway across the kitchen, and slid on the tiled floor before he could skid to a stop near the back door. Cletus opened the door and tried to toss Pudge out, but a burly guard blocked the way.

"So sorry," the guard said. "No one leaves."

"Not me," Cletus said. "The cat."

"Righto," the guard said, shrugging a bit. " 'Fraid I do have my orders. You never know what that cat could be concealing on his person."

"Half the princess's turkey," Finigan said.

"What?" the guard said.

"Nothing." Cletus slammed the door closed. Pudge hung from his arms, square body extended, all limbs pointing toward the turkey. His little jaw was still working on its last bite and his pale blue eyes were still focused on the bird, now all the way across the room.

"Great," Finigan said. "Now what do we do with him?"

"We must serve the salad," Percival said. "It's past time."

"Yeah," Georgia muttered. "We don't want to leave them alone with that soup too long."

Bubba glared at her, but she pretended not to notice. Bobby Ray peered at the gnawed drumstick. "He only took the skin off the edge. If we peel all the skin away from that part of the bone no one will notice."

"Get out of here. You're distracting me," Bubba said.

"What about Pudge?" Cletus asked.

"Cat won't get past me a second time." Bubba literally snarled the words. He spoke with such force, I actually looked around to see if there was a cleaver handy, and sighed with relief when there wasn't.

"Okay," Cletus said. He put Pudge down. The cat zoomed like a smart missile for the turkey.

"You're covered with hair!" Georgia said, and it was true. White cat hair coated the front of Cletus's tux.

"We're exceedingly late," Percival said. "The butler just gave us a look through the door."

"No one'll notice the hair in the dim lighting," Finigan said. "Let's go."

We grabbed our salad trays and hurried into the dining room. The soup bowls were empty. As I whisked Di's away and replaced it with her salad plate (another lovely, deft, almost professional maneuver which she didn't notice), I overheard the head of state's wife ask if she could get the chef's soup recipe.

Georgia snorted and Lester glared at her. "Sorry, ma'am," said Bobby Ray, who was responsible for the wife's eating enjoyment. "Closely guarded family secret."

And we all managed to stumble into the kitchen before collapsing with the giggles.

In the kitchen, Bubba was making gravy. Sweat beaded on his forehead and he bit his lower lip with the concentration of a man taking the SAT exam. He was swaying back and forth as if stirring made him dizzy.

The turkey cooled on the counter, Pudge-less.

It wasn't until I got all the way inside the room that I understood.

Bubba was standing on one booted foot. With the other, he was blocking Pudge, who was trying to get into proper position to jump onto the counter. Much of the floor was spattered with gravy, and Pudge's whiskers had some suspicious smudges.

"Someone get that cat," Bubba said. "He don't even want no gravy. Not while that turkey's in the room."

"Give him the heart," Georgia said. "That should keep him busy for a while."

"Good idea," Cletus said.

"You do it," Bubba said. "If I stop now, we're gonna get lumps."

Cletus pulled the heart, neck, and liver from their places on the turkey's side. Each movement he made left little white cat hairs all over the counter.

"Yuck," Finigan said. "Did you do that to Lester's mother's salad?"

"Sure hope so," Cletus said with a grin.

Percival had taken over blocking duties from Bubba. For each move that Percival made, Pudge made a new one, never taking his steely-eyed gaze from the turkey. From my perspective, it looked as if Pudge and Percival were involved in a ritual dance.

Finally Cletus finished carving Pudge's meal. He waved the plate under the cat's nose—

("Hey!" Bubba shouted. "That was one of my dessert plates!")

—and then carried the plate to the back door. Pudge followed, tail high, looking as proud as if he had bagged the bird himself.

"I've been thinking," Georgia said, "that we should serve the turkey and fixings as one course and dessert as the final course."

"That's only five," Bubba said, still stirring. "I was supposed ta do seven."

"I don't think anyone will miss the other two," Georgia said.

"What were you planning to serve after the, ah, cranberry course?" Percival asked.

"The bread course, what else?" Bubba wiped his forehead with the back of his left hand, revealing a sweatstain the size of California in his armpit.

"What else?" Georgia mouthed behind his back.

"Sounds good," Cletus said as he walked away from Pudge. The cat was gobbling his food so fast we could hear the sucking sounds across the room. "But I wanna go home sometime tonight. How about we just do what Georgia said? I'm sure they're not gonna mind either. I mean, how long would you want to spend with Lester's mom?"

"Good point," Bubba said. He pulled the gravy off the burner.

"Don't make no difference to me. If anyone asks, I'll just say you guys dropped the other two courses."

"Should we break some plates as a cover?" Bobby Ray asked.

"Lord, no!" Percival said. "Do you know how much these dishes are worth?"

"It was a joke, Percy," I said, unable to take the strain any longer. In two contacts, Di hadn't even looked at me. I didn't know how to get her attention without making a fool of myself. And I was getting tired of standing in this kitchen.

"Okay," Bubba said. "You guys go clear the salad and put out dinner plates. By the time you get back, I'll have everything in their proper serving stuff."

We did as we were told. Out in the formal dining room, the conversation had turned to the future of the monarchy, and Lester's father was desperately trying to turn it to something else. Di looked as if she were going to cry at any moment.

She hadn't touched her salad.

I whisked the plate away and replaced it with a larger piece of the family china.

"What is this?" Lester's mother whispered loudly to Cletus. "The invisible course?"

The butler, who was pretending to supervise, placed his hands behind his back and walked toward the table. Percival glanced in the butler's direction, and stammered, "Ah, we-we-we are br-br-bringing the main course now, ma'am."

I didn't have long to ponder what childhood memories the butler's approach raised in Percival because Di put her cool fingers on my arm. I glanced down at her manicured hand, resting so softly on my naked wrist, and I thought I had died and gone to heaven.

"Would you be so kind as to bring me a spot of tea? I do know it's out of order, but I would be ever so grateful."

Ah, gratitude. A man always likes that in a woman. It might lead her to . . . express it. "Certainly, Your Highness," I said, and cringed as I mimicked her accent.

("Is that the embarrassing moment?" Scott asks, his sneer ready.)

("No," Reuben says crossly.)

("Good," Scott says. "Because if it is, make up something better, okay?")

She didn't even notice. She returned to the discussion of the monarchy by saying that she was concerned for William and Harry's future. I didn't get to hear the rest of the thought as we carried the dirty dishes into the kitchen. A huge stack of expensive but filthy china stood on the family's American-style dishwasher.

"Ain't none of them ate their salad?" Bubba asked with obvious disappointment.

"Too pretty to touch," I said, taking pity.

No one could say that about the rest of the meal. The turkey was piled haphazardly on the platters ("Didn't anyone ever show you the old one-platter-for-white, one-platter-for-dark routine?" Georgia asked). The potatoes looked like the snowcap on Mount Shasta. The cranberries were standing in perfect, wiggly can-shaped circles on their plates ("My mom used to at least slice it," Finigan said as he picked up the cranberry dishes and put them on the tray). And the yams looked like wizened overcooked tubers in the center of perfectly white bowls (but then they always looked like that to me). There were no garden veggies because Bubba had used them all for the salads.

And to make matters worse, no one had remembered to put on water for tea.

Bubba promised to do so while we delivered the food. I hoped he would remember. He had to deal with the turkey carcass first. Pudge was done with his little dinner and it obviously had not been enough.

"Land shark," Cletus said, looking at the white cat circling Bubba's legs.

"Food's getting cold," Bubba said.

"The tea's for the princess," I said again, just in case he forgot.

"Ain't it always?" Bubba muttered.

I got the turkey platters on my large server's tray and led the charge into the dining room. "Your tea is coming, Your Highness," I said as I set a platter next to Di.

She smiled at me and I felt the look all the way to my toes. I didn't even notice when the lights went out, thinking in my dazed state that the world had simply gone dark with the force of my joy.

Lester's mother screamed. His father shouted something about getting the torch (I sure hoped that was a flashlight), and the head of state whistled for his personal bodyguard. Behind me came the sound of breaking glass. Bubba was yelling in the kitchen, and the swinging door slammed into the wall. I felt a rush of wind as something flew past me. I set the platter down quickly so I wouldn't drop it on Di. She had made not a sound.

"Get it off me! Get it off, I say!" quavered a querulous male voice that I didn't recognize.

The thin beam of a flashlight revealed a mess at the table. The head of state and his wife were quivering at the far wall. Di was sitting rigidly. Lester was running out of the room—for the bodyguards, I hoped—and the waitstaff was frozen in mid-service.

The butler was screaming and groping with his right hand at a furry white thing braced on his shoulder. Pudge whipped his little head around. He had overshot his target, but now, with the aid of the light, he saw his quarry.

The turkey platters.

He launched himself at the table.

Lester's father brought his hand up to protect his face, lost his grip on the light, and it crashed to the floor, placing us in darkness again.

Part of my brain registered the oddness of the butler's movements. Why fight a determined cat with one hand? Then the breaking glass registered.

"The butler did it!" I shouted, and ran for him. Amazingly, I reached him, grabbed him, and held him long enough for Lester's father to recover the light.

The circle of light waved around the room. At the front of the house, the bodyguards pounded on the door. Bubba was still shouting in the kitchen, accompanied by more breaking glass. The butler was struggling, and I could barely hold him. Cletus and Bobby Ray hurried to my side as the beam of light caught the butler's left hand.

He was holding the statue of Horus, the one with the ruby eyes.

"Cedric!" said Lester's father. "Whatever are you doing?"

"It fell, sir," the butler said.

Cletus and Bobby Ray grabbed the butler's arms.

"Yeah," I said. "It fell after he broke the glass."

"Good heavens," said Lester's mother as the flashlight beam wavered and went out.

"Lester!" said his father. "Didn't you replace the batteries?"

They argued for a few minutes, the front and back doors crashed in simultaneously, and then the chandeliers came back on. "The pies!" Bubba wailed.

The head of state and his wife were still cowering in the corner. Lester was standing beside the butler, holding the man's collar like a bounty hunter, Cletus and Bobby Ray holding him for real. The rest of the waitstaff still retained their various positions.

"Pudge!" Lester's mother said, her tone revealing her shock at this newest horror.

We all looked at the cat. He was standing in the potatoes and leaning over the turkey platter. A piece of white meat dangled from his dainty, overworked mouth.

Tears rolled down Diana's face, and she was shaking. I wanted to put a hand on her shoulder to comfort her, but couldn't.

"Your Highness, are you all right?" Lester's father asked.

Diana nodded, then burst into a gale of laughter. "I haven't had this much fun," she managed between chuckles, "since I quit teaching kindergarten."

The fire is burning low. The ocean rumbles behind them. Benjamin throws the last log onto the pyre.

"I don't get it," Michael says. "The butler did what?"

"He was trying to steal the Egyptian art," Scott says.

"But why?" Michael says. "He had plenty of time to do that during the day."

Reuben shakes his head. "That's what we all thought, but it actually makes a curious kind of sense. You see, any theft would be traced back to him. But he figured on that night any disturbance would be credited to the press following Princess Di. He had drugged the coffee for the guards in the sitting room and library, and had already lifted some small items from those rooms. He also did some damage to the furniture to make it look like the losses were breakage. By the time the thefts were discovered, he planned to have sold the pieces to some black-marketeers and be long gone."

"I thought you said only trusted servants were on that night," someone says from the darkness in the back.

"Well," Reuben says, "he had been with the family for decades. How much more trusted can you get?"

"What, did he just snap?" Scott asks.

"Naw," Reuben says. "I think he saw it as his last chance to get rich before he died."

Wood cracks in the bonfire. A big wave crashes against the shore. Small white clouds look like cotton against the blackness of the sky.

"I still don't get it," Scott says. "I mean, mimicking Di's accent is nowhere near as embarrassing as losing your lunch on the Homecoming Queen."

"That wasn't the embarrassing moment," Reuben says, looking down at his hands.

"That's the only one that comes close as far as I can tell," Scott says.

"Yeah, right now you kinda sound like a hero," Michael adds.

"Well, actually," Reuben says, "I left out the embarrassing part. When the flashlight went out the second time, I kissed Di."

"So what's wrong with that? I woulda done it," Benjamin says.

"Me, too."

"And me."

The rest of the group choruses their agreement. Reuben has not looked up from his hands. He clenches them into fists.

"And she said, in a very calm, mannered voice, 'Lester, I do believe one of your friends has just committed a crime against the state.'"

Someone chokes back a laugh.

"Shows she's got a sense of humor," Benjamin says at last.

"A vicious one," Reuben says. He turns his head away from the bonfire so that the group can't see his expression. " 'You should tell him,' she continued, 'that the next time he plans to kiss a princess, he should brush his teeth first.' "

"Jeez," someone says.

"And then she started laughing, only she wasn't making a sound, so I thought she was crying."

The group is silent, all imagining themselves at the side of the princess of Wales who, although she is old, is hot. Then they all imagine she is so grossed-out by their kiss that she says something about it. They shudder in unison.

Finally Scott, who feels responsible for prying this story out of Reuben, says, "Hey, man, I bet no one knew it was you. All the waiters were Lester's friends."

Reuben shakes his head. "At that very moment, the lights came up. The only waiter who was blushing was me."

Silence again. Unlike the homecoming story which has, for these men, a slight undertone of an ice goddess getting her just deserts, Reuben's story carries its own level of pity. After all, the embarrassment is on an international scale.

"Then what?" Michael asks softly.

"What do you mean, then what?" Reuben says.

"What did you do then?"

Reuben licks his lips and glances at a faraway place none of them can see. "She took my hand and, wiping the tears from her eyes, said, 'If you are a love and bring me my tea, I'll give you a right proper kiss.' "

"And did you get her tea?" Scott asks.

For the first time since dark, Reuben grins. "After I brushed my teeth," he says.

He looks at the cars parked in a line against the side of the road. Almost as if on cue, a cellular phone inside one car rings for the fifth time in the last hour.

"Aren't you ever going to answer that?" Scott asks.

Reuben shakes his head. "She'll call back," he says. "She always does."

This is for Dean and the dudes, especially Thorn B. and the other turkey mongers.

Last Tango in Tokyo

Ed Gorman

For Barbara Paul

I didn't actually see the accident, when the cat leapt from Monica's arms and ran into the street, I mean.

Monica and I had been leaving the hotel when we saw movie director John Glencannon standing there talking to his wife and producer. When Glencannon saw Monica, who'd given his last picture a bad review, he'd smirked at his producer. Then he swaggered over to Monica. Before she could quite stop him, Glencannon grabbed the beautiful white bobtail cat Ninja from her arms and tossed him up in the air. He feigned trying to catch the cat but missed. Then he swooped down and tried to pick Ninja up. Ninja got scared and darted for the street.

And that's when the car came along and hit it.

A warm, sunny morning in the chic Ginza district of Tokyo. Three Americans leaving their expensive hotel—John Glencannon, the famous action movie director (you know, the one with the famous white Stetson and famous black eyepatch); his beautiful young wife, the copper-haired actress Tracy Deeds; and Glencannon's longtime producer, dumpy, shambling Max Wylie.

Now Monica screamed and ran into the street for Ninja.

Max Wylie swore at Glencannon.

And Glencannon stood there, big and handsome as any of his own action stars, hands on hips, smiling as he watched Monica run to the injured cat. "I hate cats," he said to Max Wylie.

Now understand: at five feet five, one hundred forty-two pounds, and a dissolute forty-two years of age, I am not exactly a macho man. Indeed, several of my fellow film critics call me "Yosemite Sam," meaning I'm the sort of guy who makes a lot of noise but doesn't exactly intimidate people.

But I happen to be an animal lover, and a cat lover in particular, and I went a little crazy when I saw what Glencannon did.

He still had his hands on his hips and a smirk on his face when I reached him. He recognized me, of course. I hadn't been kind to his last two pictures either. He was going to say something but I surprised both of us by bringing up my leg and foot and kicking him squarely in his privates.

He bellowed and doubled over and I had a second clear shot so I took it, the toe of my shoe once again visiting his most cherished possessions.

He bellowed a second time, and he also sank to his knees, right in front of the hotel, right in front of a few dozen Japanese who were too polite to say anything but watched our little drama with frenzied interest.

By now, Monica had the cat in her arms. Blood trickled from the animal's mouth to the tan sleeve of Monica's dress. He was crying at least as loudly as Monica, and jerking about in his furious pain.

"A punctured lung," Monica said an hour later.

"He has a punctured lung?" I said, knowing what that meant. Very little a vet can do about a punctured lung. It's usually cruel and selfish to keep the animal alive. So you don't.

She shook her pert blonde head. She was on the downside of hysteria now—exhausted and somewhat incoherent. "That's what the vet was afraid of."

"Oh."

"But he doesn't. Have a punctured lung, I mean."

"Good."

"He has three cracked ribs."

"Poor little guy."

"But that's a lot better than pieces."

"Pieces?"

She nodded. She looked sweet and tired and young and stunned by the cruelty she'd seen visited upon her feline friend. "Sometimes when ribs break, there are pieces of bone floating around. Then they have to go in surgically and take them out. It's risky, I guess."

"But he doesn't have pieces?"

"Huh-uh. I mean, they x-rayed him three times to be sure."

She leaned against me and I was happy to slide an arm around her, something I'd been wanting to do since the flight over from New York yesterday. We were here to cover, for our respective film magazines, the Japanese Film Society's retrospective salute to the American western. Six big-name directors were here, including John Glencannon.

"I just don't understand how anybody could do anything like that," she said.

"He's a jerk, that's how."

"A lot of people are jerks but they still wouldn't do something like that."

"Yeah, but he's specially trained. He went to jerk graduate school. He's a Ph.D. jerk."

She made a damp sound that was half-laugh and half-sob. "Oh, Tobin, I like you so much. I just wish you appealed to me—you know. But I always pick the wrong guys, never the sweethearts like you."

Over several drinks of hard American liquor last evening, I'd enthusiastically promoted the idea that this little excursion of ours could possibly turn into l-u-v. Or something very much like it. But she'd said, "I'm always honest, Tobin. I like you and I think you're very cute and even sexy in your own way, but—there's just no spark there. Not for me, anyway. I'm sorry."

Now a slim Japanese man in a white medical jacket, the vet himself, came in and said to me, "*Konnichiwa*," which meant "good afternoon," and then proceeded to tell us about Ninja, the cat Monica'd bought yesterday and planned to take back to the States with her.

Ninja was very sick but was going to get better.

In a few months or so. He would have had to stay in quarantine, anyway.

Travel was out of the question.

No way she'd be taking him back to the States right away.

After leaving the vet's office, we took advantage of the warm day and walked around Ginza. Think downtown Los Angeles and Rodeo Drive combined and you've got Ginza—if you mix in an underground railway system and several monuments to various shogun and kabuki performers. There were department stores and shops and boutiques of every kind. There were people of a few dozen nationalities. There were buildings whose spires caught clouds and whose windows glowed gold with the slowly dying day. And there was a park with lawns and fountains that not even Disney could have made any more beautiful.

It was in the park, strolling past a fountain that splashed silver drops of water on the perfect puce petals of nearby flowers, that I decided that Monica needed to confront Glencannon. She'd been talking about getting a lawyer. But there's no spiritual satisfaction in legalities. Confrontation is what you need.

"Do you still have the bill from the vet?" I said.

"Sure. Why?"

"I've got an idea."

"Oh, God, Tobin, this doesn't sound so good."

"I haven't even told you what it is yet."

"I know. But the way your mind works—"

"We need to show him we're not afraid of him."

"That's what lawyers are for—"

"That's like having your older brother fight all your battles for you. This is something we need to do for ourselves."

She sighed, sweet sad face alluring as ever.

"Okay, Tobin, what's your idea?"

When we got back to the hotel, Monica finally conceding that my idea sounded like a good one, we stopped by her room where she changed into more comfortable shoes.

While we were there, somebody knocked on the door. She was in the bathroom. I answered for her.

"For Monica," the bellhop said, pointing to the card attached to the dozen roses he carried in a white vase.

He set them on the table next to the window.

When Monica came out and saw them, she frowned. "Great. That's all I need."

I wanted to ask her about her strange reaction to the flowers, but the phone rang and by the time she finished talking with her editor, we were in a hurry to get downstairs. We spent our time talking about how I was going to handle the confrontation I'd come up with.

We couldn't find Glencannon and his friends so we decided to actually attend a screening, much as that might be against the unwritten code of film critics attending the festival. The picture was *The Tall T* with Randolph Scott, directed by Budd Boetticher, written by Burt Kennedy, and based on a great pulp novelette by Elmore Leonard. There was an Old Testament fury informing characters and storyline alike. It deserved its status as a classic.

After that, we went looking for Glencannon and his entourage but still couldn't find them. We had a couple of drinks and then started our search again.

*   *   *

The three of them were in one of the four elegant bars in the hotel where most of the film festival people were staying. Their table was crowded with journalists and overeager film students and somewhat puzzled tourists. Who was this man they were all fussing about?

To be truthful, critics today make far more of action movies than they should. They start telling you that action movies are a metaphor for this or a metaphor for that. But most action movies are just what they were intended to be—diverting fun.

Glencannon's cycle of eight films about a post-Civil War drifter named Payne were as elegaic as Peckinpah's best film, *Ride the High Country*, with that same quality of male tenderness and melancholy. Hard to believe that a drunken, bullying ex-stuntman like Glencannon could have written and directed them. Even more surprising, all eight of the films had made money, performing decently in the U.S. and extraordinarily well in Europe, where critics of course saw them as a denunciation of capitalism (European critics see all our movies, even *Ernest Goes to Summer Camp*, as denunciations of capitalism).

He was drunk, Glencannon was, and Max Wylie, his longtime friend and producer, didn't look much better. Glencannon was giving one of his interminable, self-important speeches about "real men" such as himself and D. W. Griffith (a name he frequently invoked). Several times he noted that too many of today's directors were "sissies." His white Stetson was on, and so was his black eyepatch (rumors were that he didn't need it but figured an eyepatch hadn't hurt Raoul Walsh any, so he wore one) and his expensive Rodeo Drive chambray shirt with the pearl buttons. Tracy Deeds, his wife, looked beautiful and bored; Max Wylie looked drunk and bored.

The people around Glencannon were properly respectful, laughing, sighing, gasping just when they were supposed to, and Glencannon was loving it.

Until he saw me.

In eighth grade a bully named Tolliver told me he was going to meet me after school and pound my head in. I convinced him to do it over noon hour. I'd known that the suspense would be worse than the actual beating.

That's how I saw this.

I'd walk up to him, drop the vet's bill on the table, and then wait for him to start pounding me. This time I wouldn't be lucky enough to get in any groin kicks.

"You bastard," he said, and started for me so abruptly that he nearly turned over his table.

Tracy Deeds kept all the glassware from falling to the floor. Max Wylie—short, dumpy, sweaty in his thick glasses, rumpled suit, and sad-comic little bow tie—grabbed Glencannon.

I pushed the bill—and my luck—right up to his face. "This is what you owe Monica, scumbag. If she doesn't have a check by six o'clock, she'll get a lawyer involved."

And then Monica was there.

She'd been embarrassed to go up to the table with me, saying how much she hated scenes, but now she was next to me suddenly.

The first thing she did was spit in his face.

The second thing she did was slap him.

"You nearly killed that poor little cat!" she said.

And was going to slap him again, but I got hold of her arm and pulled her closer to me.

I expected either Tracy Deeds or Max Wylie to speak up in Glencannon's defense—call us names, if nothing else—but they were just silent and sour. They'd probably been walking in the debris of Glencannon's drunken life too long now.

"Remember, six o'clock," I said over my shoulder as I moved a sobbing Monica between the tables and out the door of the bar.

"*Sumimasen*," said the Japanese bellhop who brought the ice to my door.

He'd seen me help a sobbing Monica from the elevator to my

room, and he'd been intuitive and kind enough to anticipate my needs.

I gave a slight self-conscious bow and said *"Domo arigato,"* which meant "thank you" and which seriously depleted my store of Japanese words.

I took the ice bucket and went back inside.

Monica lay flat, her high heels kicked off on the floor, her eyeliner and makeup a tad smeary from her cry. I spent some time making us good strong drinks.

"Who's the picture of?" she said, sniffling tears. She meant the young man and woman in the framed photo on the bureau. My talisman.

"My son and daughter. He's a junior at Cornell; she's an intern at CBS."

"They're very good-looking."

"They got their mother's looks. She's a beauty. Still."

"Why didn't you stay together?"

I shook my head. "You know us children of the sixties. Gadabout madabout. Not to mention dope-crazed, self-absorbed creeps."

"You really hate our generation that much?"

"Hell, yes."

I carried our drinks over.

Her hands were folded, funeral-home-style, on her nice little belly. I parted her fingers and inserted the drink.

"So how should we do it?" I said.

"Do what?"

"Do what? Are you kidding? Kill the bastard, that's what."

"Don't I wish."

"Drink up."

"No offense, Tobin, but you drink a lot."

"Gee, my first AA meeting."

"Don't get defensive. I'm saying it as a friend."

"And I'm saying 'drink up' as a friend."

She sat up and drank up.

I kicked off my loafers and sat next to her back against the headboard. This reminded me of a sad wedding party years ago where

I'd ended up sleeping with the bride because she'd caught the groom (in his tux, no less) bopping her best friend in a walk-in closet a few hours after vows had been exchanged. I had been the instrument of the bride's wrath.

Dusk and neon and a moon the color of a brass pirate's coin filled the window.

We talked, but I'm not sure about what. I just spoke words. All I could think of was making love to her. All my other senses were dead. Only lust survived. It was like a high-school backseat necking session and it was great. I took her hand. She didn't spit at me. I knew this must mean something. I leaned in. I kissed her tenderly, there in the dusk and neon and pirate's coin of a moon, and she didn't spit at me then either. There really was a God.

"It'd be so nice to sleep with you," she said. She was just a little drunk; it only made her all the softer and sweeter. "Somebody I really like and respect for once instead of—you know."

"Right. Instead of somebody you just find sexy."

"Don't be hurt."

"I'm not hurt. It's just the mood. Dusk and booze—I always get like this."

"Like what?"

"Scared and lonely and—horny."

"I'll do it if you really want to. I mean, if you really need to."

"Ah. The words of love."

"You sound mad. Are you mad, Tobin?"

"No, not pissed. Not at all. But I do think it's time for you to get back to your room before I agree to your offer of mercy sex."

"I'm sorry, Tobin."

"I know."

We kissed but it was a kiss without any promises and not at all what I needed at the moment.

After she was gone, wobbling on her high heels and still carrying her empty booze glass like a little girl with a broken toy, I lay on the bed and stared up at the pirate moon and felt luxuriously sorry for myself.

* * *

There was supposed to be a panel discussion that night with several big-name directors. I stayed in bed, sleeping.

The phone rang with an urgency I wasn't just imagining. At first, I had no idea what she was saying. Her words were lost in her tears.

I rolled out of bed. All I knew for sure was that she was in Glencannon's room.

"In there. Oh, God, Tobin, is he—?"

I walked through the living room area of the fashionable hotel suite to the bedroom.

Glencannon, still in that afternoon's western duds, lay face-down across one of the wide beds. The cover was white chenille. Or had been. Now blood stained it a vulgar red. Then I noticed the black stains on three fingers of his right hand. Apparently he'd been using a Magic Marker.

I walked closer to the bed for a better look at the bullet hole in the back of his head. I thought of rabbit fur—the way it looked, stained with its own blood. The back of his head looked like that.

Close range. One shot. Instant death.

I went back to the living room. "What are you doing up here?"

She wore a crisp white blouse and dry-cleaned designer jeans. Only a dry cleaner can get the creases that sharp.

She just kept shaking her head, walking to the window, then turning back before quite reaching it.

"They'll blame me, won't they? They'll think I did it."

"You didn't answer my question."

"I didn't kill him, Tobin. I really didn't."

I grabbed her shoulders. "Answer my question, Monica. What were you doing up here?"

She looked at me, those solemn brown eyes revealing a lot more than she probably imagined.

"Oh, no," I said.

"What?"

"You did a piece on him for Esquire a year ago, right?"

"Right."

"So you had an affair with him?"

"At least give me a *little* credit for brains, Tobin."

"Then you *didn't* have an affair with him?"

"I didn't say that. I mean I had a *something* with him but it wasn't an *affair*."

"Then what was it?"

"You know, just—I wanted to go to bed with him, was all. At least that's all it was in the beginning. Then I—"

I held up my hand. "I don't want to hear anymore."

"It wasn't sleazy."

"Right."

"And he could be more sensitive than you might think."

"Yeah, I noticed the way he drop-kicked that poor little kitty. Pretty sensitive."

"He only did it because he was mad at me."

"Didn't Charles Manson say something like that at his trial?"

"He was going to ask Tracy for a divorce so we could get married."

"You were going to *marry* that jerk?"

"Tobin, please. He's right in there. Dead."

"Yeah, and it couldn't have happened to a nicer guy." Then I remembered something. "So why did you give his last picture such a trashing?"

She shrugged. "It was a bad picture—and I guess I wanted to prove that I still had some independent judgment left."

This time she made it all the way over to the window and looked out at Ginza, which was alive with night now, vampire blood in its veins.

"I wanted him to ask Tracy for a divorce but not tell her about me. I didn't want it to be sleazy."

Then she was crying again. "I loved him, Tobin, and I don't care whether you like it or not, and anyway, you're not exactly a saint yourself."

And that stopped me, all my self-righteousness.

She'd uttered an incontestable fact.

I wasn't exactly a saint myself.

We were in the bar when Tracy Deeds discovered the body and called the Tokyo police.

The ambience changed immediately. Gray-suited hotel employees were everywhere, calming guests, quickly dispelling some of the grosser rumors (no, he hadn't been beheaded), and reassuring people that there was no danger to them—though the platoon of beefy black-suited men with walkie-talkies and shoulder holsters might lead you to think otherwise.

It took an hour and fifteen minutes for the Tokyo police, in the unlikely and chunky form of a New York detective named Baily, to find us. Baily, it seemed, was on some kind of exchange program—New York got a Japanese detective for six months, and Tokyo got a beefy Irishman. He had a pug Irish face with more than a hint of violence about it—the world's most sinister altar boy.

He had a red crewcut, big smashed-up hands, and frank blue eyes that could stare down Death.

He ordered himself a Diet Pepsi and seated himself at our little corner table and said, "I understand you had a little problem with the deceased today."

"I guess you could put it that way," I said.

"I was talking to the lady."

"Oh," I said.

"Well, he put my cat Ninja in the hospital, if that's what you mean."

"Then you had a little confrontation in the lounge when you gave him your vet bill."

"Tobin gave him the vet bill."

"I don't care about Tobin."

"Oh," she said.

"I care about you. And do you know why?"

She glanced at me. She was scared. "No, why?"

"Because somebody saw you going into Glencannon's room about five minutes before the shot was fired."

"But—"

"I shouldn't have said 'somebody.' I should've said 'somebodies.' Three women getting off an elevator saw you."

"I see."

"So you don't deny it?"

"Don't say anything, Monica. You have a right to an attorney."

He glared at me. "I wasn't speaking to you, Tobin."

"She still has a right to an attorney."

He said, "I sure hope you know more about the law than you do about movies."

"What's that supposed to mean, exactly?"

"Exactly it means your review of the last Steven Segal movie was moronic."

"It was a lousy picture."

"Not to guys who have to work for a living." And with almost no pause at all, his attention swung back to Monica and he said, "And you were Glencannon's mistress."

"His mist—" Monica started to object.

But Baily stopped her. "You wanted him to leave his wife. He wouldn't. You got angry and killed him. His wife was downstairs at a screening with Max Wylie. And then you invited Tobin here up to Glencannon's room so he could figure out a way to get you out of this." His wrath was turned on me now. "You'll be lucky if you don't get accessory-to-murder out of this, pal." He smiled. "I understand they show a lot of Steven Segal movies in the slammer."

An hour and a half later, Monica was formally charged with murder and I was told to get myself a lawyer. I called the American consulate.

Next morning, Tracy Deeds and Max Wylie ate a late breakfast in the hotel coffee bar. I'd lurked in the hall outside their respective rooms and then followed them downstairs.

I pulled out a chair and sat down.

"I hope they electrocute her," Tracy Deeds said. She was all sensuality with very little beauty. On and off screen she had a sullen quality that some, me included, found mysteriously erotic. With her stern gray suit, she was trying hard to look the widow, but it was an Armani and played against the image of the humble widow grieving for her man.

"Japan doesn't have the death penalty," I said.

"I take it you don't believe she killed him?" Tracy Deeds said.

"No, as a matter of fact, I don't."

"Then who did?"

"You or Max here."

Max of the rumpled suit and pathetic little bow tie said, "I don't like you or your reviews, Tobin, and I don't want you sitting with us at a time like this."

Only then did I realize, watching him this closely, that he'd been crying not too long ago. The tears were gone but the edges of the eyes were pink and puffy. He was a sad little guy—nervous fluttery hands, kicked-dog eyes, a quick, furtive smile too eager to please— and now suddenly he looked a whole lot sadder. He was sixty and looked eighty.

"I guess I can take a hint," I said.

"I wish this was the States," Tracy Deeds said. "Then she'd get what she deserves. He was a fine man. He really was. I mean, he had a few faults but—"

She then went about some very discreet crying. Max patted her shoulder with a small hand obviously unaccustomed to lending succor.

They had willed me out of existence.

Around two that afternoon, Tracy Deeds left her room. I followed her.

She went shopping for dolls, a passion of hers that her publicist worked into every press release.

She bought two dolls, both Hakata-style (fired-clay painted dolls that represented traditional Japanese characters), and then lingered over a display of kabuki masks and figures.

As she left the shop, I fell into step next to her and guided her into a nearby lounge. She cursed me with great and creative passion.

"I called the States," I said.

"Good for you."

"A friend of your husband's I happen to know."

"So?"

"So two weeks ago, Glencannon cut you out of his life insurance. He named his daughter as sole beneficiary."

"I still say, 'So?' "

"So you killed him. You'd spent five years putting up with his bullying and now you weren't going to get anything for it."

"He was a popular director."

"He was also a fool with money. He was broke. The only money you could get out of him was his insurance."

"I didn't kill him."

"Very convenient for you and Max to be each other's alibi. You were both together while Glencannon was being murdered."

"Max had no reason to kill him either. Max loved him."

"There were rumors over the years."

"What rumors?"

"You know what rumors."

"They were lies. You know how Hollywood people are. Their only pleasure is in inflicting pain."

"But sometimes rumors are true. This one could have been."

"I hope you're through with this little meeting of ours, Tobin, because I certainly am."

And then she walked off.

Ten minutes later, Max Wylie opened his hotel room door. He had on a worn red corduroy bathrobe. His black socks had garters. He had a comic little cigar butt stuck in the corner of his mouth. He looked like a stool pigeon in a bad 1946 *film noir*.

"Oh, God. Get out of here."

He started to slam the door but I caught the edge of it and walked inside.

I knew if I asked him any questions, he wouldn't answer them.

So I skipped the amenities and went right over to the closet and opened it up and there they were. A stack of storyboards.

"Just what do you think you're doing?"

"Proving that the rumors are true."

In addition to the storyboards, I also picked up a script.

I carried them across the room and dumped them on the couch.

"Let me see your hand."

"Kiss off."

I grabbed his hand, turned it palm up. Black Magic Marker ink stained his fingers. The same kind of ink that had been on Glencannon's fingers when I'd looked at his corpse.

"They're true, aren't they?"

"What's true, Tobin? I don't even know what you're talking about."

"All those stories about how Glencannon wrote his own scripts and then storyboarded them just the way Hitchcock had so he knew exactly what to shoot and how to light it when he went on the set. You wrote the scripts and did the storyboards, didn't you?"

"That's an old story. And nobody's ever been able to prove it."

He stood at the dry bar fixing himself a drink. He looked old and sad. His garters looked ridiculous.

"They're true, aren't they, Max?"

"Yes, they're true, but so what?"

He came away from the bar, carrying his drink with great delicacy. "It was a business deal. I used to write hack western stuff for TV. That's how I met Glencannon. Then we saw the success Peckinpah had—he used to be in TV with us—and we decided we'd create the great macho creative artist John Glencannon. Most writers and directors—they're not exactly he-men, Tobin. So we created our own he-man. And it worked. I did the scripting and storyboarding and he fronted for me. Who'd believe some dumpy little guy like me was a creative macho man?"

"I notice you didn't offer me a drink."

"There's a reason for that."

"Oh?"

"You're a jerk."

"Oh."

"I didn't kill him, if that's what you're sniffing around for. Why would I kill him? We had a very profitable relationship going."

"Maybe you wanted the glory for yourself."

"You're not thinking it through, Tobin. After eighteen years, why would I want glory all of a sudden?" He belched then and tapped his chest. "Stomach acid is all the way up in my throat." He made a face. "You don't have anything, Tobin. No motive for me, no motive for Tracy. Your little lady friend—that's who killed him. She wanted him to dump Tracy and he wouldn't."

The phone rang. He pointed to it. "That's going to be for me. From Hollywood. Very private and very important. Now get out of here."

In the Ginza strip, the police station you want is Meguro. After I answered their questions and filled out their forms, the Japanese police, who were actually quite polite, let me see her.

All the natural glamor had been cried out of her. Even her blonde hair looked dull.

She sat on the other side of a plastic barrier with a microphone built into it.

"I didn't kill him."

"I believe you."

"It's starting to seem unreal. I mean, I'm beginning to wonder if I really may have killed him and just suppressed it. Not even my lawyer believes me."

"You remember what I asked you just before they took you away?"

"Uh-huh. Thinking about anything John might have said about either Tracy or Max."

"Right."

"I couldn't think of anything."

"Oh."

"Nothing really remarkable anyway." Then, "You know what's weird?"

"What is?"

"The things I think about up here. I mean, I should be thinking about what I'm going to say in my defense and everything, but I'm just thinking of really weird stuff."

"Like what?"

"Like how warm it is in Eugene, Oregon. You know, where I was born."

"Ah."

"And how Ninja's doing."

"Well, that makes sense."

"And how I wish I had those roses with me. I mean, that's what a prison cell really needs. Some beautiful flowers."

"I'll talk to the warden."

"All those dozens and dozens of roses he sent and I always threw them out right away. What a waste."

"Why would you throw the flowers away? I thought you were in love with him."

"In love with Max? Are you crazy?"

"Max sent you the flowers?"

"Sure. Who'd you think?"

"I just naturally assumed Glencannon did."

"Glencannon? He was too cheap."

"Why would Max send you flowers?"

She dropped her eyes and looked shy. "It sounds weird."

"Tell me."

"He had this thing."

"This thing?"

"Yeah. About me."

"About you?"

"Love. That's what he said anyway. I mean, he's really a sweetheart and everything but—well, you know. Me and Max together? It wasn't going to happen."

"So Max sent you the flowers."

"Yes, and so what, Tobin? You make it sound like such a big deal."

"That's the trouble, Monica."

"What is?"

"It *is* a big deal."

Thirty-seven rainy minutes later, I took the stool next to Max's at the bar. He was drinking scotch and wearing his bow tie and looking bleak.

"Scotch," I said to the bartender.

"You know that people say you're a drunk, Tobin."

"They say I'm a lot of things."

"You should watch your booze."

"Look who's talking."

When I got my drink, I turned to him in the shadows, the Americans all laughing at a dozen different dirty jokes at the tables behind us, and said, "I know why you killed him."

"I guess I may as well tell you." He stared at me. "I thought you'd figure it out. Eventually, I mean."

"I've already talked to the police."

"Pretty pathetic, huh? Me and her?" Finally he looked at me. "He treated her like hell. And you know something?"

"What?"

"I think she liked it. At least a little bit, anyway. She could've had everything with me—money, love, respect. She could've even had a few affairs on the side as long as she wasn't too obvious about them. But she wanted him. Glencannon."

"I'm sorry, Max."

He stared at his drink again. "What's funny is, I'm fifty-six years old and this is the first time in my life I've ever been in love. Pretty crazy, huh?"

"Pretty crazy," I said, and after a few minutes led him to the car where Detective Baily was waiting for us.

"This is the guy?" Baily said, sounding like an executioner sizing up his next victim.

"This is the guy," I said.

Bailey cuffed him. I felt sorry for Max. I really did.

On the way to the airport next morning, we stopped briefly at the vet's office and said goodbye to our good friend, the Japanese bobtail named Ninja. He lay in a cage on a nice warm blanket. He looked drugged.

"You really think he can bring people luck?" Monica said.

"He must've brought you some," I said. "You're not in jail anymore."

She leaned down and inserted her slender hand into the cage and started stroking him.

"Thanks for getting me out of jail, Ninja. I really appreciate it. I really do."

As we were landing in New York, Monica said, "I'll bet he really did love me."

"Max?"

"No. Glencannon."

"Oh."

"You don't think he did, huh?"

"I'll bet Max loved you more."

"Yes," she said. "He probably did, didn't he?" Then, "Poor Max."

"Yes," I said, "poor Max."

Willie's Word Against . . .

Jan Grape

When Damon and Robbie Dunlap returned to their hotel it was late afternoon, but they still would have time to rest before showering and getting ready for the cocktail party at 6:30.

The Dunlaps were attending an international symposium sponsored by the Federation of Associated Crime and Suspense Writers in Stockholm. It was a great time to be in Sweden, Damon thought. In June the country is much different from the cold, dark winters he'd often seen on TV. The days, about twenty hours long, took some getting used to, until you learned to pace yourself.

Stockholm was a city built on fourteen islands showing you water in every direction. A modern city with skyscraping twenty-first-century buildings alongside copper-roofed sixteenth-century ones. This mix of old and new gave the city a modern look, yet all the while it retained an old-world charm.

"What fun," Robbie told her husband as they crossed the lobby of the Wellington Hotel and stood waiting for the elevator. The lobby was small, decorated with English hunting scenes and leather-covered Chesterfield chairs.

The hotel, built in the 1960s, was small, only fifty-seven rooms, but each room was stylish and tastefully decorated and offered a private bath. Robbie's publisher had paid for a room, but when the hotel found out she was a mystery writer attending the symposium, the manager insisted in giving them a suite for the same price. The Dunlaps couldn't believe their good luck in staying there.

Robbie had won the writing contest sponsored by the FACSW two years ago. Her winning book, which came out last year, had been nominated for several awards. The second was due out this week and her editor promised it would be available during the symposium. Being asked by the FACSW board to attend the meeting and present a talk on writing a winning book was both exciting and intimidating. Robbie was glad Damon could take some well-deserved vacation time and come to Stockholm with her.

Robbie sneezed and continued, "I talked to Dr. Barbara Mertz for fifteen minutes. She's such a lovely person. She'd read my book and complimented me and then she introduced me to Charlotte Mac-Leod and she, Charlotte I mean, had on this beautiful blue hat with a peacock feather and I told her how much I admired her work and then up walks Sharyn McCrumb and she's as funny as—"

"Whoa, said Damon. "Slow down. These people are all mystery writers, I presume?" Damon said, turning his wife to face him. "Honey, I know you're excited," he said, "but slow down a little when you're talking to me so I'll be able to catch a word or two now and then."

Damon, a retired policeman and currently the sheriff of Adobe County, Texas, was known as an expert at subduing criminal types. Calming his wife when she got excited was a different matter altogether.

"Great Gertie's nightgown, Damon. Are we going to have to get you some hearing aids to use with those new glasses you got before we left home? I shudder to think what part of you might wear out next." Robbie sneezed again.

"My parts all work just fine. As I'll be most happy to demonstrate when we get upstairs." Damon slipped an arm around her waist in that casual manner that long-married couples sometimes master.

Robbie leaned briefly against her husband and grinned at the thought of what form his demonstration might take upstairs. She glanced at her watch and thought, we do have a little extra time. "And just where did you run off to while I was talking to some of my idols?" she asked.

"Outside. You know how stuffy those rooms get. I wandered onto the balcony and found a waiter handing out semi-cool Coca-Colas." Damon grimaced. He was an avid iced-tea drinker. But ice was obviously considered a luxury in Scandinavia, so when he felt the need for something cold he had to settle for the slightly cooled soft drinks.

"Sheriff Dunlap?" The desk clerk sang out in her British-tinged English. "We have a message for you." Damon turned and the young woman behind the desk waved an envelope at them.

"Shall I wait or go on up?" Robbie asked as the elevator came to a halt directly in front of them.

Damon pulled on the knob of the regular-looking wooden door to reveal the minuscule elevator. "You go ahead. Probably be better if only one of us gets on this little contraption at a time. I sure would hate to overload it." He gave her a quick peck on the cheek, "See you shortly, my love."

She smiled and pushed the Up button. When she reached the fourth floor, stepped off the elevator, and rounded the corner, she noticed a man standing in the hallway near the Dunlaps' suite.

"Do you like cats?" The man's quiet voice stopped her cold.

"Well, I suppose so," Robbie said, wondering why he asked. She and Damon had introduced themselves to the gentleman earlier in the day, a Mr. Folke Clausen, she thought, hoping she remembered correctly. The man's tone was polite and he wasn't alone. He was accompanied by a beautiful cat.

Mr. Clausen wasn't as tall as Robbie's husband of nearly thirty years. Not too many men over fifty matched Damon Dunlap's six feet four, but the Swedish gentleman might have tipped the scales very close to the 238 pounds that was her husband's normal weight.

He carried himself with a regal-looking air, standing military-straight, his piercing blue eyes and square jaw looking as if they belonged on a younger man despite his full head of white hair. He held a leash lightly in his left hand.

Robbie couldn't recall ever seeing a cat on a leash before. The large, regal tom had four white boots and a white bib front, making the rest of his sleek black fur look like a tuxedo. The cat sat next to and slightly behind the man's feet as if he'd come to heel. "Cats are strange, Mr. Clausen, mystical almost," she said, and shivered.

"But do you like them?" He sounded insistent.

"Yes," she said. "I've always admired the way cats let you know what they want."

The man raised an eyebrow, "Ah. You do understand, Mrs. Dunlap. But you do not now have a cat?"

"No. Not in several years."

"Pity. When you had a cat, did you talk to her and treat her like part of the family?" His Swedish accent was a bit thick. He spoke softly and Robbie strained to understand him.

"I'm afraid so."

"Good, then you might enjoy what I have to tell you." Mr. Clausen smiled at her and continued. "Remember the beginning of our conversation, when you said cats could get what they want without ever saying a word?"

"Did I say that?" A tiny tickle began in the back of her throat. She coughed and the tickle disappeared.

"Not exactly, but close enough. Do you know they sometimes speak to us? And sometimes we even understand that speech?"

"Maybe." She tilted her head, listening to her inner voice playing a memory-tape. "I think I used to understand my Suzie Q when I was a little girl."

"And when you grew up you had to put foolish things aside, did you not? She most likely talked to you and you understood. Otherwise you would have named her a silly name like Snowball or Puffy or whatever. I'm quite sure she told you her name. Cats like normal-sounding names like Willie here."

"Your cat's named Willie?" Robbie had no idea where she'd come up with the name of Susie Q but she was positive her cat hadn't told her. She fished into her purse for a tissue and wiped her nose.

"Yes. The day I brought him home from the veterinarian's office he told me his name was Willie. Not Will or William. It was Willie, no doubt about it."

Willie ignored his master and lifted up a front paw to lick briefly before he began nibbling between each toe with precise bites.

"Willie also said he would be willing to wear a leash so he could travel with me," the man said. "I bought one—five feet long—which hooked on a collar. Bought a collar, too. Right away Willie told me that was stupid."

"He told you the leash was stupid after he said he'd wear it in the first place?" Robbie was beginning to think she'd made a major mistake talking to this man, he was a bit strange. But both man and cat were standing in front of the door leading into the Dunlaps' suite. Short of shoving them aside, she was stuck.

I will not get sick, I will not get sick, she chanted to herself. *I won't give in to a cold.* But her energy level was draining almost as quickly as her nose seemed to be doing.

"Yes," said Mr. Clausen. "And Willie said if I would pay close attention, it would save us both time and trouble. I listened carefully and discovered he would wear only a harness—not a collar—and that he preferred a ten-foot leash. He wanted more freedom than a five-foot leash would allow." Mr. Clausen coughed. "I made the harness for him and you can see for yourself that he is perfectly satisfied on his leash."

Robbie inspected the cat closely. The harness went around Willie's chest and looked to be made of a soft black leather. "Yes. Willie does look smug. But I must admit it's quite disconcerting to see him sitting there calmly with that leash." She hoped then that she might be able to excuse herself politely, but the man began talking and looked as if he expected her to continue listening.

"I am a businessman and must travel all week. Willie goes with me from town to town in my automobile, but he has to stay in the hotel room all day. When I get back in the late afternoon, like today, I usually take him for a long walk."

"Rather like a dog who's been cooped up all day?"

"Not exactly. Willie has his litter box here in our room, but he needs the exercise and so do I. So we walk. We begin by walking down the stairs from the sixth floor, where we usually stay, to the lobby. Then we walk down the street. Willie often tells me what he wants for dinner, usually smorgasbord, of course, with either a specialty of Baltic herring or smoked reindeer. We mostly go to whichever restaurant he chooses."

"Willie goes into the restaurant with you?" Robbie started sneezing again. "Excuse me. Something in the air, I think."

Mr. Clausen smiled. "Oh, yes. Willie is often almost more welcome than I. Since he is on the leash the cafe owners know he will not cause any trouble. He is always a most well-behaved gentleman." Mr. Clausen beamed at Willie. "Well behaved, are you not?" he asked the cat.

And honest to pete, the cat went "Mrrrrr" at that precise moment as if saying yes sir. Robbie smiled to herself. No wonder the old man thought the cat talked to him. Things like that happened, but it didn't mean your cat was capable of talking. "And you two travel all over Sweden each week?"

"Except when I am right here in Stockholm for two weeks, like now. I am a jewelry merchant."

"I see." Although she saw nothing and only wished she could just make an exit. Mr. Clausen was obviously proud of his cat, and Willie was an attractive specimen of feline house pet. She'd humored the old man enough and now wanted to go. She felt a great need to lie down, even briefly.

Fortunately, before she had to resort to rudeness, Willie arched his back and stretched, and Robbie thought he looked impatient to be gone himself.

Mr. Clausen beamed at Robbie much in the same way he'd beamed at his cat and said, "We must go now. Willie thinks the finest salmon in the city is being offered at a special price tonight and since we've both been hungry for that lovely smoked pink fish this past week, we must leave. Very nice talking to you, Mrs. Dunlap."

Robbie, still sniffing and coughing somehow managed to say politely, "Nice talking to you, Mr. Clausen, and nice to meet you, Willie."

Willie said "Mrrrrt." Mr. Clausen gave a slight bow and they rounded the corner.

Meanwhile, when Damon Dunlap retrieved the message from the desk clerk and tried to tip her, she cut him off quickly.

"No need for that, Sheriff Dunlap. I am very happy to have a chance to practice American and I adore your accent."

Damon chuckled. "And I thought *you* had an accent. You do have me puzzled, however. You're obviously Swedish, yet you speak English like a Britisher." She had the bluest eyes Damon had ever seen and an almost square jaw. She looked exactly like the skiers on the Scandinavian Olympic ski team—long blonde hair, lithe, lovely, and athletic.

The girl smiled, showing perfect white teeth. "My teacher was from London and I always seem to pick up the accent of others when I'm around them a lot. Right now I'm living with a young man from Essex, and I'm beginning to pick up his accent."

Damon looked at the note he'd retrieved from the clerk. Another invitation to a symposium party, he noted. "Well, I've enjoyed talking with you, Miss—?"

"Call me Amalie," she said.

As Damon turned he saw a young man walking across the lobby with a big smile on his face but soon Damon discovered the smile was for the girl. The young man was slender, but his shoulders filled his jacket nicely. He had brown hair and eyes, a longish nose with a hump, and a mustache.

"Amalie, are you ready to go?" the young man asked.

"In a minute, Bob. Honey, I'd like for you to meet—"

Damon stuck out his hand. "Damon Dunlap."

"Bob Cartwright," said the young man in his strong British accent, but he wouldn't look directly at Damon. "You must be the American Amalie told me about."

"You got that right."

Cartwright's face had a brief perplexed look, then both he and the girl laughed. "A new Yank phrase. Add that one to your notebook, Amalie."

They laughed again and Damon couldn't tell what was so funny. Getting old, he thought, and glanced at his watch. But not too old for a bit of slap-and-tickle, he reminded himself. "My wife is expecting me and it was nice meeting you."

"Of course," Cartwright said. "Delighted."

The men shook again. The young man still didn't look at him, but Damon realized the lovely Amalie was much more exciting to look at and that's exactly where Cartwright's eyes stayed.

Damon walked to the elevator just as the door opened. Mr. Clausen and Willie got off and when Mr. Clausen spied Damon he mentioned the lovely conversation he'd just had with Mrs. Dunlap.

Damon, startled to see a cat on a leash, missed out on the beginning of the man's speech. And besides, his ear wasn't too keen when listening to the Swedish lilt and he picked up only part of the remaining words. Rather than make an inappropriate remark, he smiled and waved a goodbye.

Damon got onto the elevator, leaving Mr. Clausen to walk away, muttering, "*Ja*, Willie," almost under his breath. "We take our walk now. And then we go have salmon. *Ja?*"

Amalie and her young man were also on their way out Damon noticed as his elevator began its ascent.

When Damon reached the room, he was disappointed to find Robbie sound asleep but could tell she was having trouble breathing and realized she'd come down with a cold.

He opened the French door and stood outside on the balcony, which overlooked a small flower-filled courtyard, and marveled at the unique green copper roofs of the surrounding buildings. A beautiful city, he thought, yet crime was encroaching here, too. He hoped policemen here could do a better job than their American counterparts.

Inside, Damon picked up a guidebook on Scandinavia and began reading about Stockholm and marking some places he especially wanted to visit. The main tourist attraction was the royal flagship

Wasa—a seventeenth-century man-of-war originally built for the king. The ship sank on her maiden voyage in the murky city harbor. It was discovered and salvaged in 1956. Old ships held a great fascination for the small-town Texas sheriff who'd always loved the sea.

When Robbie awoke, she asked if she should cancel on the party.

"I've already called to give our regrets." He sat on the bedside and held her hand. "You want something to eat?"

"Not with this throat."

"You should eat," he said. "Feed a cold, you know."

"Well, maybe. If we can get some soup."

Damon called downstairs to ask if room service could bring some soup. In a few minutes he returned to the bedroom. "I'm not sure I understand."

"What?" Robbie asked.

"First they said they didn't have room service, then they said they'd send soup up. I'm sorry. I have so much trouble understanding the accent. I find myself in confusion half the time."

"Don't worry," said Robbie. "It'll all be clear about the time we're ready to go home."

"When I get back I probably won't be able to understand Texan."

Robbie dozed again while Damon went back to his book. Thirty minutes passed by and Damon decided maybe he should go downstairs and see if he could find out about the food.

Just as he stood and stretched, the telephone rang.

After a short conversation, Damon walked into the bedroom and found Robbie up, pulling on her robe.

"Our food's being sent up on what this gal said was a dumbwaiter," he said. "I think."

Robbie followed him into the sitting room. "Where is it?" she asked, realizing she felt hungry.

"Outside the door, the gal said."

Robbie opened the door leading to the hallway. As she did so, a bell dinged and part of the decorative wooden paneling separated and revealed a small metal door. "Look, Damon. It is a dumbwaiter. How clever."

Damon joined her in the hallway and Robbie pulled open the

handle of a stainless steel door. A large tray holding two bowls covered with stainless covers, a cloth-covered basket—probably holding bread or rolls—some silverware, napkins, two cups, and what looked to be a teapot.

"I love it," she said. "But I didn't know this thing was even here, did you?"

Damon shook his head. "No. I hadn't noticed it." He began unloading the dumbwaiter. When he closed the stainless door, the wooden panel moved slowly back into place and the opening disappeared. "Ingenious and cleverly hidden. If you didn't know it was there, there's no way you'd ever find it."

The next day, after a restless night of coughing and blowing her nose, Robbie slept late. Damon was up and gone the next morning early. Always curious and eager to learn about police techniques, especially in another country, Damon had scheduled a visit to the Stockholm police department.

When Robbie finally got up, she called downstairs and asked for hot tea and croissants. After eating she actually felt as if she might survive. She showered, dressed, and perused the symposium program schedule. A panel discussion on International Forensics caught her eye. It began in an hour; she could make it in time for the opening remarks if she hurried.

With her usual housewife's guilt over a cluttered room, even a hotel room, Robbie grabbed up her breakfast tray. She stood holding open the door to their rooms, pushed the button to summon the dumbwaiter, and waited. When it arrived, she balanced the tray with one hand, keeping the room door propped with her knee, and tugged the dumbwaiter door open.

Mr. Clausen's Willie sat on the top shelf holding something in his mouth. Before the door was fully open, he jumped out with a small "mrrrt" and ran into and through the Dunlaps' sitting room—a lightning streak of black.

"What in the world, cat? What's happening?"

Robbie went inside, closed the outside door, and began searching— wondering where Mr. Clausen could be. "Here, kitty. Here, kitty. Here, Willie."

She could see neither hide nor hair of Willie. It took a few moments before she thought to look under the bed, and when she did she found two golden eyes staring back. Willie still held the object in his mouth, but she couldn't tell what it was in the darkness underneath the bed.

She walked to the sitting room and had the operator ring Mr. Clausen's room. No one answered, and when Robbie inquired, the front desk, the clerk said Mr. Clausen was in his room. The man had obviously gone out and the maid accidentally let Willie loose.

How Willie got into the dumbwaiter was another question that Robbie didn't have an answer for.

She decided to ignore Willie, hoping his natural curiosity would bring him out before long. Great idea, but it took nearly an hour. Robbie gave up on attending the seminar and wrote postcards to friends back home. She wrote the usual *Wish you were here* cheer, because she didn't have to think about what to say.

Her brain was too busy dealing with the problem of the cat. If he didn't come out soon, she'd get food and try to entice him. She didn't know why she felt so compelled to get the cat from under the bed. Normally she would have left him until Mr. Clausen came home and just let the owner get his pet.

She kept going over in her mind what she'd seen of the object in the cat's mouth. She didn't want to swear to it, because her look had been such a brief glimpse. But unless she had somehow imagined it, Willie had a piece of jewelry in his mouth.

When Willie did finally come ambling into the room, his lovely, bushy tail was held flag-high. He came over to the sofa where she sat, and his mouth was empty.

"Hey, kitty." said Robbie. "What scared you so badly?" She held her hand low and let him sniff her fingers and thumb pad. Willie smelled then raised his head and said, "Miaow."

Robbie rose slowly and went into the bedroom. She looked around for something to thrust underneath the bed and found an umbrella that had been left in the closet. A few minutes later she pulled out the object Willie had brought in his mouth.

A woman's earring sparkled in her hand. One large stone formed the top part and two smaller ones hung from a silver filigreed backing. If those weren't diamonds, thought Robbie, they were excellent quality zircons. The earring was made for pierced ears.

Willie had followed her into the bedroom, and when she pulled out the earring and sat on the bed to inspect it, the cat jumped up beside her.

"Mrrrt," said Willie.

She reached out a hand to pat his back and that's when she realized Willie didn't have on his harness.

Willie purred and looked soulfully into her face and Robbie wished fervently the cat could talk. But what would he tell her? she wondered.

"Willie," she said. "Something is rotten in Denmark, I mean in Stockholm. And I can't just do nothing. But you'll have to stay in the bathroom until I come back."

Willie followed her into the bathroom as if he'd understood. Robbie found a shallow bowl being used for a soap dish. She cleaned it and put fresh water in it for Willie. "I hope I'll be back soon with a few answers."

"Miaow," said Willie.

She walked out the door quickly and closed it. Willie began such a screaming and howling that she thought he'd hurt himself somehow. She opened the bathroom door. Willie ran out and over to the front door. "I know you want to go with me, but until we have your harness and leash . . . I don't see how."

Robbie went to the telephone and asked the desk clerk for Mr. Clausen's room. "I'll ring for you," the operator said and disconnected before Robbie could explain why she wanted the actual room number.

"Suppose you could lead me to your room."

"Mrrrt," said Willie.

When Robbie stepped into the hall, Willie darted down the corridor and stopped to wait at the stair exit. When she opened that door, the cat scampered up the steps and she followed.

Two floors up—on the sixth floor—Willie stopped at the entry door and tried to put his paw underneath to pull it open.

"This one, huh?" She opened the door and Willie darted down the hall. He waited at the corner so she'd know which way to turn and stopped, looking at the doorknob, when he reached the room where she supposed Mr. Clausen stayed.

Robbie knocked. She didn't expect an answer and didn't get one. She turned the knob and the door swung back.

Willie streaked in, almost knocking Robbie down in the process. Mr. Clausen lay on the floor. He was unconscious, and a gash on the side of his head gaped with thick, dark blood.

Shortly after the hotel had called an ambulance and the medical people had taken Mr. Clausen to the hospital, the police showed up. A detective inspector in charge of the case was accompanied by Sheriff Damon Dunlap.

Robbie and Willie had returned to the Dunlaps' suite after she'd located Willie's harness and leash and brought them along with his food, bowls, and litter box.

"Robbie," said Damon. "This is Inspector—"

"Please call me Magnus," the officer said. Detective Inspector Magnus Zacharias was a short man with light reddish-colored hair and gray-green eyes. He walked around the room constantly, almost as if he were not paying attention when in reality he was absorbing each detail of the conversation and later, if asked, he would be able to repeat word for word as if their talk were written on Viking rune stones.

Damon and Magnus had been to Clausen's room prior to coming to talk to Robbie. Magnus chewed on an unlit pipe and had a nervous habit of clicking his fingernails. Magnus had only recently given up tobacco and the fingernail chewing was the man's way of dealing with his habit. The Texas sheriff had spent the morning with Magnus and had been most impressed with the man's keen insights and abilities.

Magnus Zacharias said he was thirty-two years old, which seemed terribly young to Damon for the man to be a detective inspector. Damon discovered later his assumption had been correct. Zacharias was one of the youngest officers in the district to have made inspector.

"You suspect Clausen was hit over the head during a robbery?" Magnus asked Robbie.

Since Magnus said he wanted to question Robbie himself. Damon sat and listened, saying nothing. Willie was asleep in their bedroom, curled up at the foot of the bed.

"Yes," said Robbie. "Mr. Clausen told me yesterday he worked as a jewelry merchant. And when I found Willie in the dumbwaiter, he had this in his mouth." She handed the diamond earring to Inspector Zacharias.

Magnus took the earring from Robbie, holding it gingerly by the edges, looked at it, and put it into a glassine envelope and then into his pocket. "What time did you find the cat?" he asked her.

She watched him and wanted to kick herself for not thinking about fingerprints; she knew better. "About ten thirty-five to ten forty."

Magnus raised an eyebrow as if to say he didn't believe she could be that precise.

"I planned to leave at eleven," Robbie said. "I wanted to attend a seminar that began at eleven-thirty and kept a close eye on the clock as I got ready." She apologized about the prints but he said not to worry. Hers could be eliminated and maybe someone's besides Clausen's could be found.

"In any case, whoever did this probably wore gloves," Magnus said. "You think Mr. Clausen was attacked and robbed sometime this morning?"

"Maybe. I do know Willie didn't have his harness on when I found him this morning. I'm assuming Clausen takes it off each night in their room and puts it back on each day." She wanted to say something else but wasn't sure how to do it.

"And?" asked Magnus.

"And what?" Robbie looked surprised. How did he know? she wondered.

"You wanted to tell me something but weren't sure if you should or not."

His attentiveness to what she said and how she was saying it made an impression. The young man's on the ball, she thought. "I'm not a nurse," said Robbie, "but I worked as an x-ray technician for years and I've seen many head wounds. The blood on that gash had begun to coagulate, so I think he'd been lying there for hours."

"Why would you hesitate to tell me that?"

"Because only a doctor should make that determination," Robbie said. "I didn't want to say something I wasn't able to prove."

"Your un-expert opinion is noted."

Damon, who had been sitting quietly, said, "So what you're saying, Robbie, is you think Mr. Clausen was probably hit on the head several hours ago?"

"I'd say sometime after midnight and before six o'clock this morning," Robbie said. "But I'm no expert, as I said."

"That all fits," said Magnus.

"What fits?" Robbie asked.

"We have a suspect who was seen leaving here last night or rather this morning around three by a reliable witness. What you just told me confirms that person's story. This time of year—so close to midsummer—it doesn't get good and dark until almost three A.M."

"Who . . ." Robbie stopped when she saw Damon shaking his head.

"I am not at liberty to say. I greatly appreciate your help, Robbie, but I must get to the hospital to talk to the victim when he awakens."

Magnus turned to Damon. "Pleasure to meet you, sir." and turned back to Robbie. "And you too, madam." Inspector Zacharias quickly left.

Damon gave Robbie a hug and ignored Willie, who'd walked into the sitting room. "Mrrrt," said Willie. The cat kept dancing around them and making noises.

"I think he wants to go for a walk," Robbie said.

"And I've been appointed, I assume," her husband said.

"We could both go. I could use some fresh air."

"You seem to be feeling much better."

"I nipped that cold or whatever it was in the bud," she said, and hooked Willie's leash onto his harness.

They walked to the stair exit and down four flights of stairs to the main level.

Damon noticed the young clerk, Amalie, and waved. She and her boyfriend, Bob, stood talking near a door that led to an office behind the front desk.

Amalie obviously didn't see or hear the Dunlaps.

"It doesn't matter what he said." Bob's voice was harsh as he spoke to Amalie. "Nothing's going to change things. The job's done, so just shut up about it." He took her arm and twisted.

Robbie also noticed the young couple and she and Damon both started towards the girl. Willie, who had been walking beside Robbie, moved slightly out ahead of them.

When Amalie saw the Americans approaching, she pasted on a smile and waved to them with her free hand. Cartwright abruptly dropped her arm and looked their way. He turned pale when he saw who it was. "Don't try it," he said to Amalie.

The girl turned, running into the office, and the young man strode towards the Dunlaps.

Willie arched his back and began growling and hissing as Cartwright approached.

When he was opposite them, Bob Cartwright made as if to kick Willie out of his way but didn't. Before Damon could react, the young man was outside the front door and gone.

"Willie," said Robbie, "what's wrong?"

The cat strained against the leash and continued growling. Willie pulled, acting as if he'd like to follow the young man.

"What's going on, Damon?" asked Robbie. She squatted next to Willie. "Calm down, Willie. You're okay." The cat still had a wild look, but he stopped pulling at the leash and looked deeply into Robbie's eyes.

Damon said, "I'm not sure, but I think I should have a little talk with Amalie."

"I think you should contact that inspector," said Robbie.

"I will, but . . ."

"No buts about it, Damon. That young man who just left here is the one who attacked and robbed Mr. Clausen. Willie knows it and he just tried to tell us."

"Could be, but the inspector will need more than a cat's word."

"Even if Willie swears to it?" She smiled up at her husband.

"Willie's right." Amalie walked out to where the Dunlaps were standing, tears streaking her face. "And your wife is right. Bob Cartwright was using me. That's what we were arguing about when you came up. I only found out a few minutes ago, but I'm willing to go to the police and tell them what I know. They'll take my sworn word even if they won't take Willie's."

The next evening Robbie and Damon brought Willie to the hospital to see Mr. Clausen. The administrator had given special permission for Willie to be allowed into the solarium on the first floor. The jewelry merchant had a skull fracture, but would make a full recovery.

Mr. Clausen and Willie both beamed with pleasure. "So you helped catch that bad guy, eh, Willie? Well, I am not surprised. I always said you were a smart cat."

"Amalie told the police everything," said Damon. "How Cartwright had questioned her about you and your routine."

"Have they caught the boy yet?" Clausen wanted to know.

Damon nodded vigorously. "He's in jail."

"And what about the girl?"

"They'll probably go easy on her. She'll lose her job," Damon said. "But I don't think she'll have to go to jail."

"Willie's a hero," Robbie said. "The newspapers want to write about him and take his picture."

"The police," said Damon, "are talking about giving him a medal or something."

"Is that right? Well, I suppose it would be okay," said Mr. Clausen, but a worried look clouded his face.

"I've saved the best news until the last," said Robbie. "Damon and I are going to stay here in Stockholm until you can come home. We will continue taking care of Willie. The hotel is letting us stay at no cost to us. The airlines will exchange our tickets home without any charge, and my book publisher is paying for our meals."

"Willie," said Mr. Clausen. "You are some smart cat."

"Mrrrt," said Willie, purring and rubbing against Mr. Clausen's hand.

"He's smart," said Robbie, "but Willie didn't figure it *all* out, did he?"

"No," said Mr. Clausen. "But I am not sure I wanted you to either."

"It took both of us muddling through it," said Damon.

"The doctor confirmed it?" Clausen asked in a quiet voice. "This old ticker is just worn out."

"Yes. Six months to a year at most," said Damon.

"You set up everything just to get me involved?" Robbie asked.

"I knew if Willie accepted you, he would be fine and I could die in peace." Willie hopped into his master's lap and looked at Clausen as if he understood what the old man was saying.

"Cartwright's already spilled his guts to the Inspector," Damon told the older man. "He says it was all your plan, but there's no proof. And no way for you to call it off, once the plan was under way. But wasn't Amalie innocent of everything except falling for a jewel thief?"

"Yes, she knew nothing. I do not care what happens to me," Clausen said. "All I want is for Willie to have a good home."

"He's got a home with us for as long as he wants," said Damon.

"A trust fund in Willie's name is available," said Clausen. "Enough until he uses up all nine of his lives."

"We don't need your money," said Robbie. "We'll be proud to accept Willie into our family."

"The money's not stolen," the old man smiled. "I was going to fence the jewelry and use part of it for his trust fund, but decided you people were much too honest. Willie should pay his own way, though, and I think enough is in the fund already."

"It's up to Willie." Robbie turned to the cat. "Shall we take the money?"

"Mrrrt," said Willie.

Cat Bay on Cat Cay

Bill Pronzini

October 21

Dear Blanche,

Well, here we are at Cat Bay on Cat Cay. Finally! Three different planes, the last one a twelve-seater, and then a forty-five-minute trip by ferry launch, and *then* Arthur had to rent a car and drive us all the way around this primitive little island to get to Tweed's Resort. Talk about remote. I was afraid it couldn't possibly be worth all that trouble. But it *is*, Blanche. This isn't just another Caribbean island—it's a vacation paradise!

Cat Bay on Cat Cay. Isn't that wonderfully alliterative? And wonderfully descriptive too. Did I show you the brochure before we left? I can't remember if I did or not. Anyway, the island is one of the outer Leewards, twenty miles long and fifteen miles wide, and from the air it really does look like a sleeping cat. There's a long, narrow, curving peninsula at the south end shaped exactly like a tail, and at the north end there's a rounded projection that resembles a head and two wedge-shaped promontories, one on either side of the head, that are perfectly symmetrical. The natives call the promontories East Ear and West Ear. Isn't that cute? They're the highest points on the cay—about one hundred fifty feet above a rocky shoreline. The rest of the island is at sea level.

Cat Bay curves in from East Ear, a mile-long sweep of brilliantly clear water and the most dazzling white coral sand beach. The photos in the brochure don't do justice to it. Wait until you see the ones I took. Tweed's Resort is at the south end, and it's just the most marvelous mix of provincial and retro-modern. Large bungalows with terraces practically hanging over the beach, and a huge main house where meals and drinks are served that you'd swear was lifted right out of one of those thirties tropical movies, like the one with Dorothy Lamour about the hurricane. I mean, there are ceiling fans instead of air-conditioning! And the grounds are fabulous. Most of Cat Cay is flat and treeless, with a lot of unattractive scrub growth, but at Tweed's there are palms and flamboyant trees and frangipani and . . . oh, every kind of exotic plant you can imagine. And old stone fences and rusty cannons from the days of the Spanish Main pirates, when Captain Kidd, Blackbeard, and Anne Bonny and Calico Jack Rackam (whoever *they* were) came all the way out here to pillage and plunder. The whole place simply *drips* atmosphere.

The owner, Jeremiah Tweed, is a delightful old graybeard, the last member of an African slave family that first settled here two or three hundred years ago. He speaks a charming native patois and tells the most breathtaking stories. His wife, Vera, does most of the cooking and is an absolute wizard—the meal we had last night was to die for. Crayfish, curried conch, and a barbecued meat they claim is beef but Arthur and I are convinced is *goat*. Not that I really want to know, Blanche, because it's delicious no matter what kind of animal it came from.

And here's the big surprise, not mentioned at all in the brochure: the place is positively teeming with cats! Dozens and dozens, nearly every variety of mixed-breed shorthair and longhair, and most as friendly as can be. Mr. Tweed says he and his wife are lifelong cat fanciers and maybe they are, or maybe they feed them and let them roam free as a promotional ploy because of Cat Bay on Cat Cay, but in any case *I* certainly approve. You know how I love cats. Of course, Arthur started grumbling as soon as he saw how many there are. He never has been able to warm up to felines, at least not the non-feral, four-footed kind.

We practically have the resort to ourselves, since the season is still a few weeks off. That would suit me just fine if it wasn't for the Tweeds' only other guest. Her name is Gloria Bartell and she's a widow from Chicago. *Claims* to be a widow, at any rate. She can't be more than thirty-five, one of those slinky blondes with ball-bearing hips and a Lauren Bacall voice. As soon as I laid eyes on her I said to myself, uh-oh, here's a woman on the make. Arthur doesn't think so, naturally. He says she's just a lonely widow with no designs on anything except crayfish and rum punches. But he doesn't fool me. I caught him ogling her in her skimpy bikini this morning, when we came out to the beach. She was lying under one of the little palm-frond lean-tos they have scattered around for shade, and without even asking me he sat down under the one closest to her. And then started a conversation that all but excluded me. Believe you me, I told him what I thought of *that* behavior when we were alone afterward.

Anyhow, Blanche, I'm not going to let myself worry about the widow or anything else. I'm here to have fun. Cuddle with Arthur, swim, go sailing, lie in the sun as much as I can stand to so I'll come home with a glorious tan that will make you green with envy, even if it is on a pudgy forty-three-year-old body. I'm not going to worry about my weight, either, not with all those scrumptious Caribbean specialties of Mrs. Tweed's and Mr. Tweed's special rum punches.

I'll write again in a day or two, whenever the mood strikes. Meanwhile, take care and be sure to let me know if and when that handsome tennis pro at the club says yes next time you ask him for a private lesson. If I wasn't a hopelessly old-fashioned, one-man woman, I'd be terribly jealous of you.

Love and kisses,
Janice

October 23

Dear Blanche,

Greetings again from beautiful Cat Bay on Cat Cay.

We went snorkeling yesterday, all the way out to the coral reef that protects the bay from sharks (the kind that live in the ocean, anyhow). The water is only about six feet deep the whole way, and so clear it's like looking down through layers of glass; you can see starfish and anemones and all sorts of other sea creatures. I worked on my tan most of the afternoon, until clouds piled up and it rained for a while. This morning I went for a lovely catamaran ride around to West Ear. Arthur didn't go along. He said he just wanted to lie on the beach and read and I couldn't talk him out of it.

Do I sound less enthusiastic than I did two days ago, Blanche? If I do, it's because I am. I'm not having near as good a time as I thought I would. You know I planned this trip as more than just a vacation, as a second honeymoon for Arthur and me. But it isn't working out that way. We don't seem to be communicating—not in *any* way, if you know what I mean. Our bungalow has two double beds and we haven't shared the same one for even a minute since we arrived.

I blame Arthur, of course. And that Bartell woman I told you about in my last letter. She hardly has a civil word for me, but she flirts shamelessly with him. He preens when she does it, too—not that I have to tell you about that annoying habit of his when he's around an attractive female.

Last night he went for a walk after dinner, without asking me to join him, and a little while later I happened to step out onto the terrace and there they were, Arthur and the widow, walking along the beach side by side, talking and laughing. One of the Tweeds' cats came bounding out of the bushes just then and ran toward them. Just being playful, the way cats are. And Arthur picked up a piece of driftwood and threw it at the poor little thing. I think he hit it, too, because I heard it cry before it ran off. Then they both laughed as if they'd shared a wonderful joke. I mean, have you ever heard of anything so cruel and heartless?

Then today, after I returned from the catamaran trip, there they were together again, in the garden at the main house, drinking rum punches with their heads about six inches apart. A few minutes ago, when we got back to our bungalow, I confronted Arthur point-blank and of course he laughed it off. All perfectly innocent, my dear—*he* says. Well, we'll see.

So that's why I'm not my usual cheery self today. I know you un-
derstand, Blanche, and I wish you were here so we could talk about it.
You're the only person I can really talk to—my one true friend.
More later. Until then,

Love and kisses,
Janice

October 24

Dear Blanche,
    Last night after dinner Arthur left on another of his walks. I tried
to join him, but he wouldn't hear of it. Well, I waited fifteen minutes
and then I went down to Gloria Bartell's bungalow. The lights were
on inside, but when I crept onto the terrace and peeked through
the jalousies, she wasn't there. I went straight to the beach. It was
a beautiful moonlit night—one of those magnificent frosty white
Caribbean moons that make everything seem as bright as day—and
I could see all the way to East Ear. There was no sign of either of
them. And no sign of them at the main house or anywhere else on
the grounds.
    It was more than two hours before Arthur came back. I asked him
where he'd been, and he said walking on the beach, enjoying the
moonlight and the peace and quiet.
    Oh, Blanche, it looks like he's at it again. I don't want to believe
it after he swore to me the last time that he'd never again be un-
faithful. I keep hoping I'm wrong, imagining things. But under the
circumstances, what else *can* I believe?

Your troubled friend,
Janice

October 25

Dear Blanche,
    I wasn't wrong. It's all true.
    Arthur *is* having a clandestine affair with that Bartell witch. And
he doesn't even care that I know it!

He disappeared this afternoon for four and a half hours. And so did she. And when he came back . . . well, one look at him and his clothes and it was painfully obvious to anyone with half a brain what he'd been doing for most of the time he was gone. I came right out and accused him of it, naturally. He didn't even bother to deny it. All he said was, "What I do is my business, Janice. I'm tired of answering to you. In fact I'm tired of *you* and of pretending I'm not just because you control the damn purse strings."

I cried my eyes out afterward. Then I swallowed the last of my pride and went to him and begged and pleaded—and he laughed at me. Exactly the way he laughed after he hit that poor little cat with the piece of driftwood. As if I were nothing to him anymore—if I ever was in the first place—except a cruel joke.

Oh, Blanche, what am I going to do?

Desperately,
Janice

October 27

Dear Blanche,

I just tried to call you. But the telephone system on Cat Cay is so hopelessly antiquated I couldn't get through. At least the Tweeds have a fax machine, one of their few concessions to modern technology. Otherwise I wouldn't be able to let you know this quickly what's happened.

Blanche, I have some ghastly news.

Arthur is dead!

It happened last night, around ten-thirty. He hardly said a word to me all day, and after supper he left me alone again and went to meet *her*, and he didn't come back. I thought . . . well, I thought he'd given up on our marriage completely and didn't care about keeping up appearances and had spent the night in her bungalow. I didn't go to check because I couldn't bear to know for sure. I just lay awake the entire night, waiting for him and crying hopelessly.

When dawn came I couldn't stand it any longer. I *had* to confront him and get it over with. So I got dressed and went to the witch's bungalow. Well, she was there alone and she claimed Arthur hadn't spent the night with her, that she hadn't seen him since nine-thirty last night. Oh, they'd been together then, she admitted that, but only for a walk over to the bottom of East Ear. He wanted to climb up onto the promontory to take in the view, she said, but she didn't because there are signs warning you the footing is treacherous and not to make the climb after dark. So she left him there and walked back alone.

I was frightened that something had happened to him and she acted as if she was too. We both ran to the main house and told Mr. Tweed, and he and two of his employees hurried out to East Ear and that was where they found Arthur. Not up on the Ear but among the jagged rocks at its base. He fell more than a hundred feet, Mr. Tweed said. He must have been a horrible sight, too, because I wasn't allowed to go and look at the body.

Everything since has just been a blur. The local police constable, a nice little man named Kitts, drove out from the village and asked a lot of questions. Then he and his men left to transport Arthur's remains to the village hopsital. He'll be back later to "attend to for-malities," as he put it.

When he does I'm going to tell him about the witch coming on to Arthur, trying to seduce him. But not that she actually succeeded, because I don't *know* that she did and because there's no reason to open up that can of worms unless it's absolutely necessary. Why say anything at all, you're wondering? Well, everybody seems to think Arthur's death was an accident, but was it, Blanche? I mean, for all I know the witch went up onto East Ear with him after all and they had some kind of argument and she *pushed* him over the edge. And if that's the way it happened, then I want her to get what's coming to her too.

More about that later. I'd better fax this right now, before the constable returns and while I still have my wits about me.

In deepest despair,
Janice

October 28

Dear Blanche,

Thank you so much, my dear friend, for the heartwarming words of solace and sympathy. You've always been there for me in my hour of need, and never more selflessly than now. I can't tell you how much it means to me.

No, you mustn't even think of flying all the way out here. By the time you arrived I'd be on my way home. Constable Kitts says I can leave tomorrow and I've already arranged to take the most direct route possible. I'm sure I can hold up well enough until I get there, and once I see you I'll let myself go and we'll have a good long cry together.

I'm sorry I wasn't able to fax this reply to you yesterday, but your fax arrived just after the constable's return. And after that, the rest of the day simply melted away for me and I was exhausted by night-fall. Constable Kitts and his "formalities," which translated into more questions and all sorts of papers to sign. Mr. and Mrs. Tweed fussing around, trying to console me. Even the witch tried to offer her sympathy, but of course I wouldn't let her anywhere near me. The sheer gall of the woman!

But evidently she's not a murderess. At least the constable doesn't think so. For one thing, she did leave Arthur when she said she did and walk back from East Ear alone. She stopped at the main house for a nightcap, and the Tweeds both remember that it was just ten when she got there. And Arthur's watch was broken in the fall and the hands were frozen at 10:34. So the official verdict is that his death was a tragic accident, which I suppose, when one takes the long view, will be much easier on me. Constable Kitts thinks one of two things must have happened. Either Arthur lost his footing on the rough ground, or he tripped over one of the Tweeds' cats—a more likely occurrence than you might think because many of them go wandering up there at night to hunt birds and rodents. Wouldn't it be ironic if he *did* trip over one of the cats, considering how he felt about them and his in-excusable cruelty on the beach the other day?

The witch has left Cat Bay and temporarily moved into a hotel in the village. Constable Kitts is letting her leave the island tomorrow too, and good riddance, even if she didn't get what was coming to her. I'm still here at the resort, though in a different bungalow than the one I shared with Arthur. The Tweeds have been marvelous, bringing me food and drinks and hovering around to see if there's anything else I need. A cynic might say they're worried that I'll sue them for negligence or something and that's why they're being so solicitous. But I'm not a cynic, Blanche, you know that. I'm just a poor, unlucky woman who seems fated to lead a tragically unful-filled life.

No, no, don't worry, I'm not *that* depressed. I'll survive this set-back and press on. Always have, always will.

One thing that is keeping me from becoming too self-pitying is that I have a part-time roommate in my new bungalow—the cutest little calico with one orange paw and the longest whiskers you've ever seen. She follows me around and coaxes me at every oppor-tunity into picking her up and cuddling her. It's as if she understands and sympathizes with me and is determined to give me comfort. Isn't it a shame that all people aren't as sweet-natured as most cats? Men particularly.

Husbands definitely.

I didn't tell Constable Kitts about Roy and George, of course. It's re-ally nobody's business but mine—and yours, dear Blanche—that Ar-thur was my third husband and the third to die in a terrible accident. Coincidences do happen, after all, and everyone knows that tragedies come in threes. It's not my fault I keep falling in love with men who turn out to be faithless fortune hunters *and* prone to fatal accidents.

I mean, you and I both know I'm not only a poor and unlucky woman, but a helpless one. Don't we, Blanche?

Love and kisses,
Janice

Cold Shoulder

Terry Black

Cats and dogs, that's how the trades described them.

Whenever *Daily Variety* wanted an eye-catching headline, they knew just what to do: check out the latest free-for-all between tough guy Larry Lydecker and Dahlia Beakstone, his volcanic wife. Move over, Tom and Roseanne—megastar Larry and the neckline-popping Dahlia were every muckraker's dream.

The wedding itself, now six months old, had seen more than its share of newsprint. When Larry "Deck 'em" Lydecker—star of *Death Warmed Over* and *The Smell of Money*—popped the question to porn-queen-turned-celeb Dahlia "Dally Ho" Beakstone, the paparazzi had a field day.

Dahlia's filmography, as *Variety* wryly noted, had its ups and downs. Her biggest hits were no-budget sex spoofs ("adaptations") of better-known movies, like *Intercourse with the Vampire* and *Star Trick 6: The Undiscovered Cindy*. Anyone who wondered what Larry saw in her had only to watch the infamous holobed scene (featuring an alien with more appendages than a Nautilus machine) to envy the lucky bastard his catch.

Unfortunately, great sex wasn't everything.

Dahlia's charms, Larry soon discovered, had a price tag. No sooner had he muttered "I do" than Larry realized just what he *had* done:

given Wifey Dearest a foothold on the rocky road to stardom. Dahlia wanted to break into movies, *real* movies. She wanted a cameo— no, a lead—no, a *co-starring* lead—in Larry's next picture, with a premiere gala at Mann's Chinese and guest shots on Leno and Letterman. She wanted her own line of skin care products ("Fresh as a Dahlia!") and later, perhaps, her own long-running TV series and syndicated talk show.

Larry could do all that for her, couldn't he?

Please?

Well, Larry's patience (never his strong suit) was already stretched bowstring-tight. He was tired of catering to Dahlia's wishes—even if just saying no meant his conjugal rights would be cut off like—well, never mind *that*. What mattered was that Larry's lifestyle would not be enhanced by a messy divorce, since Dahlia had sniffed at the very idea of a prenuptial agreement in the face of a passion like theirs.

Now her impertinent demands threatened to capsize his own future. Larry's concessions drew snickers from his fans, while his denials drew everything but gunfire—hence the trumpeting tell-all headlines and snide insider gossip. Studio execs began wondering loudly just who wore the pants in the Lydecker/Beakstone household. The final blow came when Dahlia wanted credit *above his*, as well as script approval and a first-time shot at directing.

It was too much, the final straw.

So Larry suggested they go on vacation. They could fly to Lake Tahoe, get in some skiing and gambling, have a little fun, and see if they couldn't reach a nice compromise. Larry knew she wouldn't come back with any unresolved issues.

Because Dahlia wouldn't be coming back at all.

"*Must* we bring that damned cat?" Larry groused as Stanhope pulled the plush catbox from the limo's rear seat, setting it gingerly on the curb. Behind the mesh window was a huddled form and a pair of baleful, luminous eyes.

"Where I go, Muffin goes," said Dahlia indignantly, tossing her ash-blonde hair over a creamy shoulder. "It's only fair—you've got that damned dog at the cabin, what's his name, Dracula . . . ?"

"Lugosi," said Larry, supervising the flow of luggage to the sidewalk check station. "And he's not *my* dog, he's the caretaker's. That's why we should leave your cat at the K-E-N-N-E-L," he said, noting the feline's upraised ears, "because Muffin and Lugosi don't get along any better than we do."

"Which is my fault, I suppose."

"I didn't say that—"

Thus began their journey. Dahlia was caustic as they left the tarmac at LAX, bitter as they crested the Sierra Nevadas, and downright hostile as they touched down at Lake Tahoe Airport, just three miles south of the frigid shoreline. By the time they piled into the waiting Cadillac and headed up Route 50 to Lakeshore Drive, Dahlia had lapsed into a stony silence—except for occasional cooing sounds, stage-whispered into Muffin's catbox.

The sun had risen just minutes earlier, so the spectacle of the alpine lake was stunning, even to a man preoccupied with killing his wife. Lake Tahoe straddled the border between Nevada and California, giving the upscale basin a schizoid personality. The California side was all hikers and naturalists, pinecone-munching New Agers and refugees from civilization. Not so the Nevada side; there you found acres of glitz and neon, gaudy casinos poised like vultures to pounce on the rich and unwary.

Larry's chalet was in the town of Stateline, so named because the interstate boundary passed right through it. The change was apparent within a couple of blocks; the prim, no-wagering south gave way to a fistful of high-gloss casinos—Caesar's, Harvey's, Harrah's—and a horde of one-armed bandits lurking in every corner market and gas station.

Just like my marriage, thought Larry glumly. *Cross the line, and life's a gamble.*

Dahlia was unmoved by the powdered-sugar mountains and neon skyline, mirrored in the lake's placid surface with stunning fidelity. Lake Tahoe, they said, was cleaner and purer than the drinking water in most cities. But Dahlia cared nothing for civic footnotes; she wanted to hit the slopes and then the casinos, courtesy of Larry's bankroll.

"As soon as I drop off Muffin," she said, poking a finger into the catbox. From inside came an answering purr.

I'd like to drop her off, thought Larry, picturing the sheer face of Gunbarrel, Heavenly Valley's scariest double-diamond ski slope. *Let Muffin try a four-legged freestyle—*

Instead he just sighed and said, "Honey, we're here."

"Here" was a cozy lakeside chalet, with alpine shutters and redwood trim and a stone chimney, coughing up woodsmoke. Larry crunched up to the door, his breath vaporing in the chill, and had barely cracked it open when a black juggernaut pounced on him.

"Lugosi," he snapped, *"get down!"*

Instantly the dog (who could easily have torn his throat out) dropped to the ground at Larry's feet, hanging his great head and whimpering in remorse. After a moment Larry crouched and scratched behind the Doberman's ears.

"All right, boy, take it easy." He looked up at Dahlia, just now arriving with catbox firmly in hand. "Hey, boy!" he said, pointing. "You remember my wife, and her little friend Muffin . . . ?"

Lugosi looked up with great interest. But Muffin, poking her nose up to the little mesh window, had the same reaction as Dahlia to this big, unbeautiful canine.

Muffin hissed at him.

"Why isn't that hellhound *leashed*?" Dahlia snapped. "Where's the caretaker, what are you paying him for if he's not even around to protect us from Cujo here—"

"Relax," Larry said, stooping to face the dog. "I'm sure Grissom's close by, and I know just how to find him." He took the Dobie by the ears and said clearly, *"Get . . . Grissom."*

The response was immediate. The dog leapt upward, barked, and sprang across the snow with such speed that Larry wondered if he'd been a greyhound in a former life. After just a couple of minutes (ninety-two seconds, by Larry's Rolex) Lugosi trotted back again, leading his master by the hand.

"Hi, folks," said Howard Grissom, freeing his knuckles from the dog's toothy grasp. He wiped his fingers on a fur parka, started to shake Larry's hand, then thought better of it. "I was just out back, sir, checking the plumbing. Gotta be careful, there's a cold snap coming on." He frowned. "We burst a pipe March of last year, you couldn't hardly use the toilet unless—"

"That's fine," Larry broke in. "Why don't you get our luggage and . . ." He glanced at Dahlia's catbox. ". . . find a place for Muffin, where Lugosi won't bother her."

"Cats and dogs," said Grissom knowingly. "They just don't mix. Let's put her in the guest room—and be sure to keep the door shut."

The powder was perfect, but the skiing was awful.

There were two types of skiers, Larry thought: those who looked good, and those who *skied* good. Sadly, Dahlia was strictly Type One. She looked great in her fiberfill jacket, Oakley goggles, and form-fitting Gore-Tex tights—but try and get her off the bunny slopes for some *real* skiing, and Her Ladyship was as finicky as Muffin at feeding time.

Larry sighed inwardly as he and Dahlia left the Heavenly Tram, at the highest point above Lake Tahoe. From the summit (8200 feet above sea level), you could see not only the lake far below but the sprawling Nevada Desert, on the mountain's far side. Getting down could be a treacherous, death-defying odyssey—or a milk run if, like Dahlia, you stuck to the easiest, most roundabout trails.

Larry liked to point his Rossignols bottomward and go schuss-booming down the hillside, breaking into a zigzag of tight curves and christies just at the point of suicide. But Dahlia took a more sedate approach, going miles out of her way to skirt every hazard, like a schoolmarm headed for a church social. She started to lag so far behind that Larry wondered if she'd suffered an accident.

No way, he decided. *Nothing's ever that easy.*

And sure enough, just when he'd half-convinced himself that the slippery mountain had done his job for him, here came Dahlia, her sweat unbroken, snowplowing through a series of clumsy windshield-wiper turns as the other skiers cursed and swerved around her.

"Been waiting long?" she asked, sweetly. "Don't worry, honey, I'm right behind you." She fluffed her hair, unmussed by the cautious descent. "I wouldn't want to spoil your fun."

Larry was tempted to lure her onto one of the black diamond runs (maybe he could switch trail signs?), and shove his ex-to-be down a near-vertical face. But Dahlia—with that special luck reserved for children and fools—would probably survive it, especially with the Heavenly Valley Ski Patrol poised for just such an emergency. He could picture what would happen then: Dahlia would point a ruby fingernail and shriek, *"He did it!,"* smirking as the sheriffs pounced on her husband, turning the arrest into a photo op to show off her sexy new thigh cast.

It wasn't a pretty picture.

Better to stick to the original plan, galling though it was. Larry set off down the slope again, swiftly outpacing his wife, and wished for a freak avalanche.

By the time they hit Harrah's, the sun was setting—*in more ways than one*, Larry thought. The murder wasn't due for hours, but he almost rescheduled when he toted up Dahlia's losses at the keno tables. By Larry's cocktail-napkin reckoning, the former Ms. Beakstone had already blown enough of their savings to feed a family of sixteen until the twenty-second century.

And *that* was before they hit Caesar's, Harvey's, Lakeside, and an oddly tempting one-armed bandit at the corner Chevron station.

"Hungry little bastard, isn't he?" Dahlia chirped, feeding it half her weight in quarters.

After that, you'd think Larry's not-so-beloved would retire to the cabin to sleep off all those complimentary vodkas. But Dahlia seemed impervious to alcohol, and besides, she had her nightly ritual to perform—keeping her girlish figure by jogging, without fail, at least four miles a day.

Rain or shine. Summer or winter.

Mild or freezing.

This was the cornerstone of Larry's plan. The setting was perfect:

Grissom was fast asleep, along with everyone in town except the hard-core gamblers, and *they* wouldn't notice Christ's Second Coming, let alone a quiet murder. As Dahlia slipped into her fur-lined sweats, boots, mittens, and earmuffs, as she scratched Muffin goodbye and went out to jog the shoreline, Larry threw her a jaunty wave.

And rehearsed his alibi.

My God, Sheriff, she jogs every night. I should have waited up for her, but I was just so exhausted—

Larry pulled the ski mask over his head, and shrugged into the black down jacket. He stooped to pet Lugosi, sleeping fitfully by the door, and stepped outside.

It was very cold.

She's nuts to jog in this weather, Larry thought, hugging himself against the chill. If Dahlia wasn't careful, as her mother might have said, she was going to catch her death.

The shore was still, its silence broken only by the sporadic rumble of faraway traffic noise. Dahlia was jogging along the rim of the Edgewood golf course, now utterly deserted, as far from rescue (it seemed) as a wayward astronaut. He just had to find an outcrop or something to crouch behind and lay his ambush—

He was still looking when Dahlia ran right into him.

And screamed.

I don't believe it, Larry thought, marveling (even now, in the blind panic of discovery) at the perversity of his wife. Dahlia *never* cut her jogging short, she was dependable as the sunrise, yet here she was coming back because it was too damn cold, probably, and spoiling his careful scheme.

But not really. He hadn't lost the element of surprise; his shock was nothing next to hers. Dahlia stood frozen in her tracks, goggling at him, too dumbfounded to move. Larry clamped a gloved hand over her mouth, cutting short her cries, and clumsied her into the freezing waters of Lake Tahoe. She fought like a tigress when she saw what was coming, but he kept the advantage and plunged her head under the waterline.

Dahlia bucked and thrashed, but she was cold and tired and sluggish from too many vodkas. In less time than Larry expected, the struggling ceased. He held her under a full minute longer, just in case, but there was no need; when he released her, the body was utterly still.

Just another senseless accident, folks, and a reminder not to drink and jog.

Larry found a piece of driftwood and obscured all trace of their struggle. He backed away through the water, leaving no tracks. When the Douglas County Sheriff's Office found Dahlia's body in the morning, there'd be nothing to indicate that her death wasn't an accident.

All that remained was a show of unfelt grief. Larry wasn't worried about that; despite some bad notices, he *was* an actor, and mourning Dahlia was the role of a lifetime. He actually looked forward to it, like he first time he'd assayed Shakespeare.

He was back at the cabin in less than ten minutes. Lugosi barely stirred when he let himself in; Grissom was still asleep in his room, with an irritating hacksaw snore. Larry peeked into the guest room, saw Muffin glaring at him, and fought the impulse to feed the little pest some strychnine-flavored Friskies.

All in good time . . .

He tried to sleep, but it wouldn't come.

Probably just the excitement, of course—how often does a man drown his wife? But there was something else, a lingering unease. Guilt, perhaps. Larry *was* capable of it, though memories of Dahlia (shrill, greedy, grasping Dahlia) inspired no regret. The thought of living without her filled him with little-boy eagerness, like a lifer handed a reprieve.

What, then? What was bothering him?

Could he possibly have overlooked something?

The thought of prison *did* bother him, very much indeed, and the more he wondered if he'd made some mistake, the worse this feeling troubled him. He tried to go over the crime in his mind, replaying the logic of it, putting himself in the sheriff's place. It was simple enough: Dahlia had gone jogging. She'd fallen into the water and drowned. There were no bruises, nothing to indicate force, because of the padded clothing worn by both of them.

No bruises . . .

Damn.

That was it, right there. If Dahlia had fallen and knocked herself out, there should *be* a bruise, a big one, from the impact that had rendered her senseless. With no evidence of head trauma, they could only conclude she'd been drowned on purpose, and the likeliest suspect was—

Larry sat up in bed, wide awake. He'd blundered, all right, but it was still fixable. It was 3:15 A.M., just two hours since the drowning. He could go back to the body, bash its skull with a rock or something, and hope for the best. With luck, the coroner would buy it.

He redressed and donned the ski mask, bracing himself for the cold. Lugosi had moved, presumably to a warmer napping spot. Larry opened the door—and cringed, because it was freezing out, much colder than before.

Then two things happened.

An orange streak whipped between his legs, shot outside, and vanished. Close on its heels came Lugosi, howling in pursuit. Only by flattening himself against the doorjamb did Larry keep from being bowled over.

In hindsight, he realized what had happened: he'd left the door to the guest room open. Lugosi had smelled the cat and gone hunting for it. Trapped in the cozy cabin, Muffin had hidden out, awaiting her chance—and had run like hell when it came.

Well, the hell with it. Dahlia wasn't complaining, and Larry's money was on the dog.

He sighed and left to find his wife.

Snow was falling now, patchy and cold on his face. An icy breeze blew in off the lake, raising gooseflesh even under his padded sleeves. He just wanted to be done with it, to smash that ash-blonde head and get back inside, to the warmth of his cabin. The body wasn't far; finding it should be no problem.

But something else was.

I don't believe it, Larry thought, when he came upon the prone corpse. Simplicity, that was the key—the murder had been so straightforward that an imbecile could have done it. But Larry's luck, it seemed, had deserted him. The body he needed to skull-bash, the shapely corpse lying half-underwater right where he'd left it—well, now it couldn't be moved.

Because the lake had frozen around it.

It was absurd, the final insult. Lake Tahoe *couldn't* freeze; it was the fifth-deepest lake in the world, for God's sake, impervious to the Sierran cold. At worst the edges might freeze, just a little. But freakish weather brought freakish results, and the elements (like some divine prankster) had chosen this worst of all evenings to make an exception.

Larry grabbed his wife's legs, crouching on the slippery shore, and pulled with all his might. Dahlia didn't budge. He shifted his weight, got a lockhold on those fabulous hips, and yanked until he nearly fainted from exertion.

No use.

She was stuck, and stuck tight. Larry felt like a woolly mammoth, trying to free itself from the La Brea tar pits. The clutch of the ice was rock-solid, inescapable. Larry couldn't think how to free her, unless he wanted to look in the Yellow Pages under Jackhammer Rentals, or try Dahlia's blow-dryer with one hell of an extension cord—

He was panicking, not thinking. The problem wasn't insurmountable, just an obstacle to be dealt with. Larry found a fist-sized rock and struck the ice again and again, trying to smash the glassy surface. At first he made little progress, scarcely denting the frozen half-coffin, but with each new blow he felt a little more give.

It made sense, he thought, pounding harder. The water wasn't frozen clear through; only the surface, and not much of it at that, could have iced over this quickly. If he could only penetrate this cold veneer, break through to the underlying wetness—

Larry went to work around Dahlia's head, her hair spread out on all sides like the tentacles of an ash-blonde mollusk. He couldn't see her expression, since the body was lying face-down, but he had a hunch this wasn't a good look for her.

He struck down hard; the ice splintered under the impact. Larry reared back for another blow, thinking *This should just about do it*, and that's when the lake burst under him, like a shattered windowpane.

He dropped, splashed, found himself neck-deep in ice water. The cold was unbelievable, beyond pain, so paralyzing that Larry could scarcely remember what he was even doing here, just that he wanted out and he wanted out *now*. But his limbs weren't working anymore, it was all he could do to keep his head above water as his body curled up into the fetal position, fighting to conserve heat.

Larry was no expert on hypothermia, but he seemed to recall that a man immersed in freezing water had only minutes to live. He tried to cry out but couldn't spare the breath, and who'd hear him anyway, he'd picked this spot for its remoteness—

But he wasn't alone. And his plight wasn't hopeless. Larry realized that suddenly when he heard something, a sound both harsh and, to his ears, beautiful:

Barking.

Lugosi had found him. Larry craned his neck to see the big black dog standing puzzled at the shoreline, as if waiting for instructions.

With supreme effort, Larry filled his lungs with air and managed to splutter, "Get . . . Grissom . . ."

The response was immediate. Lugosi barked, spun on his hind paws, and raced off in the direction of the cabin. If Grissom was asleep, he wouldn't stay that way; Larry knew from experience what a ruckus the Dobie could raise. Lugosi wouldn't shut up until the caretaker had stumbled out of bed and come out to see what was wrong.

Help was on the way. Grissom would save him, maybe even (for a generous fee) help to cover up this mess, make Dahlia's death look accidental again. Everything would turn out fine.

If he could just hang on until Grissom got there . . .

Eight hours later, they found him.

It wasn't hard to figure what had happened. Sheriff Eugene Pike had seen more than his share of untimely deaths, but these were especially sad because the popular couple had been so much in love, so devoted to each other till the bitter end.

"Poor bastards," he said, shaking his head. "They never had a chance."

Howard Grissom watched in somber silence, wringing his cap in his hands. "What do you think happened, Sheriff?"

"It's not hard to figure," Pike said, reconstructing the scene. "They must have gone for a moonlight stroll, though the snow covered their footprints. For some reason, Mr. Lydecker wandered out onto the ice—maybe he didn't realize, with the snow and all—and it cracked under him. If his wife had any sense, she would have run for help, but I guess she just couldn't leave her husband. That's why she stretched out into the water, to try and pull him back. But the freezing cold, well, it was too much for them."

Pike lowered his head in reverent silence. But Grissom cleared his throat.

"One thing stumps me," he said, squatting, pointing at the ground. "Here's some tracks the snow *didn't* cover—my dog's tracks. You'd think old Lugosi would have come got me, seeing 'em splash and yell like they must have. I wonder why that damned mutt ran off and let me sleep until ten-thirty this morning?"

Pike frowned, examining the tracks. Lugosi had indeed left the scene of the accident, racing for the Lydecker cabin. Not until fifty feet later did the tracks veer sideways, going wildly off course, plunging through the golf course and towards town.

"Here's your answer," said Pike judiciously, nodding at the ground. A second set of tracks cut across the dog's path, heading sideways. "Something distracted him, led him astray."

Grissom crouched for a better look, flinching at what he saw there. He sighed, shaking his head.

"I tried to tell them, Sheriff," he said wearily. "Cats and dogs, they just don't mix."

The Cat Who Knew Too Much

🧰

Dorothy Cannell

Alfred Morrison was seated in his favorite chair by the fireplace, making cheerful plans to murder his wife, when her booming voice destroyed the moment.

"Don't just sit there like a sack of flour, you great lummox, do something!"

"Yes, Edith!" Alfred planted his feet more firmly on the fine Persian carpet and opened one eye, a typical response on his part to the daily domestic crises that had enlivened six months of marriage to a woman who looked like Winston Churchill in drag.

"Is it too much to ask, Alfie," raucous sobs filled the room, "for you to take that vacant stare off your stupid mug? Just for once, look at me when I talk to you." Edith's bulldog face swam into view as Alfred strove for an expression of male sympathy suitable to whatever the current tragedy entailed, be it a broken vase or the death of someone near and dear to Edith. No, couldn't be the latter, Alfred bit down on a mirthless smile. His better half had no family, nor any friends that she wouldn't happily have traded in for a flashy rhinestone brooch. The only creature in the world for whom she

247

would gladly have laid down her life weighed nine and a half pounds and looked like the Victorian muff Alfred's grandmother had used as a hot water bottle cover.

"Ah-ha!" A congratulatory slap on the knee. "You don't have to spell it out for me, Edith. This is about Charlotte Rose, isn't it? What's the little sugar bun done? Gone and got herself run over? There, there, old girl! It's a crying shame, all right, but none of us gets to live forever."

And that's what I've got to keep telling myself if I'm not to end up losing my marbles, Alfred reflected wistfully as he stood up and patted his wife's weight-lifter shoulder. Three failed attempts in as many months on the life of the woman he had married in hope of a speedy inheritance would get any man down. But it wouldn't do to cave in and meekly accept the status quo. One of the nastier things he had discovered about his wife on the honeymoon was that her heart condition wasn't as bad as she had led him to believe. And as he had always told himself, the devil helps those who help themselves.

"Charlotte Rose isn't dead, you stupid gawp!" Edith dropped down onto the sofa with a mighty thud. "Do you bloody well think I'd be fit to put two words together if the angels had come for my little darling? She's upstairs in her canopy basket. Oh, Alfie," a series of heaving sobs, "she's got something wrong with her meow."

"What?" Alfred was shocked into joining his spouse on the sofa. Before he could inch away from her he was swallowed up in a bear hug. Edith had her grotesque moments of being cuddly. And there was nothing to do but lie still with his nose impaled in her Styrofoam bosom and pray that he would be allowed up for air before he turned as blue as his lady wife's hair.

"I noticed at lunchtime that she didn't sound herself. And what terrified me was she didn't touch her shrimp mousse or the fricassee of chicken livers. So while you were having your afternoon snooze I drove the sweet precious down to the vet's. I was sure dear Dr. Stanley would tell me Charlotte Rose had a nasty sore throat and he'd prescribe medicine, along with lots of fluids, bed rest, and perhaps a drive in the country for a blow of fresh air. But," Edith's tears plopped down on Alfred's neck as she kneaded his face into that well-sprung bosom, "we're not talking about a sore throat!"

"We're not?" Alfred mumbled as his mind leaped hopefully to proper illnesses—here he managed a squashed smile—like the Black Death.

"Charlotte Rose's trouble isn't physical. Dr. Stanley broke the news as gently as he could that she's developed a speech impediment. A stammer. Or was it a stutter? I can't remember which one he said." Edith clapped a meaty hand to her forehead, sending Alfred flying backwards so that he lay three quarters off the sofa in the manner of a magician's assistant about to be levitated to the ceiling. "It was all such a shock I blacked out and the nurse had to come in and help Dr. Stanley get me up on the examining table. A coldhearted woman. She told me to take a look at my bill and if that didn't bring me round nothing would."

"So the cat needs a course of elocution lessons, is that it?" Alfred rolled onto the floor, hobbled around on his knees until his head stopped spinning, and got to his feet. "You'll be out a few quid, but that shouldn't bother you, Edith. You've never counted the cost where dear little Charlotte Rose is concerned."

"You great dolt!" A pillow whizzed past Alfred's head, giving him a closer shave than he routinely got with his electric razor. "My angel baby's problem is psychological. We're talking about a mental illness. She's having . . . oh, I don't how I can bear to say it . . . a nervous breakdown. Could a devoted mother ever receive a worse piece of news? Any fool knows the feline mind is a perilously fragile thing, not nearly as easily cured as taking out the poor little moppet's tonsils. Dr. Stanley asked me"—heartrending sob—"if Charlotte Rose had recently suffered any sort of trauma."

"And what did you tell him, dear?" Suddenly the room tilted like the deck of the *Titanic*. Knees trembling, Alfred sat down across from his wife.

"Well," Edith's eyes shifted sideways, "I did explain that we recently changed milkmen, and Charlotte Rose doesn't readily adapt to new tradespeople. She's started taking her tea black with a squeeze of lemon. But Dr. Stanley didn't think that the new milk-man would have caused her to break down so completely. He said Charlotte Rose must have been exposed to a catastrophic event, or in all likelihood more than one, to have been robbed of normal speech."

"Watching too much telly, that's my guess. Horribly violent, most of the stuff they put on nowadays." Alfred's voice came out in a croak and he had to close his eyes to stop the room from spinning. Unfortunately, hiding out behind his lids proved no escape. His mind zoomed in on his three attempts to murder Edith. Scenes flip-flopping off kilter, as if being captured for posterity by a video cam-era in the hands of a rank amateur. The colors livid. The sounds blurred.

There was the April day when he and Edith huffed and puffed their way to the top of St. Michael's medieval tower in Riddlington, Suffolk. Realizing they were the only two idiots to have made the climb, Alfred had seized the moment to give Edith a shove that had sent her slithering headfirst down the toe-hold stone steps. She had survived that experience with a bump on the head and no memory of ever having been in the tower.

The result was much the same after her dip in the sea at Brighton. Bloody hell! Edith had been begging to be bumped off that day. Flexing her brawny arms, she had insisted on taking a rowing boat out into rain-shrouded waves in an area known, so a local had warned them, for its savage undertow. It had been a piece of cake for Alfred to fake enthusiasm. The moment they were out of sight of the beach he begged to be allowed to take an oar, and never in his fifty-seven years had he enjoyed anything more than giving his wife a bash on the back of the head and seeing her topple overboard. But talk about rotten luck! Edith had refused to sink and before Alfred could regain control of the boat a busybody Coast Guard had showed up and callously ruined what should have been the surprise funeral of the year. Edith had spent a couple of days in bed with a bad cold but no memory of why she had ended up overboard.

Poor Alfred. For several weeks he had nursed his sense of griev-ance against the guardian angel who would seem to be working overtime on Edith's behalf. A lesser man would have given up. But not Alfred. A fortnight ago he had suggested a day's shopping in London. When he and the wife were waiting to board their train home in the crush of rush hour at Liverpool Street underground station, he had maneuvered Edith to the edge of the platform and shoved her onto the line as the train rocketed into sight with hurricane velocity. This time there could be no escape! Alfred finally knew the meaning of connubial bliss when . . . the brutal reality hit him like a ton of manure. The third time was not the charm. Edith had been dragged back to safety by a Boy Scout heaven bent on doing his good deed for the day. And what did the bloody woman have to show for this near-death experience? A sprained shoulder and . . . again no memory of events after entering the tube station.

"That's right, Alfie. Sit there like a lump on a log, why don't you!" Edith's voice rivaled the roar of the train that was supposed to have made him a free and very rich man. "Here I am at my wit's end, wondering if my Charlotte Rose will ever again be a fully functioning pussycat, and what do I get from you? Not so much as a crumb of comfort. Sometimes I wonder what possessed me to marry you. Oh, I know you came on like I was the queen of Sheba, but I should have seen you for what you are. Unfeeling, that's the word. I don't suppose you'd turn a hair if my little darling should end up taking her own life before we can find out the root of her problem."

"There, there, my love!" Alfred sat down next to his wife on the sofa and patted her shoulder. The panic that had gripped him was receding. It was rubbish to worry that in mulling over the last few months Edith's eyes would be opened and she would reach the chilling conclusion that her series of mishaps had traumatized Charlotte Rose. The cat had not been present to witness any of the events, and to give his buggering wife her due, Edith had not made a major production out of recovering from her accidents. A couple of days in bed with the aspirin bottle within reach had been the extent of each convalescent period.

"I say the vet's got you worked up over nothing," Alfred spoke with increasing cheer. "My guess is Charlotte Rose will be like a cat with two tails come morning."

"That's easy for you to say." Edith gulped down a sob. "I don't think you ever really took to my baby."

Alfred almost said that the boot was on the other foot. The first time he had set eyes on the pampered Persian she had recoiled from him as if he were a viper let out of a shoebox. And after the marriage Charlotte Rose had treated him with a studied indifference that at times got under Alfred's skin.

"You're talking a lot of bosh, Edith," he said stoutly. "I'm almost as fond of the little tyke as you are. I'm just trying to put a good face on a bad situation for your sake, my love."

"Oh, Alfie!" Edith nuzzled up to him on the sofa. "I don't deserve you. I'm such a cow most of the time. I don't mean anything by it. Having pots of money can be rough on a woman, particularly"—sniff—"when she's got a face like the back of a bus. You get so's you don't trust men, even the salt-of-the-earth ones like you."

Alfred submitted to a smacking kiss without puckering his lips. "Now, Edith, you know I never wanted your money. I told you that from the word go. It was me as told you not to change your will, but you insisted!" His voice cracked convincingly. "As if any amount of money could make up for being without the love of my life. We're a family, Edith. That's what we are, you, me, and Charlotte Rose."

"Bless you!" Edith swallowed him up in a rib-cracking embrace. "You've buoyed me up so's I can face what has to be done, whatever the cost in anguish to yours truly."

At that moment Alfred experienced a flicker of admiration for the woman he had married. The old bag was dotty enough about Charlotte Rose to end the cat's misery by having her put to sleep. A pity life wasn't as simple in other ways, but there it was.

"You'll come with me, won't you, Alfie?" Edith was saying.

"To the vet's?" Alfred had his moments of squeamishness.

"Dr. Ventura isn't a vet in the usual sense of the word. He's the senior cat psychiatrist at the Royal Feline Infirmary in York. According to Dr. Stanley, the man is a giant in his field and could be Charlotte Rose's one hope of recovering from her nervous breakdown, before she slips into permanent psychosis." Edith's voice trembled like an avalanche about to let loose. "Not to scare you to death, Alfie, Dr. Stanley said there's no time to be lost and we should rush our little angel up to the institute this evening."

"But we haven't had dinner." Alfred could not keep the irritation out of his voice."

"I know, love," Edith got off the sofa like an elephant in a trance, "but it's best for you and me, not just Charlotte Rose, if we don't put this off a moment longer than needed. Dr. Stanley warned me that part of a patient's recovery program includes family therapy sessions that can be emotionally draining for everyone concerned."

"I'm not sure I like the sound of anything to do with this business." Alfred fought down the uneasiness that was worming its way up from his stomach, but he couldn't keep his hands from trembling. Edith didn't notice. She went upstairs to fetch Charlotte Rose and swaddle her in a powder blue blanket with the cat's initials monogrammed in the corner. "You drive, Alfie," she instructed in a voice that even though gentler than usual made his head spin. "What with all I'm feeling right now, I wouldn't be safe behind the wheel."

The Morrisons lived in Rotherham, so motoring to York was hardly a taxing trip under normal circumstances; but from the moment Alfred pulled away from the house, he knew he was going to have trouble keeping his mind on the dark ribbon of road. He'd been in such good spirits before Edith came in with her news about Charlotte Rose. He'd decided he hadn't been thinking on a grand enough scale in his earlier attempts to make himself a widower, and that had given him an idea. He would suggest to Edith that they go on a holiday to America to see the Grand Canyon. He'd read that every year some overly eager tourist took a fatal tumble while viewing that scenic wonder.

But now, even as he cautiously negotiated his way around a car going twenty miles an hour, Alfred felt as if he were the one falling through space down into the blackest of pits. Out the corner of his eye he could see Charlotte Rose nestled on Edith's lap. Her pose suggested she was dozing but he knew that at least one of her eyes was cracked open. He could feel her counting the hairs on his head.

Worse, he could feel her picking apart his thoughts the way she might have plucked the feathers from a sparrow had Edith ever allowed her to set her paws outdoors.

Bugger the little varmint! Alfred almost wrenched the steering wheel out of its socket. Charlotte Rose had him sized up from day one.

"Watch the road, Alfie!" Edith's bellow brought the lorry ahead of him into wavering focus. "Now look what you've done, you great clot! You've jolted our Charlotte Rose out of what was like as not the best sleep she's had all day."

"Me . . . me . . . ow . . . ow."

Bloody hell, sweat broke out on Alfred's forehead. The cat had developed a stutter! Could anything be more horrible than the humanness of the condition, particularly when coupled with that icy blue feline stare?"

"I'm sorry I shouted at you, love." Edith rubbed his knee. "It's on account of me being that worried is all."

Worried! That was a tame word for what Alfred was feeling. Charlotte Rose knew all about his attempts on Edith's life. The cat hadn't needed to be present to witness the events. On some telepathic level she had been there on the stone steps at St. Michael's tower, in the rowing boat at Brighton and at Liverpool Street tube station. She, the oversized powder puff, had been Edith's guardian angel. And now she was headed for a cat psychiatrist's couch where, under the tender care of Dr. Ventura, she would become the means of everything coming to light.

"You're not a bad old stick, Alfie," Edith rumbled affectionately. "How about we stay over a few days in York when Charlotte Rose is on the mend? Have ourselves a second honeymoon. We could go and have a gawk at the cathedral. Really do the tourist bit. You'd like to see the railway museum, wouldn't you? And to show you love me, Alfie, we could go window-shopping in the Shambles."

"Whatever you say, dear," Alfred was doing better at watching the road. His mind had suddenly become crystal clear. He could picture himself along with Edith and Charlotte Rose being ushered by a sober-faced nurse into a stark white admitting room. There waiting for them would be the world's foremost cat psychiatrist. He would be foreign, Alfred decided, with a receding hairline and a sallow complexion.

"I am not Freud." Alfie could see Dr. Ventura bowing a greeting over steepled fingers and hear the thin piping voice inside his head.

"No, of course you're not a fraud," Edith would bellow, already having trouble with the doctor's accent. "Dr. Stanley says you're a genius. And I know you can make my Charlotte Rose all well again."

"I am not Freud." Dr. Ventura's face vanished for a moment when Alfred turned on the windshield wipers, but returned seconds later with even more fanatical clarity. "What I am is a man with the mind of a cat. I understand how my patients think. I talk their language. Slowly, layer by layer, I will peel away the face that Charlotte Rose shows to the outside world and discover what torment lurks within her soul."

Rain was coming down fast now, but Alfred turned the wipers down to low in a vain attempt at blurring Dr. Ventura's face.

"Watch the road, Alfie!" Edith's voice tore through his head and Alfred drew a shaky breath. The phantom doctor was gone, but there was no escaping the real man waiting for them at the Royal Feline Infirmary. He would require full cooperation on the part of Charlotte Rose's parents in pursuit of her recovery. Edith would explain that Alfred was the little angel's stepfather. Dr. Ventura would ask how long Alfred and Edith had been married, how Charlotte Rose had reacted to the event, and if the last few months had been relatively uneventful. Edith would mention she'd had rather a run of bad luck in the way of accidents recently. Dr. Ventura would probe more deeply and express himself very interested that Edith's memory of the events was so clouded. He would mention the words *traumatic amnesia* and gently suggest that while Edith might have blotted out whatever was particularly troubling about the accidents, Charlotte Rose had been able to pick up her mistress's subliminal distress calls and had reached a point of emotional overload. Her sense of powerlessness had manifested itself in her present vocal problems.

"Alfie, are you asleep at the wheel?"

"No, dear."

"I've been thinking, Alfie," Edith kissed the top of Charlotte Rose's head, "that if Dr. Ventura is everything he's cracked up to be and does right by our precious here, I'll change my will and leave everything I've got to his infirmary. You said right from the beginning you'd never take a penny of my money."

But you weren't supposed to take me at my word, you stupid cow. Alfred could have bashed his head against the windshield.

"That day, soon after we were married and I went down to see the solicitor, he talked me into seeing I was wrong to go against your wish. And the will I made out left the lot to various charities, but this will be better. And such a nice tribute to our Charlotte Rose."

What a bloody bad joke. He could end up at the Old Bailey charged with attempted murder. And that might be preferable to what Edith would do to him if he was left to her mercy. Alfred turned his neck an inch to look at his wife, but it was Charlotte Rose's eyes that met his and he could have sworn the rotten little beast was laughing at him.

"A penny for your thoughts, Alfie?" Edith said as York Minster rose up before them in the not too far distance.

"Just watching the road." Alfred Morrison spoke with remarkable cheerfulness. His nimble brain had come up with the perfect way out. He was humming a tune as drove along thinking up ways to kill himself.